P9-BZX-846

From the very first days of our marriage Paolo brought us out of the shadows where we had been hiding our love for each other. On Sunday afternoons I'd put on my red dress and take his arm as we walked down the hill to Hartley Park, retracing our steps of that Sunday long before when he'd escorted me to the band concert for the first time.

One Sunday he told me he had a surprise for me. I was eager to know what it was and cajoled and pleaded with him, but he insisted I had to wait until we were inside the park. Once there, instead of heading toward the band shell, he led me away toward a grove of arborvitae growing in a semicircle. Within the grove he stopped and put his finger to his lips as I started to question him.

"Wait and listen," he said.

Within a few minutes I heard the tap of the bandleader's baton on the wooden podium and then the opening notes. The music was as clear as if we'd been sitting in front of the bandstand. But instead of being in the midst of a hundred others, we were alone in the grove.

He took me in his arms and swept me over the grass in time with the music. I felt his arm around my waist, his hand caressing the small of my back. His other hand was tightly entwined with mine, as if he never wanted to let me go.

A Graziuccia *e* Federigo Cardillo
Per la vita!

Acknowledgments

I am so grateful, first of all, to the members of my family who were the caretakers of Graziuccia's and Federigo's letters—my parents, Lena and Fritzie Cardillo, and my Aunt Susie Lauricella—as well as Aunt Joann Petrillo, whose kitchen-table conversations nourished my imagination.

I am blessed with a wonderful, supportive family: my husband, Stephan, who does countless loads of laundry and washes piles of dishes so that I can hole up in a library and write; my children, Luke, Nicola and Mark, who have been my champions, my techies, my fashion consultants and my photographers.

I am also indebted to my circle of Italian ladies in Springfield, Massachusetts—Christina Manzi, her daughter Rosa Anna Ronca and the assorted aunts, cousins and friends who fed me eggplant and meatballs and helped me translate many of the letters.

I thank my writing friends—Adele Bozza, Julie Winberg and Sharon Wright—who read, advised and encouraged me through many drafts and who asked the tough questions; and my agent Maura Kye-Casella, whose unfailing enthusiasm and insightful comments sustained and mentored me.

And finally, my deepest appreciation for my editor, Paula Eykelhof, who guided me through a rigorous process, mined the manuscript for the best material and helped me to shape a compelling story.

Dancing on Sunday Afternoons

Linda Cardillo

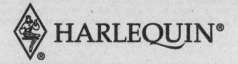

HARLEQUIN®

TORONTO • NEW YORK • LONDON
AMSTERDAM • PARIS • SYDNEY • HAMBURG
STOCKHOLM • ATHENS • TOKYO • MILAN • MADRID
PRAGUE • WARSAW • BUDAPEST • AUCKLAND

If you purchased this book without a cover you should be aware that this book is stolen property. It was reported as "unsold and destroyed" to the publisher, and neither the author nor the publisher has received any payment for this "stripped book."

ISBN-13: 978-0-373-65403-1
ISBN-10:   0-373-65403-0

DANCING ON SUNDAY AFTERNOONS

Copyright © 2007 by Linda Cardillo Platzer.

All rights reserved. Except for use in any review, the reproduction or utilization of this work in whole or in part in any form by any electronic, mechanical or other means, now known or hereafter invented, including xerography, photocopying and recording, or in any information storage or retrieval system, is forbidden without the written permission of the publisher, Harlequin Enterprises Limited, 225 Duncan Mill Road, Don Mills, Ontario, Canada M3B 3K9.

All characters in this book have no existence outside the imagination of the author and have no relation whatsoever to anyone bearing the same name or names. They are not even distantly inspired by any individual known or unknown to the author, and all incidents are pure invention.

This edition published by arrangement with Harlequin Books S.A.

® and TM are trademarks of the publisher. Trademarks indicated with ® are registered in the United States Patent and Trademark Office, the Canadian Trade Marks Office and in other countries.

www.eHarlequin.com

Printed in U.S.A.

Dear Reader,

Thank you so much for choosing *Dancing on Sunday Afternoons!* It has been a part of my life for a long while, and I hope it finds a place in yours, as well. I grew up Italian in America, surrounded by a large and tightly connected family. Like many eighteen-year-olds, I emphatically tried to distance myself from the neighborhood that had both defined and confined me growing up. I left home to go to college in Boston during the sixties (allowing me to leave was an act of courage for my parents, who were defying a culture that kept its daughters close to home). I wandered far from my Italian roots for a while, earning a master's degree at Harvard (where there weren't very many people with vowels at the end of their names), traveling to Europe and Africa, and marrying a German. It was many years later, through a serendipitous gift, that I journeyed back to that neighborhood and found the inspiration for this book you now hold in your hands.

The seeds for *Dancing on Sunday Afternoons* were a packet of letters given to me as a gift thirteen years ago. I was living in Germany at the time with my family and we had traveled back to the States for our annual Christmas visit. While I was sitting in my aunt Susie's kitchen one December afternoon drinking coffee and munching on one of her famous *mostaccioli* cookies, she told me that she'd been saving something important for me, the oldest grandchild in the family. She handed me the letters. "You'll know what to do with them," she said, smiling. I recounted the experience later that week to my parents, and to my surprise, my mother jumped up and retreated to the bedroom. "We have some, too," she told me, giving me another stack.

I flew back to Germany early in January with nearly two dozen letters and spent the winter with a notepad and an Italian dictionary, translating words that had been written seventy years before by my grandparents when they had been courting in secret, hiding their love from her family, who disapproved of him. In those letters I discovered a man I had never known—my grandfather—and a young woman I'd known only as a formidable matriarch. I sent the translations back to my father and his sister—a gift returned many times over, I realized. But I was fascinated by these two eloquent lovers and was inspired to create a story around this fragment of their history. That story is what you will find in *Dancing on Sunday Afternoons*.

I came to Harlequin Everlasting Love because the description of the new line resonated with me. I saw immediately how my story of Giulia Fiorillo and her two husbands captured the complexity and richness of lifelong love that this line intends to portray. I am especially excited that *Dancing on Sunday Afternoons* is one of its first books and I look forward to writing more.

I look forward, as well, to hearing from you. You can reach me at P.O. Box 298, Enfield, CT 06083–0298, or by logging on to my Web site at www.lindacardillo.com.

Warmly,

Linda Cardillo

PROLOGUE

Two Husbands
Giulia D'Orazio
1983

I had two husbands—Paolo and Salvatore.

Salvatore and I were married for thirty-two years. I still live in the house he bought for us; I still sleep in our bed. All around me are the signs of our life together. My bedroom window looks out over the garden he planted. In the middle of the city, he coaxed tomatoes, peppers, zucchini—even grapes for his wine—out of the ground. On weekends, he used to drive up to his cousin's farm in Waterbury and bring back manure. In the winter, he wrapped the peach tree and the fig tree with rags and black rubber hoses against the cold, his massive, coarse hands gentling those trees as if they were his fragile-skinned babies. My neighbor, Dominic Grazza, does that for me now. My boys have no time for the garden.

In the front of the house, Salvatore planted roses. The roses I take care of myself. They are giant, cream-colored, fragrant. In the afternoons, I like to sit out on the porch with my coffee, protected from the eyes of the neighborhood by that curtain of flowers.

Salvatore died in this house thirty-five years ago. In the last months, he lay on the sofa in the parlor so he could be in the middle of everything. Except for the two oldest boys, all the children were still at home and we ate together every evening. Salvatore could see the dining-room table from the sofa, and he could hear everything that was said. "I'm not dead, yet," he told me. "I want to know what's going on."

When my first grandchild, Cara, was born, we brought her to him, and he held her on his chest, stroking her tiny head. Sometimes they fell asleep together.

Over on the radiator cover in the corner of the parlor is the portrait Salvatore and I had taken on our twenty-fifth anniversary. This brooch I'm wearing today, with the diamonds— I'm wearing it in the photograph also—Salvatore gave it to me that day. Upstairs on my dresser is a jewelry box, filled with necklaces and bracelets and earrings. All from Salvatore.

I am surrounded by the things Salvatore gave me, or did for me. But, God forgive me, as I lie alone now in my bed, it is Paolo I remember.

Paolo left me nothing. Nothing, that is, that my family, especially my sisters, thought had any value. No house. No diamonds. Not even a photograph.

But after he was gone, and I could catch my breath from the pain, I knew that I still had something. In the middle of the night, I sat alone and held them in my hands, reading the words over and over until I heard his voice in my head. I had Paolo's letters.

CHAPTER 1

The Cigar Box
Cara Serafini Dedrick
1983

The phone call didn't come at two in the morning, but it might as well have. I was on my way out the door of my office at four, hoping to catch an early train out of Penn Station and make it home to New Jersey for an early start to my vacation. I run a catering company in Manhattan called Artichoke and in the last weeks of August my clients have retreated to their summer homes, giving me and my staff a breather before fall. Celeste, my secretary, waved to get my attention, receiver nestled between her ear and her capable shoulder.

"It's your mother."

"Tell her I'll call when I get home—got to make the 4:25."

"She says it can't wait. A family emergency."

My body stiffened and I could feel the color drain from my face. My mother was not the kind of woman who called with reports of every hospitalization or divorce or out-of-wedlock pregnancy in our large extended family. With eighteen aunts and uncles and twenty-nine first cousins, plus both grand-mothers, there was ample opportunity for a family emergency. But I trusted my mother's sense of what was urgent and what was merely news, and knew she wouldn't insist on talking to me now if it wasn't someone close. Had my father gone into diabetic shock? Was my brother in a car accident?

I turned back to my desk and picked up the phone. "Mom?"

"Cara, thank God you're still there! It's Nana."

My father's mother, Giulia, was a robust woman in her nineties who ran circles around most of us. Three weeks before, against the wishes of all eight of her children, she'd flown to Italy to be at the bedside of her dying older sister. Zia Letitia—we used the Italian form to refer to the aunts of my grand-mother's generation—Zia Letitia had graciously managed to wait until Nana arrived before taking her last breath. After she died, Nana had assumed the task of arranging her funeral and organizing her financial affairs. Zia Letitia had been a widow and her only son had died many years before, so there was no one left in the family to wrap up the loose ends of her long life except for Nana. As far as I knew, those tasks were almost finished and she was expected back early the next week.

"What's happened?" I couldn't imagine what could have disrupted my grandmother's determined and vigorous grasp on life.

"She fell last night. It was in Zia Letitia's house. She was alone, and no one found her until this morning. Emma, the woman who looked after Zia Letitia, called to let us know."

"Oh, my God! Is she all right? Where is she now?"

"They got her to a hospital in Avellino, but apparently she's broken her hip. She needs surgery. We thought we could fly her home, but the doctors there said it was too dangerous— the risk of an embolism's too high. Which is why I'm calling you." So it was more than just to inform me of my grand-mother's accident.

"What do you mean?"

"We don't want her to go through this alone. It was one thing for her to go off by herself to hold her sister's hand, but now it's simply out of the question. I'd go, but with Daddy needing dialysis every three days, there's no way I can leave him. Nobody else in the family has ever been to Italy—I don't think they even have passports.

"Honey, you've lived in Italy, you speak Italian, and she'd listen to you sooner than one of her children, anyway. I need you to say *yes* about this, especially for Daddy's sake. He's angry with her for going in the first place, angry with himself for letting her go, and now he's feeling helpless—although he won't admit it—because he can't go and rescue his mother. Will you do this, Cara?"

"Do you realize what you're asking me to do?" I groaned. I thought of the two weeks left of summer that I'd planned on spending with my kids. A week at the shore, then a week getting ready for school.

"If you're worried about the kids, I can look after them for a few days, and Paul and Jeannie offered to take them to her mother's house at the lake. There really is no one else who can do this, Cara. I know you think of Nana as formidable and in-destructible, but she's in a precarious state."

I listened in silence, watching the minutes pass on the clock on my desk. I'd already missed any chance of making my train. I was both dismayed at my grandmother's situation and frus-trated that the competence and independence I had developed in my life apart from my family were now the very things pulling me back. I did not want to go. But I knew I would. I fought the resentment that I was the one my mother had turned to—me, with a very full plate of full-time job and four children—when she could have asked my sister or my cousin, both younger, freer, teachers with summers off and no children. But I was also proud that she'd called on me, knowing she was right when she said I was the only one who could do this.

"I'll need to talk to Andrew and sort everything out with the kids. I'll ask Celeste to book me on a flight to Rome tomorrow and I'll take the train from there to Avellino. Do you have some contact information for me—the hospital, Emma?"

I heard my mother exhale in relief.

"Thank you, honey. I knew I could count on you. I've got all the numbers right here. Let me read them off to you."

I spent the next half hour writing down the information provided by my mother, phoning my husband and giving Celeste the task of getting me to Italy within the next forty-eight hours. I finally collapsed in a seat in the second-to-last car on the 5:43 to Princeton, scribbling lists to myself and trying to remember a language I had not spoken regularly in seventeen years.

The next afternoon, with my husband and children heading off to Beach Haven, my bag packed and my passport in my purse, I drove up to my parents' house in Mount Vernon, just outside New York City. When my mother had called Giulia that morning to tell her I was coming, Giulia had dictated a list for me—things to do, things to bring. I picked up the list and the key to Giulia's house from my parents and said my goodbyes, recognizing the gratitude in my father's eyes despite his gruff warnings about watching out for both my grandmother and myself.

I left my parents' neighborhood of manicured lawns and stately colonials and drove south to the neighborhood my grandmother had lived in since she'd arrived in America. I climbed the steep steps to Giulia's front porch, past the rose garden her husband Salvatore—my father's stepfather—had planted for her in the middle years of their marriage, well before I was born. With Giulia in Italy for the last three weeks, many of the blooms were long past their peak. Had Giulia been here, I know she would've trimmed the flopping, untidy heads.

I let myself in the front door, but not before glancing up and down this so-familiar street. To my right, a row of pale stucco houses, many of which Giulia owned. To my left, the beginnings of commerce—the butcher, the barber, Skippy's Bar & Grill—and on the corner, Our Lady of Victory elementary school. I remembered how one frigid November morning, when I was in kindergarten, I had dutifully exited in a silent, straight line as we'd been trained by the nuns to do when the fire alarm sounded. I'd been careful to line up along the side of the building, trying to keep still in the cold. It had been at that moment that Giulia had emerged from Lauricella's grocery store across the street and observed the shivering children and the sisters bundled in their black shawls.

"Where is your coat? How could that nun let you outside in this weather without your coat?" Giulia stood on the sidewalk and scolded me from across the street.

She was making a spectacle and I was mortified. The only modestly saving grace was that she was speaking in Italian, but her gesturing and agitation were clearly understood by the nuns and my classmates.

"Go back inside this minute and get your coat!"

I wanted to explain to her that this was a fire drill, but was afraid to speak, afraid to break the rules so dramatically presented to us by Sister Agatha as a matter of life and death. Six hundred children had burned to death at Our Lady of the Angels in Chicago because they hadn't followed the rules.

My grandmother knew none of this. She knew only that her grandchild was shivering and the woman responsible for her was ignoring that.

I had watched in horror as Giulia crossed the street, removing her own coat and ready to wrap it around me, when the bell rang and we began to retrace our steps back into the building.

Now, inside Giulia's house, I adjusted to the dim light of the long front hall. The portrait of the Sacred Heart, his hands spreading his cloak to reveal his throbbing scarlet heart, still hung in its place of honor above the radiator.

The house smelled of ammonia and wax and lemon oil. I was sure Giulia had scrubbed and polished meticulously before she left, leaving the house spotless, reflecting her own sense of order.

My sandaled feet echoed in the silent house as I walked down the hall. Although what I'd come for was upstairs in Giulia's bedroom, I went first to the kitchen.

Check the sink, the freezer, the pilot light on the stove, she had instructed. Make sure the back door is secured. Dominic Grazza, her neighbor who was supposed to be watching the house, wasn't as reliable as she would like.

But all was as it should be. I drew myself a glass of water and sat in the red vinyl chair at the small table tucked into the alcove formed by the chimney wall. The table was only large enough for two. Through an archway was the larger table where supper was served, but at noon, when it had only been my grandmother and me, it was at this small table that we'd eaten together. I attended the morning session of kindergarten and came to her house every school day for lunch and to spend the afternoon. She always had ready a warm bowl of her homemade chicken soup or *pasta e fagioli*.

After lunch, when the dishes were dried and put away, I had remained at the table, my back against the warm wall, and watched and listened as women from the neighborhood came for my grandmother's magic.

We called it the "eyes"—her spells to ward off headaches and stomach cramps; to bring on a late period; to counteract whatever curse had been set upon the suffering soul knocking at my grandmother's back door.

It wasn't just the immigrants who came. My own mother, my aunts, women who worked in banks and offices and got dressed in suits and stockings and high heels every day, made their way to her kitchen. There she'd lay her hands on them and dispel the pain with her incantations. When I was sick, the fever and nausea and loneliness flew from my troubled body into my grandmother's open and welcoming arms.

Later in the afternoon, she always went upstairs to sleep, exhausted and without words.

I would retreat to the living room, knowing it was time to be quiet, and watch "The Mickey Mouse Club" until my father came to pick me up at the end of the day.

My afternoons with Giulia were an arrangement put in place because my own neighborhood had no Catholic school. Sending me to kindergarten in a public school was not an option in our family, so I spent the first year of my education in Giulia's parish until my family moved uptown. Everyone seemed happy with the solution, especially my mother, home with two younger children and relieved of the burden of getting me to and from school every day.

I finished my water, carefully rinsed and dried my glass and replaced it in the cupboard. My responsibilities in the kitchen were fulfilled, and I walked slowly up the stairs to the back of the house, where Giulia's bedroom overlooked the backyard and the garden. On her dresser were propped more images of saints. In front of them were three small red glass pots holding votive candles. It was the first time I'd been in the house when

Giulia wasn't there, and it was a disturbing reminder of her absence that the candles were unlit. I pulled out Giulia's list and began to open drawers, tugging at the wood swollen with August humidity. Her checkbook and accounts ledger were in the top drawer, as expected. I had to hunt for the sweater she thought she'd need now that the evening air in the mountains was beginning to chill with the approach of September. A few more small articles of clothing were easier to find. The last item on the list was identified simply as a "cigar box" that was supposed to be in the bottom drawer under some bed linens. I was expecting another set of the flower-sprigged percale sheets and pillowcases that were on her neatly made bed, but these bed linens were heavy white cotton, elaborately tucked and embroidered with Giulia's large and graceful monogram. I had never seen them on her bed. Small packets of cedar were scattered in the drawer and the pungent smell indicated to me that the drawer had not been opened in a long time. I lifted the linens and found a box-like shape wrapped in another embroidered cloth. When I unwrapped the cloth, I saw that I had indeed found the cigar box.

It was papered in garish yellow and brown with the portrait of some nineteenth-century barrel-chested tobacco mogul on the cover, and a Spanish label. The box had once held Cuban cigars, but I was sure it wasn't cigars I was bringing to Giulia.

I sat on the floor and carefully lifted the cover. Inside the box were stacks of letters on pale blue notepaper, each stack tied with a thin strand of satin ribbon. I could see that the letters had been written in a flowing hand in Italian and signed *Paolo,* the father my father had been too young to know, the grandfather whose red hair I had inherited.

I closed the box, feeling I'd already gone too far, that I had violated the privacy of a very private woman. Why she would want me to remove these letters from what appeared to be a hiding place and carry them across the Atlantic to her was both perplexing and intriguing. The woman who was asking me to do this was not the woman I knew my grandmother to be— the matriarch of our very large family, who had not only her sons and daughters, but her nieces and nephews, grown men and women in their fifties and sixties, listening to her and deferring to her as if they were still children; the businesswoman who'd asked me to collect her mail as well as her checkbook so she could manage her real-estate investments from her hospital bed; the woman who could be counted on to have a sharp opinion and directive about everything that touched the lives of her children and grandchildren.

Perhaps because I'd been a baby when her husband Salvatore had died and I had only known Giulia as a widow, I could not fathom her ever being in love. I knew, of course, that she'd been married before Salvatore to Paolo Serafini. But that had been long ago, and whatever traces of him remaining in her memory were well hidden. We did not even have a photograph of Paolo.

Giulia had never seemed to have much use for love. She had warned me away from romantic entanglements more than once when I was a teenager.

"Stay away from Joey Costello," she told me one evening as we were shelling peas on her front porch. I was thirteen; Joey lived next door to her. He was a year older, full of the swagger and bravado of the good-looking Italian teenage boy. But he had noticed me and was paying attention to me in ways that I, bookish and reserved, found thrilling.

"He's nothing but trouble. You don't need to be hanging around the likes of him. At the very least, you'll get a reputation, like that *putana* of a sister he has. And at the worst, he'll break your heart as soon as somebody who can sway her hips better than you walks by him. You're too smart, Cara *mia*. Don't waste your time on boys like that."

Later, when I was sixteen and spending a week with her while my parents were away, I developed a crush on a neighbor who lived nearby, one of her tenants. He was married and in his twenties, with two small children. But he did chores for Giulia around the garden and the house, so he was around to talk to as he fixed a faucet or dug up some rosebushes she wanted to transplant. He was cute and funny and attentive and, in the short time I'd been there, it seemed to me he was finding quite a few things to do for Giulia. When his wife went to visit her mother with the kids, I suggested to my grandmother that we invite him to Sunday dinner.

"Phil's all alone today. Wouldn't it be nice to ask him to eat with us?" I was trying to sound like the gracious lady of the manor, bestowing kindness on the hired help, rather than the infatuated teenager I was, looking for any reason to be in his presence. I was nonchalant, mentioning it as an afterthought as she and I cleaned up after breakfast.

Giulia looked me in the eye, put her hands on her hips, and said, "Absolutely not. Don't think I don't know what's going on in your head. He's a married man. He stays in his house and eats what his wife left for him, and you put your daydreams in the garbage where they belong."

And that was that. I spent the day sulking at the lost opportunity and marveling at Giulia's ability to sense even the most subtle vibrations of sexual attraction. She was the watchdog at the gates of my virginity, the impenetrable shield that would keep me from becoming a tramp.

Now I gathered up Giulia's possessions and stowed them in the zippered tote bag I planned to take onboard the plane. After a final glance around the room, I shut the door and headed down the stairs and out to my car. I pulled away from the curb and the memories and headed for the airport and Italy.

CHAPTER 2

Journey to the Mezzogiorno

The cacophony of the Naples train station assaulted me as soon as I stepped off the express train from Rome. Announcements of departing trains reverberated across the vaulted space; mothers scolded misbehaving children; whistles shrieked; a group of yellow-shirted boys kicked a soccer ball near the far end of Platform 22.

As I adjusted the strap of my bag, I also adjusted my mental state—from efficient New York manager and organized mother of four—to Italian. It was more than recalling the lyrical language that had surrounded me in Giulia's house. I knew I had to pour myself quickly into the fluid, staccato pace of Campania in August or I would be trampled—by the surging population, the Vespas leaping curbs, the suspicion of strangers and by my own sense of oppression.

I knew this because I'd been here seventeen years before, a bright-eyed high-school art student who'd spent the summer in the rarefied atmosphere of Florence, living in a *cinquecento* villa, painting in the Uffizi on Mondays when it was closed to the hordes of summer tourists, reading Dante and Boccaccio. I had believed that I knew Italy. But then I had come south, to visit Zia Letitia.

I had traveled by rail then as well, through Rome to Naples. A stifling heat had encroached on the overcrowded train as it journeyed farther south, toward an Italy that I didn't recognize. The blue-greens and purples of the Tuscan landscape, warmed by a honeyed light, had given way to an unrelenting sunshine that had seared the earth to an ocher barrenness.

Everything I saw seemed to be the same color—the rough-hewn cliffs, the crumbling houses, the worn faces.

When I'd arrived at midday in Naples—sweaty and cranky—I felt myself to be in a foreign country. For the first time in my life, I had felt menaced—by the drivers in minuscule Fiats who ignored traffic signals, by the barricaded expressions of the people massing and knotting around me, by the heat and clamor and stench that had so unraveled the beauty and civility of this once-splendid city. The life of Naples was in the streets—raw, intemperate, flamboyant—and to the eyes of strangers, emotionally closed and hostile.

That day seventeen years ago, I had escaped on the two o'clock bus to Avellino, arriving two hours later in front of a bar named the Arcobaleno. In contrast to the press of humanity in Naples, a melancholy emptiness greeted me here. In the bar, where I bought a Coke and sought a telephone, I was the only woman. Two old men in the corner interrupted their card game to stare openly; the younger men, playing pinball, were more surreptitious but watched just as closely.

I called a phone number given to me by Giulia to make arrangements with a distant relative who could take me to Letitia. But the woman who answered was irritable. She had no time and could not help me. I would have to manage on my own. Take the bus, she barked. Just tell the driver you need to go to Venticano. And she hung up.

Shaken and feeling increasingly alone, I'd found a bus that could take me up the mountain. Later than I'd hoped, the driver cranked the door closed and began the laborious climb out of the valley. He'd brought the bus to a halt in a deserted piazza and thrust his chin at the door to announce my destination. Within seconds I stood alone in the road, facing shuttered houses and an overwhelming sense of abandonment. Why had I even considered making this journey? I had naively traversed half the length of Italy expecting to be welcomed in my ancestral home but instead the doors were locked and no one was willing to acknowledge me as their own.

With only Zia Letitia's name—no address—I had approached a woman darning in the doorway of a nearby house, whose wary eyes had been upon me since I'd descended from the bus.

"I am looking for Signora Letitia Rassina," I had explained, proud of my flawless High Italian, the only thing that stood between me and panic.

"You come from the north." It was a statement, spat out in distrust and contempt, not a question requiring confirmation.

"I studied in Firenze, but I come from America. I am the granddaughter of Signora Rassina's sister." Unwittingly, I had uttered the magic formula.

The guardedness and suspicion fled from her face. She took me by the arm.

"Come, I'll show you where the signora lives."

As we turned to walk down the hill, I saw faces appearing at suddenly unshuttered windows and heard voices calling out to the woman. Within minutes, nearly thirty people crowded around us, jostling for a glimpse of the Americana as we arrived at Letitia's house.

The house—ancient, once elegant—presented a silent facade to the tumult in the street below. No one responded to our energetic knocks and shouts.

"She must be sleeping. Giorgio, go around and get Emma."

"Emma takes care of your aunt, and she has a key to the house," she explained to me.

A few minutes later, smoothing down what seemed to be a hastily donned black dress, a middle-aged woman had hustled breathlessly after Giorgio with a key ring in her hand.

"No one sent me word from America that someone was coming!" She was both suspicious and injured to have been left out of the preparations for my visit.

Horrified that I'd been allowed by my family to travel alone, she was nevertheless satisfied that I was indeed Giulia's grand-daughter. With a shriek of pleasure, she inserted an iron key into the massive arched doorway of the house.

Inside was a musty vestibule, lit by the late-afternoon sun streaming through a window on the rear wall where a stone staircase led to a landing on the second floor. Emma led me up the stairs. Behind us came the rest of the villagers.

Once again, our knocks were met by silence. Emma called out Letitia's name in a loud voice. "She's old. She doesn't hear so well anymore," she murmured to me.

Finally, the door opened and a woman appeared, her face marked by confusion. She stared uncomprehending into my face. I stared back at a woman who could have been my grand-mother's twin. Letitia's confusion receded as she listened to me identify myself, ignoring the commotion that surrounded her. Then she reached out and stroked the opal hanging from my ear. It was Giulia's, and she'd given it to me on my sixteenth birthday. I'd been wearing the earrings all summer, and they had become so much a part of me that I'd forgotten their origins.

"Giulia's earrings," she whispered. "You are my blood."

Letitia had pulled me into the apartment, embracing me with the mingled old-woman aromas of garlic and anise and must. She sent Emma down to the shop to purchase ingredients for dinner and told the villagers lining the stairs to go home to their own kitchens. Alone together, we sat with a glass of very strong wine as she hung on every word I brought her of her distant family.

After dinner a group of young women from the village had arrived at the door to take me for the evening *passeggiata*—a walk around the village. Letitia had shooed me away with them. Severia, the young woman who'd been my tour guide, was the schoolteacher in the village. I was stunned when she told me she was only twenty. Like Emma, and nearly every other woman in the village, she was dressed in a severe black dress that extended below her knees. She wore her hair in the style of my mother's generation.

The village was a grid of two or three streets clinging to the side of the mountain. Only the main road from Avellino that continued farther up the mountain was paved. Few of the stone buildings had electricity, and all of them showed the ravages of centuries of wind and earthquake. Dust swirled at our feet as we crossed the meager piazza, shared with a goatherd leading his scraggly flock back to a lean-to for the evening. Severia had pointed out with pride the small schoolroom where she taught from first through sixth grade. If parents wanted more schooling for their children, they had to send them down the mountain to Avellino.

I had recognized that what I was seeing and the lives that

were enclosed here were little different from what Giulia had experienced as a girl. In that instant, I had understood that it might have been my life as well.

"Thank God," I had whispered to myself. "Thank God that my grandmother got out."

The next morning I left, as I had come, on a dusty bus that had stopped when Emma flagged it down. She'd packed me a cloth-wrapped sandwich of bread and pungent cheese, with some tomatoes and figs from the garden behind Letitia's stone house. She had clucked and worried about the long trip ahead of me to Milan and my flight home and had given me stern instructions to speak to no one on the way to Naples.

"Girls alone disappear," she had said.

As the bus pulled away, I had looked out the window. Letitia stood waving from her balcony. She had changed from her morning housecoat to a green silk dress. In her hand was a lace-trimmed handkerchief that she dabbed at her eyes.

I stood now in the rotunda of the Naples *Stazione Centrale,* about to make the same journey. This time, instead of depending on SITA buses to get me up to the mountains, I had reserved a car. But before picking it up, I detoured to the flower shop, hoping to find something that would survive until I reached Avellino. The saleswoman recommended a potted hydrangea and wrapped it extravagantly in layers of purple cellophane and a massive bow, wishing my grandmother *buona sante* as she handed me the gift with a nod of approval.

Armed with a map and directions outlined for me by the clerk at Avis, I located my Fiat in the parking lot, took a deep breath and plunged into the late Sunday afternoon traffic, keeping an eye out for the Autostrada symbol and signs for the A16, the east-west highway that connected Naples with Bari on the Adriatic. About a quarter of the way across the ankle of

Italy's boot, I knew I'd leave the highway and head south into the mountains and Avellino.

I was tired and hungry. My jetlag was catching up with me. A part of me longed to stop at the Agip motel on the broad avenue leading toward the entrance ramp of the Autostrada. Its familiar sign, a black, six-legged, fire-breathing mythical creature on a yellow background, beckoned like a McDonald's Golden Arch, promising a cheap, clean room. But Giulia was expecting me at the hospital Sunday evening, and even though there'd be little I could do for her at that time—no surgeon to confer with, only a night nurse on duty—I pushed myself past the fatigue to be at my grandmother's side.

The highway had not existed seventeen years ago, and I was astounded that I was able to cover the hundred kilometers to Avellino in under an hour, compared to the nearly three hours it had taken the bus on my last trip. When I exited the highway, a sign welcomed me in four different languages.

When I drove onto the grounds of the hospital of San Giuseppe Moscati, the doctor saint of Naples, it was nearly sunset.

I grabbed the hydrangea and my tote bag from the back seat and headed into the hospital, moving from the brilliance and shimmer of light and heat that had surrounded me all day into shadowed dimness. Everything in the lobby was in shades of brown, like the sepia tones Renaissance artists used to create the sinopia, the preliminary sketch under a fresco. The highly polished linoleum, the wooden paneling that climbed three-quarters of the way up the whitewashed walls, the tattered seats in the waiting room, even the habit of the Franciscan nun sitting at the reception desk, created an aura of subdued and quiet sanctuary.

She looked up as I approached. When I asked for my grandmother, she jumped up.

"Oh, we've been expecting you! The *signora* was telling

everyone that you were coming. Let me call Reverend Mother. She can explain your grandmother's condition before you go up to see her."

Within minutes, Reverend Mother, an energetic and ageless woman and the director of the hospital, swooped into the lobby and kissed me on both cheeks.

"Can I get you some tea, my dear, while we talk about your grandmother? Come, let's go to my office."

I sank into the chair she offered and gratefully accepted the hot cup of tea that she produced within a minute.

On her desk was a file on which I could read my grandmother's name. I was beginning to feel—with some relief, given my fatigue—that Giulia had things under control here, if she had the hospital so well prepared for my arrival.

"Your grandmother is quite a formidable woman, as I'm sure you know. She was very busy the last two days keeping us all informed of your coming. I believe she feels a need to protect and watch out for you. But I must tell you, my dear, she needs *you* to watch over *her,* although she'd be the last to admit it. She's in a weakened state because of the night she spent alone after her fall—we've been replenishing her fluids with an IV, but at her age, even twelve hours of dehydration can be damaging. She was disoriented when she got here. She has recovered her faculties enough to issue edicts and lists, I understand, but I have to caution you that your grandmother has a long road ahead to recover from this fall. In many cases, with patients of this age, we would not even be considering a hip replacement."

I absorbed Reverend Mother's report in silence, gradually comprehending the gravity of my grandmother's condition.

"I hadn't realized how serious this fall was," I murmured. "I naively believed I was asked to be here as a companion to her."

"I'm not trying to overwhelm you and burden you so soon after your arrival, but I felt it was important for you to understand the severity of her injury and to warn you before you see her. She's quite bruised and also very angry with herself for falling. We've also had to increase her morphine dosage because of the pain, so she may begin to drift.

"The surgeon will be in tomorrow morning at eight o'clock and can give you the details about her operation. More than likely he will operate on Tuesday morning."

I nodded, understanding that I would need to be an advocate for my grandmother.

"May I ask you if you've booked a place to stay? If not, I'd like to encourage you to stay here with your grandmother. We can have a cot set up in her room. In my opinion, it would be a blessing for her to have you so close."

I set down my teacup because my hand was shaking. With four children, I'd seen my share of emergency rooms, and my youngest had been hospitalized for four days with pneumonia, so I was no stranger to the emotional fragility caused by illness and the need for a family member to be close at hand. But despite my confidence in Giulia's ability to control even this situation, Reverend Mother had quickly and authoritatively set me straight.

I leaned my elbows on her desk and put my head in my hands. I felt the adrenaline of the last two days seeping out of me and tears of exhaustion and doubt well up. Reverend Mother came around her desk with a handkerchief and put an arm around me.

"Everything Signora D'Orazio has said about you convinces me that your family has sent the right person. Why don't I show you where you can wash your face and then let's go see your grandmother."

Once again, she whisked me down the hall, this time to the ladies' room. When I was ready, we took the elevator up to the orthopedic floor. As we passed open doors, I saw and heard clusters of people gathered around patients' beds, family members taking advantage of the Sunday-evening visiting hours, and was relieved that now Giulia would have someone at her bedside, too, even if what I could offer was simply a voice and a face from home.

Reverend Mother knocked at a partially opened door.

"Signora D'Orazio, she's here! Your granddaughter is here!"

I willed a smile to my face and walked into the room.

"Nana," I said. "It's me, Cara."

She turned toward the door and reached out her hand. I was glad Reverend Mother had prepared me, but even so, her bruised and swollen face and the black-and-blue marks on her arm appalled me. She looked as if someone had beaten her, and then I remembered the stone steps in Letitia's house.

I went to her, put the hydrangea on the floor and threw my arms around her, careful of the IV and reluctant to hold her too tightly for fear of hurting her sore body.

"How good you are to be here!" she whispered.

I sat on the side of her bed and she stroked my hair, by now flying out of its ponytail. She rubbed my bare arms, as if assuring herself that I was truly there.

Reverend Mother left us, letting me know that she was going to order the cot.

Shortly afterward, Giulia's supper tray arrived. When the nun bringing the food saw that I was there, she said she'd call down to the kitchen and have them send something for me. In the meantime, I busied myself with cutting meat and buttering bread for Giulia. She waved me away when I lifted a spoonful of soup to her mouth.

"I didn't break my arm, for God's sake. Just help me sit up a little higher so I don't dribble all over myself."

This was the Giulia I knew, and it was a relief to have her scold me.

By the time we'd both eaten, an aide had delivered a cot, sheets and pillows and made up a bed by Giulia's side. I went down to my car and retrieved my suitcase and then stole a few minutes to peel off the clothes I'd been wearing for two days and take a shower in a bathroom down the hall from Giulia's room that the aide had pointed out to me.

When I rejoined Giulia, she'd had her evening medication, and some of the strain I'd seen in her face was eased. She beamed at me. I was now scrubbed, my hair neatly braided, and wearing fresh clothes.

"Sweetheart, did you bring the things I asked for?"

I patted the tote bag. "It's all in here, Nana. Do you want anything now?"

She wavered, but then threw up her hands as if surrendering to an irresistible need.

"The box. The cigar box. You found it, where I said to look?"

I nodded and dug it out of the bag. "Here it is, Nana."

She took the box and stroked the outside of it, tracing the colorful image of Francisco Fonseca. Then she held the box to her breast, cradling it with her eyes shut. At last, she lifted the cover and stared at the stacks of letters before slipping one out from its ribbon binding. She closed the box and brought the single letter to her lips before unfolding it.

For a few moments I watched as she scanned the lines. I thought she was reading, but then she turned to me in restless exasperation.

"My eyes are no good at night. I can't see the words. Sweetheart, you've done so much, just to come, but do this for me. Read to me. Read me the letter."

She handed me the blue sheet of paper.

I took it hesitantly.

"Are you sure you want me to read this, Nana?"

She looked at me and the letter in my hand, agitation rising in her as she struggled between the absolute sanctity of the message in the letter and the urgency she felt to hear it again.

"I need to hear it tonight, Cara. Go ahead. I trust you."

And so I began to read the words on the page—an elegant, flowing Italian script. At first, my brain attempted to translate silently for myself as I read the Italian out loud, but after a few minutes, I stopped trying to decipher the meaning and simply pronounced the words. I felt as if I were singing a song whose soul and emotion were in the music, not the lyrics.

Dearest Giulia,

Don't forget what I asked you last night—to find five or ten minutes before noon. I have the most important things to communicate to you. If you only knew how much I suffered this morning, to go to work without even seeing you or telling you that I love you.

I am crazy with love. I have never loved with so much devotion. You are the star that shines brightly, a sparkling beam, and you adorn my poor heart with infinite madness. Now that I am writing to you, I believe I have you near me. It seems as if we are talking. How I long to embrace you!

I cover your face with my tears, and dry them with my kisses.
Most faithfully,
Paolo

When I finished, I glanced up. Giulia's eyes were closed and the agitation that had disturbed her earlier was gone. I gently removed the cigar box from her lap and put it on her bedside table. As I reached to turn out the light, she stirred and touched my wrist.

"*Grazie, figlia mia.*"

I slipped into the cot, the words of my grandfather Paolo echoing in my head.

CHAPTER 3

The Beginning

The next morning I accustomed myself to the weekday pace of San Giuseppe Moscati. Breakfast trays, medication, bath, changes of bed linen. I could see the distress in my grandmother's face, the tension in her body, as the procession of nurses' aides and nuns moved in and out of her room. She scolded a cleaning woman who attempted to move the cigar box of letters that I had placed on the bedside table.

"I'll put it in a safe place, Nana," I reassured her as the bustle around her continued. "We can read more later, when it's not so busy."

The surgeon showed up around ten. He was in his late thirties, a trim, athletic-looking man, wearing a stylish blue shirt under his white coat. His eyes, also blue, conveyed intelligence and compassion. After he'd checked on my grandmother, I conferred with him in the hall, along with Reverend Mother and the sister in charge of the orthopedic ward.

He had scheduled Giulia's surgery for Tuesday morning and felt she'd need at least ten days of recuperation before I could take her home. He explained the details of the operation and his expectations for her recovery. I brought up my concerns about her medication and the discomfort I was witnessing, and he agreed to make adjustments, giving the sisters some latitude in monitoring her painkillers. Within ten minutes he was gone.

Before returning to Giulia's room, I leaned against the wall in the corridor and considered what I had just heard. Ten days. This was more than I'd bargained for. More than I thought I could handle. I chafed at missing my family and our long-awaited week at the beach; I worried about upcoming projects at work; I wondered how I'd fill the long hours sitting at Giulia's bedside. But I'd made my choice. I'd said yes, I could do this. I walked back into Giulia's room.

She turned her head as I pushed open the door and she smiled.

"I was wondering where you were, sweetheart. I thought maybe I'd only dreamed you were here. But then I saw your valise in the corner and I told myself, 'You may be an old woman, but you're not a confused one.'"

I glanced at her IV and assured myself that it was flowing smoothly. Then I sat in the chair by her bedside. We talked about what the doctor had told me and I pressed her to be vocal when she was in too much pain.

"Don't suffer in silence, Nana. He's written orders to give you more painkillers if you need them, so speak up."

"I don't want to be in a haze, not knowing what's going on around me. Letitia didn't even know I was there at the end."

"This isn't the end for you, Nana! You have a broken hip,

not a terminal disease. Dr. Campobasso can replace it and you'll walk again, back in your own home."

"Okay. Okay. But if I start babbling like my crazy cousin Elena, you make them reduce the morphine. I'd rather have a little pain than be seeing visions at the foot of my bed."

I smiled and promised her as I stroked her hand. As I did so, her clenched fingers released their hold on the bedcovers.

"How about a cup of tea and I'll read you another letter?" She drew my hand to her lips and kissed it.

I went down the hall to the ward kitchen and poured two cups of tea into china cups and brought them back to her room on a tray. When she was settled, I retrieved the box and passed it to her so she could select a letter. She spent some time sifting through the fragile sheets. None of the letters were dated, and the envelopes had no postage or street address, only her name in a flourishing, emphatic script.

She finally pulled one out and gave it to me.

"This one." She leaned her head back and closed her eyes and I began to read.

Adorata Giulia,
I cannot explain in words how my heart beats for you. I dream of you all the time. If you love me as I love you, we would never suffer. We would always be happy. You have become the owner of my heart. I am yours. How can I give back all the love you show me? My love for you grows day by day and nothing can stop it, not even the anger and disapproval of your family. What have I done to these people that they don't want me?

My heart is full of love for you. I adore you and want to kneel at your feet. I will love you always, in spite of what others say.
I await your reply.
Paolo

I folded the letter again. Who was this passionate, intemperate man whose blood I carried in my veins? I gazed at my grandmother, the woman he had loved so desperately, who had so consumed him.

"Tell me about my grandfather, Nana. Why did he write you these letters?"

"We had secrets in those days, Paolo and I. Secrets we kept hidden, concealed. But that wasn't the beginning. The beginning was open and innocent, because I was not aware of what lay ahead—with him or my family. I was just a girl. A girl newly arrived in America who didn't want to be there. I believed my parents were punishing me by sending me to America. It was killing me, breaking my heart, to leave Italy."

She turned her face to the window; the late-morning light filtered through white curtains. Beyond lay the rock-strewn hills of her childhood.

"The beginning, the girl I was when I met Paolo, started out there." She thrust out her chin and gestured toward the window.

"My own grandmother Giuseppina was a *maga*. I suppose now people would call her a sorceress," Giulia began, and I listened.

CHAPTER 4

The Convent of Santa Margareta
Giulia

In my grandmother Giuseppina's garden grew the plants she mixed into her medicines; in her head lived the magic words she sang to release her spells; in her fingertips danced the powers she used to heal. She cured the pains and the sorrows of those who came to her, who asked her to speak for them to the saints.

She was known outside our village of Venticano. People came from Pietradefusi and Pano di Greci, some even from as far as Avellino. She turned no one away.

I have a distant memory—sometimes I think it was a dream. In it, Giuseppina, speaking to my mother, raised her very dark eyebrows and nodded in my direction. "I'm watching that one."

I was three years old, feeling only Giuseppina's eyes—loving and burning—upon me. Not long after, my mother was confined to bed with the twins she was carrying and everyone was sure she would lose. Giuseppina came that day with her daily infusion for my mother, which she always swallowed reluctantly. Giuseppina saw the state of affairs: my mother exhausted, sleepless, with barely enough will to get herself through the pregnancy, let alone pay attention to the youngest of her six children. My brother Claudio was the oldest, followed by my sisters, Letitia, Philippina (whom we called Pip), and Domitilla (whom we called Tilly) and then my brother Aldo and me. Even with my father's sister, Pasqualina, helping in the household, this seventh pregnancy was tapping all my mother's strength.

"You need more rest and less worry, Anna. It's Giulia. She's too much for you right now. The others, they're old enough, they take care of themselves, they obey Pasqualina, but not that one. You need peace and quiet, not listening with one ear to what's going on in the rest of the house.

"I'll bring Giulia to my house. I can take care of her better than Pasqualina with everything she has to do here. Now close your eyes. Don't even think about it. In a few months you'll have your babies and everything will be back to normal."

My mother, too drained to fight, acquiesced. That night, Giuseppina took me home with her. My mother delivered the twins—Giovanni and Frankie—early, but Giovanni was sickly and did not survive more than three months.

My mother's loss and subsequent depression gave Giuseppina more reason to keep me, and ultimately I stayed for seven years.

From my very first day in her house, I barely left her side. If we happened to be separated and she wanted me, she never called me. Somehow, whether she was across the room or across the courtyard, a voice inside my head spoke the name *Giuseppina* and I knew to look for her.

When I found her, she'd nod and touch my head with her hand, smudged with dirt from the roots of her plants and smelling of garlic and fennel. Maybe it was my nose that led me to Giuseppina. Giuseppina told me I had a "good" nose, that it was important to smell the sickness in order to identify it.

So many people came to her aching, unable to sleep, unable to eat. She put poultices on their sore muscles, gave them powders to bring on sleep or stimulate their appetites, and coaxed the pains out of their bodies with the touch of her hands. But as she murmured her spells, she was also listening to their stories, the secrets they knew were safe with her. Giuseppina absorbed their suffering, drawing it out of their bodies and taking it into her own.

Giuseppina's house was on the other side of the village piazza from my parents'. When they were first married, Papa and my mother had lived with Giuseppina. But my mother, distressed by the constant parade of sick and troubled people through the place, had cried to Papa that she needed her own house. My mother, too, had a sensitive nose, and she could not bear the smells so vital to Giuseppina's healing ways.

There were many other things my mother could not bear— untidiness, or inelegance, or ignorance. Especially ignorance. That's why she sent me to the Convent of Santa Margareta, with all my sisters—Letitia and Pip and Tilly—and took me away from Giuseppina.

"I let Giuseppina take Giulia seven years ago, but now it is time to reclaim my daughter," she told Papa.

My mother wanted us to be educated, to learn to read and write as she did. My Zia Pasqualina, Papa's sister, did not understand my mother's influence over Papa. My mother was not a woman who drew other women to rally around her—at least, not other women from Venticano. She came from the city, from Benevento. Every summer, she left my brothers and sisters with Zia Pasqualina, a childless widow, and Zia Teresia, her simple-minded younger sister. For all of August, my mother took the baths in Ischia with her childhood friends from Benevento. Papa's business provided the family with a comfortable life; he was the proprietor of the only livery stable in the mountains south of Avellino, with carriages that made deliveries and carried passengers. But Zia Pasqualina believed he indulged my mother in "extravagances."

My mother and Giuseppina argued about me. Giuseppina could see no use for the nuns and their teaching. She wanted Papa to let me stay in Venticano, but my mother was insistent.

"Felice, who can teach her here, in this pitiful school?" my mother demanded of Papa one night before he went off to his card game. "I want only the best for our children!"

Giuseppina, who could not read or write, stalked off from that battle with her head shaking. She told Papa he could bring me to the nuns, but he was a fool if he believed I'd learn anything from them. Papa's cousin Elisabetta was a sister at Santa Margareta. "Everybody knows how stupid she is," Giuseppina reminded Papa.

And so in August of 1900, even though much still needed to be harvested in Giuseppina's garden, Papa hitched up his best wagon, the one he used in his business for the daily trip to Napoli, and headed south with us to Sorrento. I did not cry as we departed the piazza and Giuseppina turned her back on my mother's dream. I did not cry as we rode through the gate of the Convent of Santa Margareta and were surrounded by walls twice as high as my head.

I never cried. Instead, I counted beans.

Beans like stones. We all took a handful from the bowl by the holy water when we came into the chapel at six in the morning. Sister Philomena watched. My hands were small. One morning, the beans spilled; Sister Philomena frowned and grunted. She was too fat to get down to help me pick them up. The big girls up front turned to frown also, except Pip, who buried her face in her hands, pretending to pray, trying to hide her shame that I was her sister.

I got on my knees, looking for all the beans. One had rolled far under the corner of the last pew, in the dark near the confessional where the padre sat on Friday mornings. I left it. Perhaps it would sprout in the dirt and the damp, send its tendrils out around the ankle of a sinner.

I went to my place in the row with the rest of my class. Sister Philomena followed me, watched as I set my beans in two piles on the stone floor and then knelt on top of the beans. Satisfied, she heaved herself into her priedieu and made the sign of the cross.

The beans were supposed to be a reminder to us of Christ's suffering on the cross; a small sacrifice to offer up as penance for whatever transgressions we had committed as sinful girls.

Nobody else wriggled or shifted against the hard white lumps biting into our knees. But I felt them. I didn't pretend they weren't there. Sometimes, when Sister Philomena wasn't paying attention, I scooped the beans into my pocket and stuck my tongue out at anyone who noticed. In the classroom, I was just as fidgety. I hated sitting still to recite lessons or listen to the endless droning of the nuns. To relieve my boredom I drew caricatures of Reverend Mother in the margins of my notebook. The girls sitting nearby would whisper and point and giggle, breaking up the monotony of the day, even if it meant a scolding.

One morning after breakfast, it was gray outside the high windows of the refectory. In that entire convent, there were no windows low enough to sit by and look out to see the garden, the trees or the hills beyond the walls.

I cleared away my dish and cup and took the broom from the cupboard. It was my day to sweep. I swept the crumbs from the corners and under the tables and moved toward the door to the loggia. Sister Elisabetta, Papa's cousin, unlocked the bolt so I could push the crumbs outside. She was supposed to wait and then bolt the door again when I was finished. But there was a crash from the kitchen and the hysterical screams of too many girls, so she rushed off with the keys in her hand and I was still outside, listening to the drizzle beyond the loggia, breathing in air that wasn't stale with the sleep and whispers of all the girls in that house.

The kitchen garden was on this side—clumps of basil and parsley and rosemary and oregano, just like Giuseppina's. It had always been my job to pick the basil for her gravy, parsley for the brazziola and the meatballs.

I peeked back into the building and saw no sign of Elisabetta. She was still fixing the disaster in the kitchen. So I dragged the heavy door closed behind me and turned, stepping off the loggia and into the garden.

The path was brick, slippery from the rain and the snails, but I raced along it, faster and faster the farther I got from the house. I raced past the garden and then off the path through the orchard of oranges and apricots and olives.

It began to rain harder. The raindrops pummeled my face, washing away the milk that had dried above my lip. Pip always gestured, exasperated, across the refectory, trying to get my attention. She'd pick up her napkin and in large gestures, demonstrate how I was to wipe my mouth like a lady.

My legs kept moving, carrying me beyond the orchard to the pond. I unbuttoned my shoes and peeled off my stockings and sank into the mud at the edge of the water. A family of ducks rose up squawking. I waded into the water. My dress billowed around me. I leaned back and floated, my arms stretched out, my mouth open to the rain, the clouds in my mind cleared away by the stillness. I was alone. I was free.

I don't know how long I floated before Aurelio, the old gardener, came along the path trundling his muddy wheelbarrow, singing hoarsely. He was not bent like the old men in our village, but stood tall and straight. His yellow-white hair stuck out from beneath a brown wool cap.

He sang his song—a hymn we sometimes sang to the Blessed Virgin—over and over again until he stopped suddenly in the middle of a verse. His hoe and scythe fell to the rocks and his boots sloshed into the water.

The mud at the bottom sucked at his feet and turned the water into a murky soup the color of lentils. When the water became too deep, he thrashed and pushed his way toward me and scooped me up in his arms. All this time, I had listened with my eyes shut tight against the rain, against this rescue.

Aurelio carried me through the water and put me down tenderly on the matted reeds near where I'd left my shoes and stockings. He placed two fingers on my neck and bent his ear to listen for my breath. Although I could hold my breath for a long time (I always won in contests with my brothers), I did not know how to stop my heart from beating. So I couldn't pretend to be dead. I fluttered my eyes and opened them and Aurelio knelt by my side and sobbed. I could see the skin around his neck, rubbed raw by the blackened chain he wore as a penance for some long-forgotten sin.

"*Mi dispiace,*" I whispered. *I am sorry.* I hadn't meant to frighten him. I had only wanted to be outside. To smell the earth. To feel the water holding me.

He reached into his pocket and pulled out an orange. He peeled it with his fingers, digging into the center to tear back the skin with his thumbnail, broken and embedded with the loam of the garden. When it was all peeled—a single spiral coil—he broke the orange into sections and held them out in his palm. I took one and bit into it, the juice exploding into my mouth and dribbling down my chin. I hadn't tasted an orange since I'd been at home with Giuseppina. Giuseppina sliced her oranges across with a knife, making circles of different sizes. Aurelio didn't use a knife, just his hands.

The rain was coming down harder, filling my shoes and the wheelbarrow, sticking my muddy dress to my back and flattening my curly hair. I was happy. For the first time since I'd been at Santa Margareta.

In the distance, past the fruit trees, toward the house, I heard the sound of the bell and then the muffled notes of my own name. They were looking for me.

Aurelio heard it, too. He got up from his haunches and tossed the orange skin onto a pile of rotting weeds. He dumped the water out of my shoes and placed them with my stockings in the wheelbarrow, then piled his tools on top.

He held out his hand and helped me to my feet. Together we walked back to the convent, leaving the quiet of the rain dancing on the surface of the pond, slowly crossing the orchard toward the clamor and agitation around the house. Up ahead, Elisabetta—her veil drenched and heavy—and Sister Philomena with an umbrella, searched the bushes for me.

When Elisabetta saw me she gasped, fell to her knees with the sign of the cross and just as quickly rose and ran to me, the key ring jangling at her waist.

"Thank God! Thank God! You're safe!" She embraced me, then stepped back and slapped me across the face.

"Well, this time you've gone and done it! I can't protect you from Reverend Mother now. The house is in an uproar, your sisters are all in tears, no one's settled down for lessons because of worry over you, and Reverend Mother is pacing the hallways in a fury."

Aurelio bent down into the wheelbarrow and got out my shoes and stockings. He passed them to me with a wink.

Elisabetta finally noticed that I was shivering.

"*Grazie, grazie, Fratello* Aurelio, for bringing her back."

As we walked back toward the house, I turned to the old man and curtsied.

"*Addio!*" I whispered.

He touched his hand to his hat, lifted the wheelbarrow and returned to the orchard.

Papa came to fetch me after Aurelio found me. I waited for him in the hallway outside the Reverend Mother's office, listening to the rise and fall of her complaints. Despite my mother's hastily worded letter of entreaty and promises of generous gifts to the convent, Reverend Mother refused to let me stay at school with Letitia and Pip and Tilly.

"I am throwing up my hands, Signore Fiorillo! I can do nothing with the child. Not only does she disrupt classes and— Mother of God—Holy Mass, making the other girls giggle at her antics. But this running away is the limit. For the sake of the other girls, I have no choice but to send Giulia home."

CHAPTER 5

Signore Ventuolo's Lessons

I returned to Giuseppina's house after Reverend Mother had
sent me away from the convent. Papa had gotten my mother
to agree that Giuseppina needed someone to help her. Since
she was unwilling to give up either Pasqualina or Teresia, she
acquiesced to my resuming my role as Giuseppina's helpmate.

Giuseppina greeted me with tears in her eyes the night Papa
brought me home. She checked me carefully for fever and
other ailments she was certain I'd contracted from the pond.
She also examined my head for lice, since no bed was as clean
as my own—although we brought our bed linens home from
school every week for Teresia to boil and starch before we went
back on Monday.

Then she sat me down at the table by the stove, warm from

a day of baking and cooking. She fed me *pastina in brodo, mani-cotti,* chicken *salmi, rabe* and *zeppula con alice.* All my favorite foods in the same meal. Papa ate with us, but my mother had declined. She was disappointed in me, since I'd displeased the Reverend Mother so much. I had disgraced my family. I knew my sisters were holding their heads high, ignoring the whispers that followed them through the hallways, but inside they were mortified by my shameful disobedience. The nuns now eyed them suspiciously, waiting for any one of them to exhibit the family trait so flagrant in me. Their embarrassment had triggered a renewal of my mother's headaches. She had one the evening Papa brought me home. I was permitted into her room to greet her upon my return. The curtains were drawn against the late-afternoon sunlight and the air smelled faintly of eau de cologne. My mother lay propped up against several pillows, a dampened linen cloth pressed over her eyes.

"I cannot say that I am glad to see you, Giulia."

"I know, Mother, but I am glad to be back."

"In a few days, we'll talk about this. Now run along and get yourself settled at your grandmother's place."

It took my mother more than a few days to recover and decide what to do with me. So in the meantime, I was just happy to be home in Giuseppina's house. I took off the scratchy uniform we'd had to wear at the convent and worked barefoot in Giuseppina's garden, pulling up the stalks of harvested veg-etables, turning over the soil, chasing away the crows from what was still left on the vine. At noon, Giuseppina called me in for soup and bread and I washed the earth from my hands in the bucket outside the kitchen door. After siesta, I played with my little brothers and we ate figs from Giuseppina's tree.

Every day I also went to visit my mother, and when she was feeling better she began to question me about what I'd learned from the nuns. I didn't think it was much. My letters, my prayers, my sums. I recited for my mother, read to her from the prayer book she'd given me at my First Communion, showed her the small piece of embroidery I had begun—blue cornflowers, along a border. She nodded in satisfaction.

"Well, despite the Reverend Mother's complaints about how little you paid attention, you seem to have learned something. You are by no means a stupid child, Giulia. And I do not intend that you remain an ignorant one."

My mother eyed me firmly.

"But what did I learn?" I stamped my foot. "It was all so boring and so mean. I would rather be ignorant than go to a school like that again."

"To be ignorant is to waste the talents you were born with. To be ignorant is to confine your life to a path no different than the generations before you. We have embarked on a new century, Giulia! Don't turn your back on the higher things— music, art, literature. When you learn to read, you can read more than the holy words between the black covers of that prayer book. Oh, I know the nuns think those words are the only reason to learn how to read. That's their job. But believe me, you will be enthralled by what you discover, how big your world will become…. I am simply heartbroken that you have lost that opportunity."

I could not comprehend my mother's heartbreak. Instead, I peered out the window at my younger brothers throwing clumps of manure at one another in the stable yard as they mucked out stalls.

"Perhaps…perhaps it's simply that the nuns were the wrong teachers for you. They didn't bother me as a girl, but you and I are very different, aren't we?"

I turned back from the window, surprised by my mother's understanding that she and I were different. In the past, I'd been acutely aware that she had disapproved of the life I was leading with Giuseppina. But this time, she seemed to accept that she could not force me to embrace the things she held so dear.

"I must think about this for a few more days, Giulia. Find a solution that does not waste your gifts but doesn't confine you, either. The answer is more difficult, of course, because the school here is far worse than the nuns, and Papa will not allow me to send you away again."

I smiled to myself at my wonderful Papa, but my joy was short-lived, for my mother solved the dilemma of keeping me in Venticano by finding Signore Ventuolo. She enlisted the help of her lady friends who went with her to Ischia every summer—women she'd known since childhood whose lives revolved around salons and balls. It was Leonora Esposito, who had known Signore Ventuolo's mother before she died, who suggested him. She made all the arrangements, assuring my mother of both his good background and needy circumstances. And so my mother took her summer money and hired me a tutor from the University of Napoli. Instead of soaking in the sulfur baths at Ischia the following August, she endured the mountain heat so that I might be educated.

I hated it when Signore Ventuolo arrived in Venticano. The nuns were by then only a bad taste in my mouth—a kind of suffocating taste, but well behind me. It was January when he first entered my parents' house.

He had ridden home with Papa on the Monday evening carriage, carrying a scuffed and tattered satchel stuffed with books, a copy of the newspaper *Il Corriere della Sera* and a threadbare shirt.

I watched, sullen, from an upstairs window as the carriage rolled into the stable courtyard. Signore Ventuolo climbed awkwardly down from the seat, his short, stocky legs stretching tentatively for the hard-packed earth. Once on the ground, he backed quickly away from the panting, restless horses, who knew that they were home. The climb from the valley had been accomplished, and their grain bags were waiting in the stable.

For Signore Ventuolo, the climb was still ahead—convincing my mother that she had invested wisely, persuading Papa that a daughter's education was worth this much trouble, and, most challenging of all, bringing me down from my angry perch.

I had been summoned from the warmth and familiarity of Giuseppina's kitchen to greet Signore Ventuolo and have dinner with him and my parents. My hair had been freshly braided, my hands were scrubbed, my pinafore was starched. Zia Pasqualina had fed my younger brothers, Frankie and Sandro, earlier, and the older boys, Claudio and Aldo, had found some urgent work in the stables that required their attention (although not so urgent that they couldn't leave it later to peer through the dining-room windows at our unusual guest). My sisters, of course, were all at Santa Margareta on their knees.

Having escaped the horses, Signore Ventuolo gratefully accepted the washbasin offered to him by Zia Pasqualina before greeting my mother, who waited in the parlor, with me called from upstairs to stand by her side. He managed to remove the grime of the journey, but not the beads of sweat that continued to trickle down the sides of his face and onto his frayed collar. Pasqualina's water likewise had little effect on his unruly black hair and untrimmed beard. Shoving his handkerchief back into a pocket, he finally followed Zia Pasqualina out of the kitchen and into the parlor. When he approached my mother, he took the hand she held out and brought it to his lips. Papa had a carefully groomed and waxed mustache, and I watched for my fastidious mother's reaction to the bristling, tightly kinked hairs surrounding Signore Ventuolo's eager mouth. But I detected no distaste on her part.

"Welcome to Venticano, Signore Ventuolo. I'd like you to meet my daughter, Giulia."

I curtsied quickly, but kept my hands behind my back.

My mother inquired about the journey, the health of Leonora Esposito and the weather in Napoli. By the time my father appeared, I was sure there was no other topic to discuss and was grateful for his presence, which signaled that food was now on the dining-room table. Zia Pasqualina always orchestrated the serving of a meal with Papa's readiness for it, and, sure enough, she was just setting a steaming bowl of rabbit stew on the table as we entered the dining room.

My mother directed Signore Ventuolo to sit at her right. My usual seat when I ate at my parents' house put me directly across from Signore Ventuolo, where I had a clear view of him throughout the meal. Despite his shabby appearance, I recognized that Signore Ventuolo knew how to conduct himself at a table. I realized, to my dismay, that my mother would note his manners positively as well. The more he did correctly in my mother's eyes, the less likely he would be on the return carriage to Napoli the next morning.

From my point of view, that first evening could not have gone worse. Papa's suspicions of a man who was eking out a living as a scholar had already been expressed in the house before Signore Ventuolo's arrival, and I was hopeful that he'd be even more dismissive once the man was under his roof. But Signore Ventuolo had clearly read the newspaper that day.

"Signore Fiorillo, has the unrest on the waterfront affected your business? Are you finding it difficult to reach the port?"

Papa's eyes narrowed as he measured a man he had previously imagined in a ruffled shirt, smoking opium and reading Robert Browning. That this scholar could possibly understand the obstacles standing in the way of a businessman's success was unsettling. But even he could hold Papa's attention for just so long, and Papa went off to his card game as soon as he had finished eating.

Signore Ventuolo did not accompany Papa to Auteri's tavern. He stayed behind with my mother and me, drinking black coffee and anisette, entertaining her with stories about the plays he'd seen over the weekend and the art exhibit at the National Gallery. Pasqualina remained in the kitchen after she'd washed up, listening to their conversation with the door half-opened. I was supposed to be listening in the dining room, but I had come into the kitchen for more cookies and something to drink.

"Why are you so interested in what they're saying? It's so boring," I told her.

"It's what they're *not* saying that interests me," she answered, watching intently through the crack in the door. My mother laughed and inclined her head as she poured Signore Ventuolo more anisette.

My mother finally excused me for the evening, and Claudio accompanied me back to Giuseppina's house across the piazza. The next morning, the work for which Signore Ventuolo had been hired began in earnest. I grudgingly retraced my steps to my parents' house, sullen and resistant. I was grouchy and tired the first morning. I didn't like going from the bustle and activity of Giuseppina's house to the stiff-backed chairs and silence of my mother's parlor.

"It is too distracting at Giuseppina's house," said my mother. "Too many people going in and out, too many questions about the stranger."

My mother hovered in the corner with her spectacles, reading while I learned, but listening to every false word I uttered. Signore Ventuolo, after acknowledging her presence, focused all his attention to me. When he read aloud, he used different voices for each character. Listening to him was like watching an entire company of actors on a stage.

After that first week, I had lessons with Signore Ventuolo

every Tuesday and Wednesday in my parents' parlor. I began to look forward to them.

In my whole life, I had never spent so much time with my mother. She was full of sparkle those days, smiling, sitting up with Signore Ventuolo both nights talking instead of going to her room in silence when Papa left for Auteri's. She ordered crates of books from Napoli and began to paint. She set up her easel and her parasol on the balcony and painted the hills or arranged a bowl of peaches on the dining-room table and fussed with the lace at the window until the light slanted across the bowl "just so."

On the days Signore Ventuolo wasn't there, she listened to me read or had me practice my multiplication tables. Pasqualina took the little ones for a walk so my mother and I could study.

My mother said that Signore Ventuolo lived alone in rooms in Napoli, with no mother or wife to cook and wash for him. She told him to bring his laundry when he came, and Zia Teresia starched and ironed so that his shirts, though old, were neat and white.

Zia Pasqualina and Zi'Yolanda, my uncle Tony's wife, sat in the courtyard at Giuseppina's house peeling eggplants one day, several months after Signore Ventuolo had become my tutor.

"Anna would adopt Signore Ventuolo if she could. I don't know what else he's good for. Who ever heard of making a living teaching little girls? Why isn't he out working for his father? I know for a fact that his family is in the textile business. So why is he here instead of in the mill? Did they disown him? Is he one of those anarchists, throwing bombs at his father's factory? Is that why Anna brought him here?" Zia Pasqualina jabbed at the skin of the eggplant as she continued.

"He feeds his belly on my cooking, dumps his dirty clothes in Teresia's wash bucket, drinks Felice's wine. All for such nonsense as teaching Giulia to read and write. Why couldn't they leave well enough alone when the Reverend Mother sent her home? Couldn't they see Giulia wasn't meant to be schooled? Wasn't it enough that the sisters think she's uncontrollable? Do they want her to run away from here, too, for the entire village to see? How long does Anna think Giulia will sit still for these lessons she'll never use? She should be in the kitchen with me, or better yet, here in Giuseppina's garden, helping her grandmother who needs her eyes, her ears and her sturdy legs."

Zi'Yolanda nodded her head in agreement. "All these books will give her too many ideas, make her lazy and useless. Look at Anna, for heaven's sake!"

I had been in my room, reading one of the books from Napoli. I wanted to tell them that I did sit still. I was back in Giuseppina's house, but now a desk stood under the window, stacked with texts and copybooks and ink pots.

"Look at me now, turning the pages of this book, laughing at the stories, going far away in my mind to the places I read about," I wanted to shout at them.

But Pasqualina and Yolanda moved on to another topic, their opinions of my mother and her passion for education falling in a heap with the eggplant skins at their feet.

I wanted to tell them that Signore Ventuolo was not at all like Sister Philomena. He brought me sweets from the *conditoria* in his neighborhood in Napoli. After I read my lessons to him with no mistakes, he rewarded me with a bonbon. Every week he had something different in the white-and-gold bag. Sugarcoated almonds in pale colors of pink and green and lilac, cherries dipped in chocolate, colored fruits and flowers made of almond paste.

The only thing I didn't like about Signore Ventuolo teaching me was the look on Giuseppina's face—her annoyance when I left with my packet of books to walk to my mother's house and her pain when I returned, full of lightheartedness and excitement that I could not share with her.

CHAPTER 6

A Game Called "America"

The changes my mother initiated by educating her daughters were only the beginning. Within two years, the foundation upon which we based our lives began to shift, creating tremors as real as the earthquakes that sent whole villages toppling down the mountainside in our valley. My brother Claudio decided to leave Venticano right after the feast of the Ascension, as soon as he turned eighteen. He wanted to be someone other than what Papa wanted for him. He told us all, in that voice of his that was always so sure, so smart, that there was no better place for him than New York.

In the last months before his leave-taking, Claudio and Papa had done nothing but argue with each other—thunderous shouting matches that began out in the courtyard and carried into the house at dinner.

"Small potatoes," he called Papa's business.

"The world is wider than the road from Venticano to Napoli," Claudio told him. "This is the twentieth century, for God's sake. This region is dying. Pretty soon you'll only be hauling caskets to the graveyard."

"Hasn't this life given you enough?" Papa demanded. "You, with your fancy suit and the respect you get just because of your name. What do you think bought you that respect? Who built this house that stands higher than any other in Venticano, so that you, too, can hold your head higher? From living over a stable with your grandmother's herbs hanging from the rafters, I have brought all of you to *this*. Stone by stone, this house was built because every day I traveled that road to Napoli—that road you say is so narrow. Every morsel you put in your mouth, every thread on your body…"

"And just as living over a stable wasn't enough for you, staying here in Venticano isn't enough for me! Every day I drive into Napoli I hear the same stories at the docks—the opportunity, the immensity and fertility of the land—that's what I want for myself, a future in America!" Claudio shouted back at Papa.

"You think America is going to give you this and more? You think you're not going to have to work hard? You think you can turn your back on your family, on your heritage, and succeed? Then go. Get out of my sight!"

Papa slammed his fist on the table, my mother caught his flying wineglass, and Claudio grabbed his hat and bolted out the door and down the hill to Auteri's for a glass of grappa. The rest of my brothers and sisters watched wide-eyed and swallowed silently, not wanting to draw Papa's notice and take Claudio's place as the object of his wrath.

"There will come a time he won't come back," warned my mother, mopping up spilled wine.

"Then good riddance. Let him go." And by the middle of June go he did, driven by his own dreams, my Papa's stubbornness, my mother's pride. It was my mother who paid for his passage, selling some of her jewelry to finance his journey.

On the day he left, my mother dressed in her most elegant gown, put on her ruby earrings and stood on the balcony over the front door of her house—the balcony that looks out on the main street of our village and beyond, to the entire valley below. The balcony from which anyone can see and be seen.

She stood there without tears while everyone else wailed and sobbed, her face shielded from the scorching sun by her wide-brimmed silk hat with the blue feathers, as Claudio walked out of the village and down into the valley on his way to America. She stayed there hours after he was no longer visible to us, but I think she saw him in a way no one else could—his safe journey, his arrival, his triumph. I remember the look on her face, her belief in the rightness of what Claudio was doing.

For Papa, however, Claudio's leaving was a defeat. Claudio *walked* away because Papa refused to take him in his own carriage. Papa spent the day in a darkened corner of Auteri's tavern and spit on what he called Claudio's worthless dreams. Claudio had wanted nothing that Papa could give him.

My parents' house was very quiet in the days after Claudio went.

But his going left a hole in our lives. My family had been in Venticano for nearly five hundred years. How many times had I heard Giuseppina recite the litany that began with Alessandro Fiorillo, the crossbowman who'd sailed from Barcelona to invade Napoli under Alfonso the Magnanimous of Aragon? He never returned to Spain. Instead, he fell in love with the beautiful Maria and remained to cultivate a patch of earth and father her babies.

Giuseppina could not comprehend Claudio's leaving Italy. When he set off from Venticano, Giuseppina had taken a lock of his dark hair, his fingernail clippings and a milk tooth she'd saved since his babyhood. She kept them in a pouch, blessing them every year on the anniversary of his departure.

For us children, the pain of Claudio's departure had been much simpler. We could not understand, could not forgive his leaving *us*. The only people before Claudio who'd left Venticano, never to return, were the dead. What was this place America—farther than Avellino in the valley, farther than Napoli on the sea—that had swallowed up our brother?

In America, Claudio was successful right away. The money began arriving that August. I think my mother knew how well it would go for Claudio—how well it would go for all of us. When Claudio started sending us money, he also sent us letters filled with stories. He recreated for us the streets of New York, teeming with people and commerce. It was the commerce, especially, that fascinated Claudio and presented him with opportunity. In Little Italy, he saw the pushcarts laden with vegetables and fish and shoes and pots that provided the daily necessities to the tenements. Uptown, he saw the glass-fronted shops, their shelves filled with goods—goods he knew had to come from somewhere outside the city. Goods that had to be hauled from where they were made to where they were sold. And so, after a few months of laboring for someone else, Claudio turned in his shovel, and with the money he'd saved, together with what remained of the money my mother had given him, he bought a horse and wagon and began hauling everything the city needed. He had found a place that, unlike Venticano, was not shriveling in the sun but was expanding, exploding.

What we gleaned from Claudio's letters was the sheer immensity of America. So many people, so many streets, long vistas that stretched as far as the eye could see or dream. And one by one, my brothers—first Aldo, and then Frankie and Sandro, who are even younger than me—begged to join him. The hole created by Claudio's departure did not close. Instead, it widened, tearing apart the life my family had known.

My oldest sister, Letitia, had married six months before, a marriage arranged by my parents with the jeweler Samuel Rassina, the son of one of Papa's business associates. She was eighteen and already bitter. She seemed to spend most of her time in the church, "praying for babies, instead of staying home making them," her mother-in-law complained.

I knew, from observing other girls in the village, what lay ahead for me. A year or two of meeting stiff and boring boys at gatherings with families like ours, always under the extremely watchful eye of my mother. And then, after the families nodded and whispered, the women sitting on the sofa and hiding their conversations behind painted fans, the men out on the porch with their cigars and their eyes narrowed, estimating the worth of the girl's family or the boy's land—then, the banns of marriage would be announced in both churches. A string of novenas would follow, the girl's grandmothers and aunts praying that no unforeseen obstacles would tumble into the couple's path, like the loose boulders that had slid off the mountain, crushing five of the village goats and blocking the road to Pano di Greci for three days. Praying that the wedding would take place before the girl had a chance to disgrace the family with a baby born too soon, like Constanza Berti. She'd come to the doorstep of my cousin Arturo's house and thrown the baby into the arms of Arturo's mother, screaming, "Here, this is yours!" My aunt and uncle had made Arturo marry her and take her and the baby away.

My mother wanted no Constanza Bertis in our family.

"You are not peasants! You are the daughters of Felice Fiorillo." Her greatest weapon in her defense of our honor was our pride. From the time we were small, she had Zia

Pasqualina scrubbing us and dressing us in starched white dresses while the other children in the village ran around barefoot and in tatters. When the money from Claudio began coming, the dresses became finer, and we ordered fabrics from Napoli for the bed linens we were to take to our marriage beds.

Painstakingly, under the instruction of Zia Pasqualina, I embroidered red silk *GF*s on the elaborate pillowcases I sewed, festooned with tucks and elegant lace. My fingers cramped from the tiny stitches. My mother held up these beautiful objects to us like Giuseppina's talismans. If we wanted a life filled with beauty and elegance, a life where we could rest our heads on an embroidered pillowcase, rather than a life spent washing someone else's pillowcases, then we had to remember that its cost was far more than the silver she'd paid for this linen. How would we be able to put our heads on these pristine objects if we ourselves were soiled?

My sisters soaked up these lessons without question. They were willing to sit for hours with their needles and thread, gossiping about wedding dresses and arguing over the placement of a flower. They looked at the not-married and the married in our family, in our village, and had decided which side they wanted to be on. I was not so sure.

I was haunted by Letitia's heartache. How lonely she seemed! Her husband had no brothers and sisters, and he was often away, leaving Letitia alone with his nagging mother. "No wonder she seeks refuge in the church," my mother muttered one day.

The lonelier and more withdrawn Letitia became, the more I began to share my brothers' growing excitement with each letter from Claudio. I was still young enough to be granted an occasional excuse from the sewing circle, and then I went off with Aldo and Frankie and Sandro to the hills and played "America"—the rules defined by whatever wonders Claudio had described in his most recent letter. The more I learned from Claudio, the less willing I was to do as my mother expected.

I wanted to laugh, I wanted to dance. I did not want to spend the rest of my life praying to the Blessed Virgin in a village church.

CHAPTER 7

The Spell

On Christmas eve every year the entire family gathered at
my parents' house to celebrate—my grandmother, Giuseppina; my sister Letitia, her husband and his widowed
mother; Papa's estranged brother Tony, who had begun to talk
about following Claudio to America with his wife Yolanda and
their son Peppino; Zia Pasqualina and Zia Teresia, who did all
the cooking for the feast of seven fishes, the traditional Christmas eve meal; and all my brothers and sisters who were still at
home. In the two years since he'd been gone, my mother had
set also a place for Claudio on Christmas eve, an empty chair
she allowed no one else to sit in. She did not set a place for
the wife Claudio had written us about in October of that year.

The house was ablaze with light. Every candlestick in the

house had been polished and arranged on the table, the credenza, even the windowsills. My mother and Pip had laid the table with a damask cloth, heavy silver and platters painted with cherubs and goddesses. For one night, everyone put aside grudges and resentments, ate abundantly and then walked across the piazza to attend midnight Mass together. At the end of the service, as the bells chimed "Adeste Fidelis" and the snow swirled around our feet, we bid one another *"Buon Natale"* and separated.

After we returned to my grandmother's house, I started toward my bed, but Giuseppina reached out for me with her blue-veined hand. My Christmas eve was not yet over.

"Wait," she said. "I want to show you something, *figlia mia.*"

She gestured for me to follow her to the kitchen, where she stirred the coal embers in the grate and then sat on her chair— the stool where she sat every day when "the parade of the afflicted," as my mother called them, came for her ministrations and her medicines.

"How old are you, Giulia?"

She asked a question she knew the answer to. This was just like Giuseppina. She often asked the simplest of questions, questions whose answers seemed so commonplace, so obvious, that at first you worried she was becoming feeble-minded and forgetful. But then, when you answered her question, scoffing, "But, *Nonna,* you know already!" you found that your answer meant something else entirely.

"I'm fourteen, *Nonna,*" I answered, puzzled by what Giuseppina was seeking, by what my answer would reveal to us both.

"Ah," she sighed. "Fourteen. Yes, I thought so."

Giuseppina did not keep track of time the way my mother did. She could not read the baptismal certificates pressed between the thin pages of my mother's Bible that recorded our names and the years of our births. She had no calendar hanging on the wall next to the washbasin advertising the granary in

Avellino. She had no gold-leafed clock sitting on a mantel that needed winding with a key. Giuseppina measured time by the season. Planting, tending, harvesting. She measured time by the length and warmth of the day. She measured time by the flame in her votive candles.

She looked at me then and measured another kind of time—one that marks the distance between the three-year-old chatterbox she took under her roof and her wing, and the almost-woman who, cicada-like, filled the silences in her house with words, questions, songs and stories. She eyed me, in my fine Christmas dress, my face still flushed from wine, the walk home in the cold air, the warmth rising up from the stove.

"When I was fourteen, I had already been promised to your grandfather Antonio," she mused.

Has she found me a husband? I wondered. Was that it? I was old enough to be married off? What about Tilly and Pip? Weren't they supposed to go before me? I wasn't prepared for this, if this was what fourteen meant to my grandmother.

"When I was fourteen, I also sat with my *nonna* on Christmas eve." She waved a hand in front of her eyes as if to clear away the clouds that obscured the memory of another old woman and her granddaughter. I was more comfortable with this image. A girl sits at the feet of her *nonna*, listening and watching.

"It's a sacred time," whispered Giuseppina, "for the *maghe*."

A shiver of recognition rippled its way from my hairline down my spine. I was no longer comfortable, but I was also not unwilling. With relief, I realized that Giuseppina did not see me on the threshold of marriage, as she had been at fourteen. But I understood that she did see me as her heir in something far more mysterious, far more powerful. My heart was pounding.

"You are ready," she announced to me, taking my hands in hers. "Ready to learn the first spells."

We were facing each other and she moved closer, so that our knees touched. She then guided my right hand to her forehead and flattened my thumb against her brown and spotted skin, starting my hand in a rotating motion.

"First, you must listen with your *skin*, your *blood*. Hear the blood of the other, take in its message through your fingertips."

My eyes were wide open, staring into hers, looking for what I was supposed to find.

"No," she said, "not with your eyes." She passed her hand over my eyelids, brushing them closed. This time I clenched them tightly shut, trying very hard to do what she'd told me. I felt her hand again, hovering lightly over my eyes.

"You are trying too hard, *figlia mia*. Do not try at all. Do not think. Just listen."

We sat quietly for many minutes, her hand at first suspended in front of my eyes and then no longer there. I don't remember the moment when she took it away. In the beginning I heard the hiss of the fire, the rustle of the wind, the banging of a loose shutter, even the braying of the padre's mule. My hand continued to move in the gentle rhythm she had set for it, across the fragile folds of her aged face. Again at a point I don't remember, the sounds of the night receded and I heard nothing; and then I heard something. Not words. Not direction, or explanation, or even *yes* or *no*. But I know what I heard was Giuseppina.

Then for the first time in my life I began to speak aloud the words of the spell. I had heard them since I was an infant, so Giuseppina did not have to say them to teach or even remind me. But that night they became *my* words. I said the names in order, the list of the saints and spirits called upon to provide protection and blessing. I made the request for help, for the ring of goodness to surround her. I offered the honor and gratitude for their assistance, and then I repeated the names again, beginning with the least and ending with the Great Intercessor, the Holy Virgin herself.

I was trembling and breathless when I finished. I waited for Giuseppina's judgment. But it did not come. I cautiously opened my eyes. Her head had fallen forward, her heavy silver earrings resting on the crocheted shawl she always wore draped across her shoulders, her chin pressed into the large cameo at her neck. Her eyes were closed and fluttering under the folds of her eyelids. Her breasts rose and fell in the rhythm of my circles. She had fallen asleep, brought to a place of peace and repose by *my* spell. By *my* words. I covered her with a blanket, banked the fire and made myself a bed at her feet.

After that night, she allowed me to do the spell for the colicky babies brought to her by distraught and exhausted mothers, and for the mothers themselves. Soon they no longer waited for Giuseppina, or turned to me reluctantly when Giuseppina was overwhelmed by the numbers seeking assistance. They began to ask first for me.

CHAPTER 8

La Danza

The summer I turned sixteen, a group of us—cousins and friends who had played together since we were children—gathered in the late evenings behind the Cucino brothers' barn. Mario Cucino had a fiddle, and on moonlit nights, amid the crickets and fireflies, someone would signal with the rhythmic cadence of clapping hands and the music began. We danced. Whirling, wild, joyous, the letting go of winter's confinement and—for me—my mother's constrictions.

I lived for those summer nights. For the moist darkness, a reprieve from the scorching heat and the eyes of the village gossips; for the feeling of breathlessness and weightlessness that overcame me as I spun in circles, my arms outstretched and my castanets alive; for the smells of wine, honeysuckle, hay, sweat. For the aching nearness of Vito Cipriano, shirtless, brown from his endless days in the fields. For what I felt coursing through me—new, delicious and forbidden. For what I had discovered with Vito.

One searing day, Giuseppina and I had gone up into the hills to gather angelica when the heat overwhelmed her and she sought refuge in a small grove. I gave her a few sips of water to drink. She leaned back against a tree and fell immediately into her customary snoring sleep.

I sat with her for a while, but I was neither hot nor tired, so I picked up my basket and continued over the rise to the meadow where the last of the angelica grew. I was crouched there, cutting the stems with my knife, when I saw the shadow. I turned quickly, my knife ready to plunge, to protect myself. But it was Vito.

The grass was very tall; there was no one to see us except the hawks. Vito and I had kissed before that day—sweet kisses on the path back from Cucino's in the half darkness, hurried and cautious, always listening for the sound of footsteps or a shutter opening as one of the sleepless sought the relief of the night air. But in the meadow was different. In the meadow...I let him touch me.

I knew the length and depth of Giuseppina's siestas. And I could still hear her snoring. At first, Vito's kisses were as urgent as the night and I kissed him back with the hunger that had been building to a frenzy all summer long. But then we stopped for breath. He tilted his head to gaze at me and began to stroke my hair and my face. I have a vein in my neck that always swells and pumps visibly when I am nervous. I felt it surging, revealing my emotions. He touched it with his fingertips, then buried his face in the hollow right below it. I could smell the earth on his hands. He had had no time to wash, had come to me directly from the fields when he'd seen me with my basket walking up the rocky path. I felt his hand glide from my neck, along my arm and back up again to the drawstring of my blouse. My hand closed over his as he attempted to loosen the string. *"Per favore,"* he whispered, begging me with his eyes. I hesitated. He released the string, but then brushed his hand across my blouse, over my breast. No one had ever touched me there before. I hadn't known how it would feel, had not known the ripple of desire it could set off. I struggled with the warnings and admonitions of my mother. But this discovery was so extraordinary to me, this moment of our unexpected solitude so magical, that I pushed aside the voice of my mother and bent my ear once again to the voice of Vito.

"I want to touch you," he told me.

"Yes," I answered.

He undid the string and lifted my blouse over my head, then my camisole. This nakedness in the brilliance of midday, in the presence of Vito, was so surprising and so thrilling that I lost my breath. Then I felt his hands, callused and eager. That my body could feel this way! I reached out for him and pulled him toward me and gasped when I felt his own naked chest for the first time against mine. I had watched since childhood the calm and the absolute pleasure on the faces of babies when they nestled against the bare breasts of their mothers, and that's what I knew when Vito extended his body over mine. For a few abandoned moments, surrounded by the drone of the cicadas, the biting fragrance of the grass crushed beneath us, I was aware only of my longing. But in the distance, in a place inside my head that stayed apart, I still listened for Giuseppina's snores and I still measured Vito's every move. I knew I was in danger—from discovery, from desire.

I stopped Vito when his hand reached under my skirt. His face clouded with frustration and anger. I felt a sharp twinge of fear—that I might not be able to hold him back, might not want to. But then we both heard the sound of my name, frantic, wild. He rolled off me, cursing, staying low, and I grabbed for my clothes and wriggled into them.

"Stay down," I hissed, and then rose with my basket to see the top of Giuseppina's head coming up over the rise. I waved and hurried toward her, brushing the grass from my hair, my back.

"Are you crazy to wander off by yourself! Never again, do you hear me!" She vented the fear she must have felt when she woke to find me missing." You look flushed, feverish," she observed as I came nearer. "You've been too long in the sun." She saw the mound of flowers in my basket. "That's enough for today. The fright you gave me has worn me out."

We set off down to the village. I didn't turn to look back.

But that night I couldn't wait to return to the dance and Vito's arms. Those hours contained everything my mother had tried to keep me from. I danced barefoot, like the daughters of Tomasino the goat herder, feeling the earth, damp with dew, between my toes. In the early hours of morning, when I returned in exhaustion to Giuseppina's, I poured water into the speckled washbasin and thoroughly scrubbed my feet before slipping back between the sheets of my bed. Giuseppina might not have seen the smudged evidence, but she would certainly have smelled the loamy traces still clinging to my skin.

But my ablutions were not enough to hide my secret life.

Mario Cucino's cousin Clara betrayed me. Clara had watched Vito and me all summer from the corners and the shadows, a skinny, sallow-faced girl who was always chewing on a strand of her hair and did not know how to laugh.

She shrewdly enlisted my brother Aldo as her accomplice. Aldo had embraced his position as Papa's favored son after Claudio left us. He postured in front of the hallway mirror, mimicking Papa's elegant style of dress. He passionately remade himself in Papa's image, taking meticulous care not only of his wardrobe but also of the wagons and horses. He polished, he groomed. He seemed determined to earn Papa's respect, eagerly volunteering for the hardest routes, even passing up the usual entertainments of the other boys in the village to pore over the ledger books late into the night. Papa rewarded him when he turned eighteen, entrusting him with the busy Avellino route.

Aldo had never ventured to Cucino's. He had never experienced the need to break free of the confining Fiorillo name— not as Claudio had by leaving Venticano altogether, nor as I had, in my own fledgling way, by dancing, by dreaming. If he knew about Cucino's, he'd chosen to ignore it, until Clara, recognizing in Aldo a younger version of Felice Fiorillo, whispered in his ear one day. My little brother Sandro, who sometimes tagged after Aldo, witnessed that encounter and later told me about it.

Clara had been invisible to young men, especially young men like Aldo. But then, Clara realized she had something Aldo might want, something that would earn him more favor with the father he seemed so intent on pleasing. She pushed that perpetually loose strand of hair behind her ear, smoothed her dress and approached him.

"You're Giulia's older brother, aren't you?"

Aldo nodded, but eyed her quizzically. "How do *you* know Giulia?" he asked, the surprise in his voice undisguised.

Clara smiled disingenuously. "She comes dancing at Cucino's sometimes. Weren't you aware? I had heard she was hiding it from her grandmother, but I thought she might have trusted you. You must know about Vito?" She looked at Aldo, offering her sympathy to the shocked brother. "Oh, no, I haven't said too much, have I?"

"Not at all. I'm grateful to you, Signorina."

Very few young men had addressed her as *Signorina*.

That night, Aldo waited under Giuseppina's mulberry tree and watched me lower myself over the ledge of the window. When my feet touched the ground he sprang forward and tackled me, knocking me breathless into the flower bed. I shrieked and kicked, not knowing it was my own brother. Our scuffling, of course, roused Giuseppina, who threw open her shuttered window, muttering and cursing the disturbance until she saw who it was and—more pertinently—how I was dressed. I was no longer in the nightgown I'd been wearing when I'd said good night to her an hour earlier, but rather in my flounced skirt and bodice, with no blouse underneath. My arms and shoulders were bare. My hair, now unbraided, tumbled loosely down my back, somewhat unkempt thanks to the tousle with Aldo. As Giuseppina took in my appearance and realized what it meant, she began to wail and keen as if it were my stiff and lifeless corpse lying beneath her window. It might as well have been, given the catastrophic aftermath of Giuseppina's discovery.

In the midst of her lamentation, she ordered me into the house. But she could not prevent Aldo from running to fetch Papa. I cursed at his retreating footsteps. Papa arrived from his card game in a frenzy.

"You whore," he roared and slapped me twice, once on each cheek. "I forbid you to go to Cucino's again. If you disobey me, I swear I'll bring you back to my house and keep you under lock and key."

I spent the rest of the night in Giuseppina's bed with her. When she finally fell asleep, I crept over to the window. Not to escape again, but merely to catch a glimpse of the night and hope that Vito was hovering somewhere in the shadows.

The next morning my mother made her entrance. (No one had dared wake her the night before.) Her outrage was focused not so much on the dishonor that had provoked my father's anger as on the company I had chosen to keep and the manner in which I'd chosen to keep it.

"Dancing in the mud with a Cipriano! Haven't I taught you to expect more? Will you throw your life away to bear the squalling babies of an uneducated peasant, just because you admire the shape of his buttocks?" she shrieked at me. Then she quieted and narrowed her eyes as a question—more a demand—formed in her head.

"Are you pregnant?"

"Mama! I've only danced with him!" I protested quickly, knowing that dancing alone was enough to anger her, hoping it was enough to keep her from suspecting more.

"Well, thank the Blessed Virgin for that."

My mother did not know—and I did not reveal to her—what I felt when I danced. She could never have known the force of the yearning and urgency that propelled me. She shifted her fury to Giuseppina, not for failing to guard me or seal me in, but for making me susceptible to the night.

"It's you who've cultivated this wildness in her! You've encouraged her to befriend these people, to partake in their primitive pleasures. You let her go off into the hills alone to gather your weeds and look what she brings back! She should've been reading books, not mixing potions for the lovesick."

Giuseppina was no less upset with me than my mother was, but for other reasons. Giuseppina understood the longing. She had taught me the power of the feelings, the dreams that burned inside of people. She believed that to disown what you felt made you sick—sick at heart, sick in the head.

Over the years, most often in arguments about me, Giuseppina and my mother had done their own dance around each other. This time was no exception. My mother, normally decorous and contained, unleashed her words, her pitch, her pace. She brimmed with uncontrollable passion. Giuseppina, on the other hand, became impassive, impenetrable. My mother shrilled her words as if they were fists beating, hammering in futility at the wall of Giuseppina's silence. When my mother finished her tirade, Giuseppina dismissed her with the peremptory gesture of impatience she reserved for the truly stupid with whom she wouldn't even deign to speak. Once again, my mother was forced to retreat.

When she was gone, Giuseppina said, "Before you find yourself pregnant, come to me first."

She turned away from me without her customary penetrating glance. I was expected to understand; she would protect me, as she'd been unable to protect me the night before from Aldo's spying and its consequences. She was angry with me for exposing her lapse, for making her look like a fool and for taking risks with my reputation. But she was also letting me know that she forgave me.

My parents, however, were not ready to forgive. My mother, especially, was determined to protect me in her own way from the dangers she saw lurking behind the eyes of every young man in the village, and within my own emerging womanhood.

Her solution came quickly.

My sister Pip had made a rash promise to a young man in Pano di Greci. She was nearly twenty, but she had no experience of men, as I did. Her embroidery stitches were neat; she followed all the rules at the convent of Santa Margareta; she would make someone an obedient, if foolish wife. But not this someone in Pano di Greci, my mother decided. Not knowing her own heart, Pip was relieved at my mother's intervention. She floated this way and that, always doing what she was told. The family of the young man, however, was enraged, raining curses and threats upon Pip's empty head.

My mother and father conferred noisily, Papa at first resisting my mother's radical suggestion. Ever since Claudio had left,

Papa had refused to even read any of the letters from America, let alone respond. But my mother, summoning all her emotional power, prevailed. A letter was hurriedly sent to Claudio.

Pip, in the meantime, was kept at home, not even allowed to go to the market for fear she would be kidnapped in broad daylight crossing the piazza.

To all outward appearances, life in the Fiorillo households—my parents' and my grandmother's—remained as it had been, except for Pip's and my confinement. But my mother's days had taken on a kind of silent intensity as she worked out in elaborate detail what she considered to be the rescue not only of Pip, but of me and Tilly as well.

She told none of us, for fear of alerting the enemy in Pano di Greci or arousing the rebel in me.

She did not tell me, in fact, until she had the passage booked, the steamship tickets in her hand, my father's horses practically bridled and ready to drive me to the pier.

"Aiuta me!" I wailed to Giuseppina when my mother marched to her house and ordered me to pack my trunks. *Help me.*

"She cannot help you this time. Your sister will be killed or worse if she remains here, and she can't go alone. She and Tilly can't manage such a journey by themselves. You're the only one with enough sense to see you all safely to Claudio. Venticano is no life for any of my daughters, but believe me, Giulia, it is especially no life for you. You are going now, before you're ruined by what you have clearly never learned to control."

She stood over me while I gathered my belongings together. The tears flooded my cheeks, spilling over onto my clothes. Giuseppina wandered around the house, muttering her incantations, burning incense, tucking her blessings among my possessions as I packed.

"You'll leave before sunrise tomorrow, on your father's normal run to Napoli, so as not to arouse suspicion. The boys will come this evening after dark to take your trunks to the house, and you will come with them. You'll sleep with Tilly in her bed tonight. I forbid you to breathe a word of this to anyone, especially Cipriano or any of the Cucinos. If you do, you threaten not only your sister's life, but your own as well."

My mother's voice was taut; her face revealed the sleepless-ness and strain of the last few weeks. But just below the surface of her exhaustion, her rigid instructions, I thought I saw a kind of rejoicing—that she was going to be successful in getting us out of here, this village and this life that had been such a trap for her. And I hated her for it.

"I don't want to go!" I screamed at her. "What about Giu-seppina? Who will help her?"

"Don't make me laugh! You don't want Giuseppina's life any more than I do! I know you, Giulia. Giuseppina may have taken you from my side, but she can't take me out of you. You are *my* blood. Your tears are not for Giuseppina, but for something walking around out there with bulging pants. Believe me, you'll find a hundred just like him in America. And—like your brother Claudio—they will have money, they will have a future, they will have a life to offer you."

Giuseppina's mutterings became louder, more intense.

My mother simply could not understand my heartache. I didn't want a hundred other boyfriends. I wanted Vito.

When my trunks were packed, my mother had no patience to listen to my sobs for the rest of the day. She locked the trunks herself after she was satisfied that they contained everything I'd need in the life she was sending me to. She took the keys and added them to her own ring of household keys, telling me she'd return them to me before we departed in the morning. What did she believe? That I would forget them? That I would add unsuitable items to the trunks after she left—talismans and powders from Giuseppina's trove? That I would dump the contents of the trunks in the mud of the piazza in a fury of final rebellion? Perhaps that was it. But I felt her taking the keys as another slap.

The trunks sat all day in the middle of my bedroom as an affront, an immovable reminder of my mother's resolve.

I could not stop my tears. At times they were simply silent streams, slick on my cheeks, trickling down my neck. At other times they were wild sobs, engulfing my entire body, starting in some place so deep inside me that I'd never felt it before— deeper even than the longing that had entered me this summer when I'd danced with Vito. I did not know myself. Did not know I could feel such sorrow, such fear.

Giuseppina fed me broth at midday, holding me in her arms like a baby, spooning the warmth into my mouth where it mingled with the salt of my sorrows.

She put me in her own bed at siesta to keep my emotions from being heightened by the massive trunks near my bedside. She lay with me, murmuring the words of her simplest spell.

In her bed, awaiting the evening and its further agonies, I didn't think I'd be able to let go of the thoughts crowding my head. But her words washed over me until they were no longer words. Her hands stroked at the pain until they were no longer hands. I fell asleep.

When I woke it was nearly dusk. Giuseppina was gone from the bed and I heard her in the kitchen, clattering pots and pans. I smelled the extraordinary smells of roasting lamb and freshly cut oranges. I went into the kitchen and then helped Giuseppina in silence, slicing tomatoes and unwrapping the mozzarella. A small bowl of figs sat on the table. She must have walked down to the orchard to pick them in the afternoon, while I'd slept. She was now trimming the shank of prosciutto, shaving thin slices from the cut end. The kitchen was stifling from the fire in the oven, combined with the oppressive July heat. No one cooked like this in summer. The aromas of rosemary and garlic mingled with the red wine she had poured over the lamb. Despite my sadness and my unwillingness to eat at midday, my body now gave in to hunger.

I devoured the meal, savoring every mouthful. Giuseppina sat across from me, watching me eat silently.

I helped her clear away the meal and wash up. By the time we finished, the darkness was spreading and deepening. My brothers would be arriving soon. She took me into her room. We stood in front of her shrine, before the flickering candles in their red pots, the faces of Mary, the Sacred Heart, Saint Anne, Saint Joseph—her own saint—glowing and gazing out at us. She blessed me and whispered her strongest spell of protection. Then she kissed me, unfastened the clasp of the amulet she wore and draped it around my neck.

There was a knock at the door. I began to shake and my tears returned.

Aldo and Frankie were here, neither of them understanding my grief and both wishing it was they who were on their way to America and not their sisters. Giuseppina had decided not to come to my parents' house. As the boys hoisted the trunks onto their shoulders, she cast one final blessing upon my things and then took me in her arms.

I wanted to collapse at her feet, throw my arms around her knees and not let go. But she held me up—for an old woman she had moments of surprising strength.

"*Figlia mia,* don't do this to yourself. Don't shame yourself in front of your brothers, who will only drag you to your father's house. Go now. Remember everything I have taught you. My blessings are with you. You will find what you long for in your life. Cherish it. Protect it. You carry my gifts within you, too, not just the blood of your mother."

It was the first and only occasion Giuseppina had openly countered my mother's words to me. She released me into the protection of my brothers.

We walked silently across the piazza. Aldo kept one hand in his pocket, closed over a bulge I soon recognized as my father's gun. Both boys kept glancing from side to side. Frankie's baby face twitched every time we heard a cat wail or a bucket of dishwater splash upon the stones. But we met no one else. Before we left the piazza, I glanced back. Giuseppina stood in the light of her doorway, still watching us. I could no longer see her face, only the outline of her body standing sentinel until we turned the corner. I lifted my arm in farewell and saw hers go up in response.

At my parents' house, a brittle calm filled every room, every face. Pip twittered nervously, remembering every five minutes yet one more item she'd forgotten. She babbled about the outfit she was going to wear tomorrow, couldn't decide which hat, fretted about her tendency to become nauseated when traveling. Tilly sat in the kitchen, baffled and frightened by this extraordinary change in our lives.

In contrast to Pip's chatter and Tilly's confusion, I was sullen. The boys joked and teased, but their resentment was unmistakable. My aunts—Pasqualina, the childless widow who wasn't sure whether she adored Papa or my brother Sandro more, and Teresia, the one whose mind had never grown beyond childhood—hovered anxiously, saying their prayers and jumping every time they heard a noise outside. I secretly hoped that one of those noises was Vito, somehow aware of my predicament, emboldened to rescue me. But I was not allowed near a window, and they were all shuttered anyway.

My mother, still tense, sent Pip and Tilly and me to bed with the admonition that we were to be up and ready to depart at 4:00 a.m. I slept very little without the solace of Giuseppina and with my own heartache. I awoke to a smoky lamp in my face, my mother's voice urging me to get dressed. Tilly's side of the bed was already empty. I moved unwillingly, but I moved, remembering Giuseppina's warning not to disgrace myself. I dressed in the dim light, half listening to Pip's whimpering from her bed. Silly Pip, whose thoughts had been filled with fashion the night before, had suddenly realized what was going to happen today. So it was Pip my mother had to struggle with, had to coax, and soothe and finally order out of bed. Tilly and I were at the kitchen table, forcing down cups of Pasqualina's coffee and a slice of bread, when Pip came downstairs, her eyes swollen and red, her nose running, her shoes unbuttoned.

My father and Aldo, who was to accompany us to Napoli, were out in the courtyard preparing the horses and loading the carriage. Teresia wiped the tears from her face with the edge of her apron. Pasqualina finished wrapping the provolone she was adding to a basket densely packed with provisions—salami, soprasatta, olives, bread, figs, even a glass jar of last year's eggplant. She handed it over to me, rattling off a list of instructions that began with when and what to eat, but rapidly advanced to the dangers that lay ahead of us among strangers and how we were to protect ourselves. Pasqualina, who had never ventured farther than Avellino in her entire thirty-eight years, was giving us travel advice.

My father's command from the courtyard interrupted her, and we all scrambled to gather together the last of what we were taking with us, to put on our hats and gloves, to kiss one another goodbye. Frankie and Sandro, sleepy-eyed and not completely dressed, had tumbled down the stairs for a final hug. My mother handed me the keys to my trunks.

"Your father has all the papers. He will give them to you at the pier. Claudio will be waiting for you in New York. Go with no one else, no matter what they say to you. Stay in your cabin except for meals. We've bought you first-class tickets so there's no need for you to have anything to do with the unfortunates in steerage. Take care of one another. Don't venture anywhere without the others. Do us honor when you arrive. Be good girls. You know that we'll hear about it if you are not. Write to us. Now, off you go. God be with you."

She held each one of us in a strong, swift embrace.

Pip's chin began to tremble again, but my father barked his final order and she climbed into the carriage. The first pink streaks of dawn were edging over the horizon and my father wanted to be well over the mountain by daylight.

Aldo hopped up onto the seat next to my father in front. I parted the curtain in the carriage to grab one last look at my family before we headed out of the courtyard and onto the Avellino road. My mother shed no tears, just as she hadn't four years ago when Claudio had left. She closed the gate after us, a look of satisfaction, the fulfillment of a dream, on her face.

I drew the curtain back and settled into a numbing doze. I was in a temporary state of resignation, following my parents' wishes by sitting in this carriage, but unable to bring myself to feel any emotion other than a silent rage.

My mother's plans were so carefully constructed, my father's carrying out of them so thorough, that we arrived in Napoli early that afternoon without incident. My mother later wrote us that no one in the village even suspected we were gone until nearly a week had passed.

We ate with my father at a restaurant run by a friend of his and then drove on to the harbor. I had never been to Napoli before. By this time, safe from curious eyes, we were allowed to open the curtains and glimpse the city. It was huge, teeming, loud, confusing. Everywhere there were people. Soldiers on horseback with plumed hats, ladies with brightly colored faces, beggars.

As we approached the wide expanse of the Bay, we were stalled in a river of wagons, carts, men on foot with awkwardly shaped bundles strapped to their backs or bulging valises in their hands, women struggling with wailing babies in their arms and small children clinging to their skirts, dressed in several layers of clothing. Lining the avenue to the harbor were food vendors of all sorts, men in suits and hats offering their assistance with the paperwork required for passage, *capos* shouting for able-bodied men who wanted work on the rails, on the roads. Pip cowered in her corner of the carriage. "They're all so dirty!" She acted as if merely looking at them would defile her.

I leaned forward at the window, straining to see ahead, to catch a glimpse of bay or smokestack, but nothing was visible. I smelled raw fish, roasting chestnuts, rotting fruit, horse droppings, grilled sausages and peppers, the sweat of a thousand people. I could not yet smell the sea.

The carriage suddenly lurched forward. Wagons and carts ahead of us had begun to move. I leaned back and closed my eyes to shut out what I could of my anger. I saw Vito's face— laughing, coaxing, teasing. I saw him dancing, his bare arms raised above his head, clapping out the rhythm. I saw him coming in from the fields, wiping his face with a large blue bandanna. I saw him at the feast of the Madonna, dressed in a starched shirt, hoisting the statue onto his shoulder in the piazza. I saw him lying in the meadow with me.

The carriage jolted to a halt, and I heard the voice of my father in heated discussion with someone on the street. I opened my eyes, returned to the present, to the aching in my heart, the aching between my legs. We had reached the pier. Ahead of us loomed the steamship, swarming with activity. Beyond it shimmered the dazzling vastness of the light upon the Bay. Behind us towered Vesuvio, the layered hills, my own dreams. I opened the carriage door and stepped out, setting one foot ahead of the other in the direction of America.

CHAPTER 9

Laughter

Paolo Serafini heard my laughter before he saw me—a cascade of joy, he told me later, rising above the jabbering of the women behind the house of my brother Claudio, his friend and business partner, the man he loved more than a brother. That I was laughing at all was a miracle. It protected me from the desolation I felt at being uprooted from Italy.

Claudio and Paolo were partners in one of Claudio's business ventures—a saloon that provided them both with some income. Claudio had told Paolo that his three unmarried sisters had arrived from Italy, but Paolo had been so busy that he hadn't gotten over to make his "welcome to America" speech until we'd been there almost a month. He did not knock on Claudio's door panting with expectation, or even curiosity. It was purely a duty call: offer his services to the family of his best friend as if they were his friends. Before that day, he believed that he would have done anything for Claudio. But he had not realized that "anything" could include loving his sister.

We were all out in the back of Claudio's house in Mount Vernon—Pip and Tilly and I, Claudio's wife, Angelina, her sister and a couple of her cousins—sitting on a little spit of stone between the kitchen door and the pathetic garden Angelina had tried to plant. With our sleeves rolled up and knives flailing, great mounds of purple-black eggplants fell victim to our energies. Like Paolo's mother in Napoli, like our aunts up in the hills, we were slicing and salting, laying up *melanzane* in big crocks that Angelina had somehow managed to cram onto that tiny terrace.

I had my back to him, my whole body relaxed with mirth, wisps of my hair escaping from its clasp. When I lifted my right arm—the one without the knife—and wiped away tears of merriment with my outstretched palm, Paolo watched the soft curve of my breasts beneath my flower-sprigged cotton dress.

He reached his hand into his pocket, withdrew his handkerchief—freshly laundered by his sister Flora—and held it out to me.

I turned my face toward him, for the first time registering his presence, and swallowed him with my eyes without once losing the rhythm of my laughter.

Una bella figura. A handsome man with hair the color of Zia Pasqualina's polished copper pots and eyes a transparent, dreamy blue. He was dressed in a brown suit, and his fingernails were clean. Not at all like Claudio.

"Ooh, Paolo!" shrieked one of the others, but I didn't hesitate or even lower my gaze.

I took the handkerchief, brushing my eggplant-stained fingertips along his hand—lightly enough to escape the notice of the others, but long enough for him to recognize that it was deliberate.

He was not a man from the hills, with little experience of the world and even less to say about it. And he was no greenhorn—he'd been in America for ten years. He knew the life, he knew the streets, he knew women. He knew the words they liked to hear.

But he stood before me, watching me press my face into his handkerchief, and imagining himself taking that same handkerchief in his hands and drinking in my fragrance, tasting the salt of my tears—and every sound he had ever uttered to a woman failed him. This is what he told me later.

"So you're Paolo. Claudio wrote us about you. I'm Giulia."

"Claudio's *baby* sister," Angelina put in, wiping her hands on her apron, about to take charge. Angelina didn't like him. She jumped up, all tense and formal and placed herself between us. So just to give her a little more *agita* (as if she didn't create enough for herself every day), I played up to him with my eyes. Didn't say anything. Just looked. Boldly. It made the other girls giggle and Angelina furious. Claudio had told her why I'd been sent away by my mother, so Angelina believed that if she didn't watch me every minute, I would disgrace her.

Paolo saw from Angelina's stance that she would have built a fortress around me, the same way she pulled her baby boys close when danger was near. Angelina, whether she wanted to be or not, was mother-in-absentia to us, and she had just realized that, with me, this was going to be no easy task. *Keep away, Paolo,* she was ordering him.

"This is Philippina." Angelina laid her hand on Pip's shoulder. "And this is Tilly." Paolo took in the funhouse-mirror images of my two sisters. Pip was all bony and angular, a skeleton on which her clothes fluttered, and Tilly was as lumpy and pasty as gnocchi—but they both had the square-jawed Fiorillo face. Tilly seemed planted in her seat, as if she wanted to take root in her corner of the terrace like a waxy palmetto, not move out into the world at all.

By then, Paolo had regained his words. He upended one of the empty eggplant crates and sat down—to Angelina's visible relief—across from rather than next to me. He, too, needed some distance. He chatted with everyone, asked the expected questions about the land left behind, the journey completed, the strange new world encountered since we'd set foot on Ellis Island. The other women in the group, all worldly veterans of two or three years here, teased us newcomers for our wide-eyed wonder. But not without a tinge of homesickness, an evanescent longing that all of them, even Paolo, at one time or another experienced, and sometimes denied. For him, it was the memory of walking along the jetty at Santa Lucia; ahead of him was the light—lavish and prodigal upon the Bay—and to the east, over the city, the shadow of Vesuvio, hovering.

I said almost nothing as the others talked. But my eyes, glistening with interest and amusement, never left Paolo's face—a caress, I knew, that was as deft as that of my fingertips.

Not only was he unlike Claudio, there had been no one in all of Venticano to compare to him. Not even my father—the coddled brother of his widowed and never-married sisters, the successful businessman, the product of my mother's ever-intensifying drive for betterment—not even he possessed Paolo's elegance. Claudio said that Paolo was an educated man, a man of letters, with piles of books in his rooms and the manner of a scholar. But it was more than his culture and refinement that set him apart from the life that had surrounded me in Italy. He was also different in the way he returned my gaze. Neither red-cheeked and flustered nor swaggering like the boys back home, who teased or made crude jokes when they thought you were interested in them. Paolo looked at me deeply, without embarrassment, with candor. I could tell that he admired me. I enjoyed such attention.

But what would I do with it, with him? He was older than Claudio, almost thirty, a man of the New World. Too old for me. Letitia's husband was much older than she was, and that had brought her only dissatisfaction.

I looked, but I was not ready to feel. There was too much of this new life to understand. The voices were so strange and raucous, the streets so numerous and confusing. There were so many people whose faces I didn't know, who did not even nod in greeting. I laughed in the garden with the women during the day; I poked fun at Angelina and her proprieties. But at night I was still terrified. I missed both the stillness and the music of Venticano; the faces of Giuseppina and my little brothers; and I missed Vito Cipriano—the roughness of his coarsely shaven cheek and the apple scent of the pomade he wore too thickly on his curly black hair.

I didn't want to be here.

The morning was passing rapidly, and the pile of eggplants had not diminished noticeably since Paolo had appeared in our midst. He could sense, once again, Angelina's slightly veiled impatience. He knew he was going to need Angelina on his side. So he rose from his perch, ready to make his farewell, and with a grin and a flourish, invited all of us sisters for a stroll and then the band concert in Hartley Park on Sunday. Pip and Tilly beamed and giggled. Angelina shot a look of gratitude at Paolo for the gift of a Sunday afternoon free of her sisters-in-law. And I, a smile of acknowledgment spreading across my face, leaned my head back and laughed.

As Paolo walked away, he slipped his hand inside his pocket and clutched the handkerchief, still damp with my laughter.

CHAPTER 10

Hartley Park

Paolo took us three sisters to Hartley Park, as he had promised. On Sunday afternoons the footpaths in the park were crowded, the crunch of leather on stone a backdrop to the German and Yiddish and Italian conversations wending their circuitous way to the band shell.

That Sunday, the musicians were performing selections from Scott Joplin and George M. Cohan. Paolo picked us up promptly at three. Angelina had not invited him to Sunday dinner, which I thought was ungracious, but I was learning after only a few weeks in America that customs were different here.

Paolo lived alone in a rooming house a few blocks from Claudio's. His married sister Flora also lived in Mount Vernon, and he'd borrowed a blanket from her that she did not object to our spreading on the grass. He had also stopped at Barletta's on the way to Claudio's and picked up three small nosegays of lilies of the valley and forget-me-nots—identical, except that he'd askedVinnie Barletta to put a single red rose in the middle of one.

When he got to the house, Tilly and Pip were waiting, gloved and anxious. He swept off his hat and presented them with the bouquets, careful to hold back the one with the rose.

"Oh, Paolo! *Grazie!* How thoughtful! What a gentleman!"

A few minutes later I came down the stairs.

"*Come sta,* Paolo! You're here so soon! You don't give a girl a chance to take off her apron."

Paolo turned to me with the flowers. I noticed that my bouquet was unusual—not a match to the others now in the hands of my sisters—but I didn't react. Instead, I took it with a smile and a curtsy. Although I'd flirted with him yesterday over the eggplants, I couldn't imagine him as anything more than a *simpatico* friend of my brother's, a man who was showing me some kindness in this strange new land.

We walked down to the park, Paolo in the middle between my sisters, me on the periphery, laughing, almost skipping, relishing my freedom from Angelina's kitchen and laundry and damp babies.

When we got to the park, we looked for a comfortable patch of grass. I wanted to be near the music and strode toward the band shell, stepping carefully around the early arrivals sprawled around their picnic baskets.

Pip didn't want to sit on the ground, not even on Flora's blanket; she didn't want to be so close to other people—to the smells of their food and their unfamiliar bodies, to the sounds of their unrecognizable tongues. She hung back near a bench by the path. Tilly was torn between my pleasure in the outing and Pip's fears and disdain. She was following me, somewhat breathlessly and clumsily, when Pip's bony hand stretched out to hold her back.

Paolo was coming up in the rear, carrying the blanket as well as a cardboard box tied with multicolored string and filled with cannoli from Artuso's bakery. Pip stood in rigid exasperation; Tilly in flustered confusion.

"Oh, Paolo, stop her!" I heard Pip say. "Look at her parading up there. Who does she think she is? A child at a carnival? Isn't there some quiet bench we can sit on out of the way? Look, over there under the trees."

I was up ahead, waving to indicate that I'd found a spot.

Paolo moved toward me, not seeming to care if Pip stood waiting on the path, arms crossed and foot tapping, for the entire concert.

"Paolo, Paolo, over here," I called. "This is a good spot, don't you think? Let me help you with the blanket. I'm so excited! This is the first time I've heard music since I left Italy—what a wonderful idea! Claudio doesn't think of things like this. He doesn't understand that people need more than work, more than money. Did you know that he almost didn't let us come when Tilly told him you'd invited us? We've been so cooped up in that house, barely allowed out to do the marketing. He's worse than my Zia Pasqualina with his worries and warnings."

I couldn't stop babbling, I was so thrilled to be away from everything that had oppressed me since coming to America. I shook out the blanket with a vigorous snap.

"Oh, I've been longing for a day like this! To be outdoors among the trees and flowers, to smell the air, feel the sun, to put on my fine dress instead of trudging around day after day in a housedress and apron with my hair tied up in a rag. Angelina thinks we're her servants. She either doesn't know or doesn't want to know what we came from, how we lived in Venticano."

I finally noticed that my sisters were still not as eager as I was to embrace the day in the park in the midst of strangers.

"Pip, Tilly, over here!" I stood again and waved. Pip, red-faced, lips set in a taut line, came gingerly toward us.

"Giulia, this is not appropriate. I will not stay here in front of all these strange people and I do not want to sit on the ground. And why must you always bring such attention to yourself—chattering and waving like a silly child. You continue to be an absolute embarrassment to me, no matter where we are."

She turned to Paolo to seek his agreement.

"Paolo, I expected you, of all people, to behave in keeping with the trust Claudio placed in you as our escort," she said sternly.

I was annoyed. "Oh, Mother of God, Pip, sit down and enjoy yourself and leave Paolo alone. If it really disturbs you to sit on the blanket, go find a bench. You do manage to drain the last ounce of pleasure out of your life, don't you? Why did you even come? To torment me?"

The people seated around us were beginning to notice. Although they probably couldn't understand a word Pip and I were saying, they could surely hear the scolding in our voices. The concert was about to begin. People were coughing, re-settling themselves, gathering their children into quiet heaps, and packing away the remnants of cold chicken and pickles.

Tilly, an expression of hopefulness on her face, piped in blithely, "So we're sitting here after all, are we? I do think we'll hear the music better. Oh, look, there's the concertmaster already. We'd better all sit down or we'll block the view of the people behind us."

Paolo and I took the opportunity of Tilly's timely arrival to find our places on the blanket and join in the overall hushing that whispered across the lawn. Paolo took care not to sit too close to me and made space for Tilly, who seemed relieved to finally be at rest.

Pip remained standing, her defeat spreading up her face. She took a half turn, looking back over her shoulder at the bench, now half-occupied by an elderly couple with cane and parasol. There was room for Pip, but it was unthinkable that she'd sit alone.

From her stance of rigid refusal, Pip crumpled into an awkward pile on the blanket. She sat as far apart from us as she could, first brushing away small flecks of dried leaves and tiny pebbles before she arranged herself, smoothing her skirt over and over. She did not speak to us for the rest of the afternoon, not even to take a cannoli when Paolo finally opened the box during intermission.

I quickly forgot about the unpleasantness and absorbed myself in the music. In contrast to my sisters, I couldn't sit still. I was in motion even as I sat, legs tucked under me. My hands lightly tapped out a rhythm at times on my thigh, at times on the blanket beside me. I swayed, my shoulders loose, fluid, an elixir of life running beneath my clothing, animating the dress like some puppeteer bringing a costumed marionette to life.

My fingers played the blanket like a keyboard or the strings of a guitar; my body danced; I breathed the music into my lungs and exhaled it as joyous movement.

Once or twice I glanced at Paolo, acknowledging his presence and sending him a smile of appreciation. He had chosen well: the music wafting through the early September air, the afternoon sunlight filtering through the trees, the aromas of freshly mowed grass and chrysanthemums filling our lungs. Not Italy, no, I can't say that it resembled closely any Sunday memory that I carried. But the afternoon held some familiarity for me, some joy, some spark that reunited me with home. Paolo had given me a small gift by bringing me here.

CHAPTER 11

The Palace

About a year before Pip and Tilly and I arrived in America, Claudio and Paolo had stumbled across a building. It was a place nobody had wanted then—filthy, abandoned, something without any value to those who saw it only with the eyes of realists, not with the eyes of dreamers. But Claudio and Paolo were dreamers. That was why they'd come to America.

Claudio's dreams were all about money and doing better than Papa. He fled across the ocean to a land where no one knew him, no one expected something from him just because he was Felice Fiorillo's oldest son—and what did he do? He bought himself a bay and a black horse and started hauling goods in a wagon, just like Papa. But before you knew it, it wasn't just one wagon, it was four. And a stable on Fourth

Avenue to house the horses he picked up, one or two at a time when he had the cash. Driving all over New York, bringing the stone, the wood, the bricks that were building the city, he met people, he talked them up, he imagined the possibilities. Anything with a dollar sign in its future, Claudio latched onto, cut himself into the deal. That was why he bought the decaying place he and Paolo named the Palace of Dreams. But Claudio was shrewd. He knew he didn't have the patience to run it once he'd created it, so he made a three-way deal—Claudio, Paolo and Willie Rupert, who owned a brewery.

The Palace was a dump in the beginning, but a dump in the right place, close to the factories and the rail line. Claudio and Paolo cleaned it up, hauling away the debris in Claudio's wagons, bringing in furniture and fixtures that Claudio was able to trade for—a chandelier to hang over the bar, even an old piano. Willie's brewery provided the beer. Paolo did the books and managed the place. He was usually at the Palace every evening after he finished work as a union secretary with the IWW.

Before long, they started getting customers—the men coming off their shifts at Ward Leonard and Pioneer Watch-works, the conductors and engineers from the New Haven and Hartford Railroad, Claudio's business associates from around the city. As the whistles blew, you could hear them.

"Stop by the Palace for a round."

"Meet me at the Palace."

"Comin' to the Palace tonight, lad?"

They came for a couple of drinks and a card game, just like the men in Venticano had made their way to Auteri's every night. They unwound, looking for a little time for themselves before they plodded home. They left some of their worries on the table; they left a few dollars, too. Soon, like everything Claudio touched, it was a success.

CHAPTER 12

The Blouse Factory

Not long after we'd arrived in Mount Vernon, Claudio got us jobs at the blouse factory over on the South Side. Claudio's businesses were expanding, but with our three additional mouths to feed, plus his own growing family, his resentment at having to support us was mounting. It had all started with Claudio's wife. I was out sweeping the front stoop when our ignorant neighbor across the street, Carmella Polito, leaned out her window to shake her dust mop.

"Eh, enjoy what you're doing now, because it won't be long," she called.

I pretended not to hear her, but she went on anyway.

"Just you wait. That wife of your brother's ain't gonna stay quiet about you girls not bringing any money into the house. He's gonna make you go to work."

The know-it-all slammed her window shut when I continued to ignore her, but I didn't forget what she'd said. A couple of weeks later, I walked past Claudio and Angelina's bedroom one evening and heard them fighting. Angelina's voice was rapid, complaining. Once or twice she said my name. Claudio was gruff and irritable. Finally, he silenced her with an explosive and exasperated "*Va bene!* Okay, okay, I'll see what I can do. But I don't think there's much of a market for anything those nuns taught them." I tiptoed quickly down the hall before he opened the door.

Within a couple of days he'd made the rounds of those who owed him favors and came up with three seats behind the sewing machines on John Molloy's shift at the blouse factory. Tilly, Pip and I were to start right away.

It was not what my mother had imagined for us when she sent us to America. Claudio's descriptions of his success in his letters to her had ignored the tough, gritty work that had produced that success. For Claudio, our jobs at the factory were the equivalent of the pick and shovel that had been thrust into his hands when he'd first set foot on American soil.

We had trouble from the first day. I had never sewn on a machine before. Zia Pasqualina and, later, the nuns in Sorrento, had taught me fine hand-stitching, embroidery, elegant work for objects of quality. In America, they didn't know about such things. You looked at the American girls on the streets; their clothes had none of the finer details. The rich ones, they went to the immigrant dressmakers, schooled like us in convents. But those factory-made clothes! We were sewing women's blouses. Fifty of us in a room, the din of the machines unbearable, the dust, the unending piles of fabric arriving constantly from the cutters, the squabbles between girls from different neighborhoods, the ever-watchful eyes of Molloy. This was not the life my mother had imagined for us.

I had headaches by the end of the day. My shoulders and neck were in knots. My fingertips felt numb. Sometimes, in the afternoons, when the sun came through the dirt-caked windows and beat on my back, when the drone of the machines filled my ears so that I couldn't hear even my own daydreams, when Molloy was at the other end of the room with his clipboard—I allowed myself a few minutes of escape, pressed my head against the enameled black metal of my Singer and closed my eyes.

I thought about being someplace else. Sometimes it was back in Venticano, working with Giuseppina in the garden, the earth clinging to my hands, getting under my fingernails. I pulled up a carrot, its feathery greens brushing my bare arm. I rinsed the carrot in the metal water bucket and bit into it, tasting the soil and the sun, tasting Italy.

Or I thought about Saturday nights—the one just past or the one to come—and dancing at the Hillcrest Hotel with Roberto Scarpa. His sister Antonietta worked the machine next to mine and she was the one who'd told Tilly and Pip and me about the dances. I had to beg Claudio for weeks to take us, pleading with him as if he were Papa, reminding him that this was America now. If he could send us to work in a factory like the American girls, then he could let us dance like the American girls on Saturday night! He finally gave in, but full of rules and orders about how we were to behave and who we could associate with. He took us there around eight and then hung out on the porch smoking with his friends, poking his head inside every now and then to make sure we were still there and hadn't sneaked out with some boy he didn't approve of. If he only knew!

"Where's Giulia?" he barked one night to Tilly when he

stepped in to make his hourly check and I was nowhere to be seen among the swirling skirts and tapping feet.

"She's gone to the toilet." She gave her well-rehearsed reply, for once not fumbling in anticipation of his rage should he realize she was covering for me. She took a deep breath when he apparently believed her and went back to his friends. But she came scurrying to the small parlor, where I was sitting in deep conversation with Roberto, who was holding my hand and whispering in my ear.

"Claudio's looking for you!" she hissed. "You'd better get back soon or he won't let us come next week!"

I rolled my eyes at Roberto to let him know how miffed I was by the interruption. "Okay, okay, I'll be there in a minute," I said and shooed her back to the dance floor. I turned back to Roberto. "She's right, you know. Claudio's very strict. I don't want to provoke him." I got up off the sofa, but continued to hold his hand. I squeezed it and whispered, "I don't want to lose the opportunity to be with you."

I meant what I said. But I also didn't want him to think I was going to be easy. I sat with him in the back parlor, but you wouldn't catch me like some of the girls I knew from the factory. They went out with men alone; they didn't just meet them at dances. They didn't live with their families. They had no protection. Claudio's vigilance irritated me, but because the men knew he was my brother, they didn't try anything.

Roberto and I walked separately to the dance floor and I stopped to talk with his sister, who had introduced us. Antonietta had talked incessantly about Roberto at work. He was the oldest of her brothers, the tallest, the handsomest. I hadn't believed her until I saw him for myself. He was blond, with long arms and legs and powerful hands. When he danced with me (and by then, I was the only one he danced with), I felt the strength of his grip around my waist. I saw my hand disappear inside his. I'd always been small for my age. Even then, at sixteen, I still wore a child's-size shoe and glove.

People watched us when we danced. Roberto was so big that everyone gave him room. But despite his size, he was very graceful.

Dancing at the Hillcrest was different from dancing at Cucino's. People were more *watchful*—of others and of themselves. They cared more about what other people thought than we had dancing in the dirt in our bare feet. In Mount Vernon, all the girls spent hours during the week talking about what they'd wear, who they hoped to dance with. We then spent more hours Saturday evening getting ready, borrowing from one another, coaxing our hair into the styles we saw in the magazines that got passed around at lunchtime, trying to find some happy medium in the way we were dressed so that we'd be allowed out of the house but still look stylish. So much energy went into these preparations! It made Tilly giddy and brought nervous shrieks even to Pip's serious countenance.

The other difference between Cucino's and the Hillcrest, like everything else in America, was how big these dances were. At Cucino's, we were maybe a dozen, and all of us had grown up together. Here, the ballroom was a crush of people—fifty, a hundred sometimes. So many strangers. People came up from the city, from the Bronx mostly, because of the Hillcrest's reputation. The musicians were the best. Paolo Serafini played the piano. Claudio said it was a way for him to pick up a few extra dollars every week, since he was never going to get rich working for "that union." But the way Paolo played, you could hear that it wasn't just for the money. He knew all the popular songs. Claudio said he even wrote songs himself, but I'd never heard him play them at the dances. What he did play was wonderful dance music, music that had people moving and laughing and clapping their hands. The ballroom at the Hillcrest on Saturday nights was a blur of color, a haze of voices, a release of all that weariness and longing from the week before. What would we have done without those dances? Nothing to relieve the chill of my sister-in-law's house, the loneliness of my new life, the tedium of broadcloth that faced me every day.

I felt a kick abruptly interrupt my thoughts, a warning from Tilly, who sat at the machine behind me, that Molloy was on his way back here. We had, each of us, already been caught dozing at our tables. Molloy cautioned us not to do it again. So we took turns, one watching out and warning while the others slept.

We had other troubles with Molloy as well. Getting to work on time was a struggle. There was no peace in my brother's household in the morning. Claudio and Angelina's babies clamored from hunger and dampness. Pip and Tilly and I groped for clothing, for the hairbrush, for coffee. Still in his bed, Claudio muttered at the noise, exhausted from a day at work and a night at the Palace. He stayed hidden until we were all gone and the boys were fed and dry. Pip would snatch the broom, Tilly washed the dishes, I chopped the onions and the garlic for that night's marinara and sliced bread and provolone for us to take to work.

One early November morning, I poured some olive oil into Angelina's heavy pot. It was good quality oil, thick and green. Claudio got it from the DiDonato family, the ones with the importing business. Back then, Americans didn't know what olive oil was. I got the onions started, then ran out to pluck some *basilico*. It was almost finished, all scrawny and leggy. Any night soon we'd have a frost. But even in the intensity of summer, this basil hadn't grown. I hadn't been in Mount Vernon long enough to figure out if it was Angelina or America. But this was not a garden I knew. When I had stood in the middle of Giuseppina's garden, I found myself in a fresco, like the one imbedded in the wall of Santa Maria dei Miracoli. All around me was color: the red tomatoes and peppers, the purple eggplants and fava beans, six different shades of green—zucchini, *broccoli rabe, basilico,* artichoke, escarole, *fagiolini.* Perhaps it was the sun, which was so different from the sun in America. I asked myself, isn't it the same? How can the light, the warmth, be so alien to me? In Italy, the sun released, set free the growing things, splurged itself in unrelenting generosity. In America, the sun was wan, stingy, exacting. It was no wonder these basil plants had to stretch themselves, strain for their meager ration.

I pulled my sweater tighter around me against the cold morning and raced back to my onions. Tilly had, thankfully, finished washing up and was crushing and straining the tomatoes.

"Be careful that no seeds get through. You know how bitter they'll make the gravy and I don't want to listen to Claudio complain after I've had a long day at work."

"Maybe *you* want to strain, to make sure it's perfect?" There was an edge to Tilly's voice. As sweet as she was, she didn't like to take direction from me. But they all knew I was the better cook. Giuseppina had taught me. In my mother's house, Pasqualina had hoarded her skills, unwilling to share Papa's appreciation for a well-cooked meal. And my mother believed there were better things to learn than how to cook.

Of course, here in America, Pip and Tilly had no Pasqualina to bury her arms in flour and eggs every Saturday morning to make the pasta. In fact the three of us were Angelina's Pasqualina. The sisters of her husband, given refuge, a roof, in exchange for our domestic services.

I chopped the basil and threw it together with the tomatoes into the pot. I jumped back as the contents of the pot flashed and sizzled, sending up a hot red spray. I didn't want to have to change my blouse. A flick or two with my spoon and I set the pot on the back burner for Angelina to watch during the day.

I raced upstairs to wash and run a brush through my hair.

"Hurry up! We're going to be late again and Molloy will be furious! He'll go right to Claudio, too. Why can't you ever be ready when it's time to leave?"

Pip and Tilly waited for me in the front hall. I slipped in the last hairpin on my way down the stairs, the soles of my boots slapping urgently against the wood as Claudio grumbled in annoyance. Coat and hat, a last glance in the mirror by the door, and we were off—coffee and tomato and warm stove left behind in Angelina's kitchen, a ten-block walk ahead of us, Molloy and his clock waiting.

I hated that walk. I hated the dim early morning light and the chill that put an ache in my toes. I hated leaving the familiar streets of the neighborhood. We walked down to the corner, past Our Lady of Victory and the tenements on the other side. Then the houses started to dwindle as we approached the New Haven Railroad line. Because there was no bridge at the bottom of this street, we had to turn left down by the tracks and walk east to the bridge at Fourth Avenue. On the other side of the tracks, we had to walk two blocks west again and then another three blocks south to the factory.

Sometimes we walked with a couple of other girls from the neighborhood and then it was not so bad. We joked along the way about Molloy or talked about the dance, or even stopped to look in the window of the Tabu dress shop on the corner. But this morning we were so late that Annunziata and Carmen hadn't waited for us and we were trudging alone, our steps quickening to a run when we passed the clock in the window of Ruggiero's Shoe Repair.

"We can't be late again. Molloy said—"

"I know what Molloy said. Don't talk. Keep moving."

Just then we heard the screech of the five-to-seven whistle. From this side of the tracks we wouldn't make it in five minutes.

Tilly, Pip and I looked at one another and agreed without speaking to take our shortcut. Instead of turning toward the Fourth Avenue bridge, we wriggled through the fencing and raced down the rocky slope toward the railroad tracks. We had done this many times before. Milkweed and the shriveled blossoms of goldenrod and thistle caught and clung to our skirts and sleeves. My boots skidded on the crumbled dirt and gravel, and I slid the rest of the way down on my backside. Tilly and Pip reached the bottom ahead of me and started over the tracks. We were a few blocks west of the station, where the tracks branched out five across. I brushed myself off and followed them.

I was almost across the third track when I stumbled, falling to my knees as I tripped over the hem of my skirt. *Va Napoli,* I muttered to myself as I heard it rip. Something else to mend, as if there weren't enough of Claudio's shirts and my nephews' overalls in the basket that waited for me every night. I pulled myself to my feet. My hands stung from where they'd slammed against the gravel bed and my chin felt wet and raw. I knew Molloy would send me to the washroom to clean my bloody face—and dock my pay before he'd let me near his blouses. For the second time that morning, I brushed myself off and started off. But I couldn't move. My left foot remained rooted to the ground, like an unfamiliar weight at the end of my leg when I tried to lift it and take a step. I raised my skirt.

My boot heel had become wedged in the space between the ties, clutched by the resin-soaked wood. A chill climbed its frantic way up my back. My hand reached without thought for Giuseppina's medal around my neck. Then I pulled at the boot with all my strength and will, but it wouldn't budge. I tried wriggling my foot as if I were about to dance. I was so distracted, so consumed by my entrapment, that I didn't notice Tilly and Pip, who'd already made it to the other side and begun to scramble up the embankment. Suddenly, I heard Pip's voice, but not in the scolding tone she used when I lagged behind and she was nervous about Molloy's clock.

"Giulia! Giulia!" she shrieked, a knife edge of hysteria, a bow drawn across a tightly strung violin. "The train! The train!"

I jerked my head up, first in Tilly and Pip's direction, then to the left, where Pip was frantically gesturing. A locomotive was heading toward me from the station. I couldn't see if it was traveling on the middle track.

I grabbed Giuseppina's medal once again as it dangled over the boot, kissed it and rapidly mumbled a prayer. Then I placed both my hands around my ankle and struggled again to lift the boot free. But it still wouldn't come loose.

"Untie the boot! Untie the boot!" Pip's hands stabbed the air in a pantomime.

But I didn't want to. My boot! My mother had sent them, exquisite butter-yellow boots with black trim and laces. They fit me perfectly, narrow and graceful around the ankles, the leather as soft as the satin bags my sisters and I embroidered to hold our wedding tributes. Those boots were my memento of all that I'd left behind in Italy.

The locomotive was looming; I could feel the tracks starting to heave; I could hear the hiss and clang. My fingers somehow found the ends of the laces and pulled them loose. I lifted out my foot and hobbled to the other side where Pip and Tilly waited, white-faced. I flung myself into the bushes at the edge of the southern slope as the train passed.

CHAPTER 13

The Keys to the Store

Things happen for a reason. My scratched and bleeding face, my lost boot, cost Tilly and Pip and me our jobs with Molloy. Claudio roared for a few days—first at our insanity in crossing the tracks, next for our inability to get to work on time and keep Molloy happy. Angelina sulked to have us back in the house all day, but I think she was also secretly pleased that my boot had been destroyed. I kept busy, washing and starching the curtains, beating the carpets, emptying the cupboard of all the glassware and dishes and washing everything till it gleamed. The house reeked of ammonia and lemon oil.

By that time, wooed by Claudio's success and his own dis-affection with Papa, my uncle Tony had brought his wife,

Yolanda, and their son, Peppino, to America. Claudio had found both Tony and Peppino jobs on a construction crew and they lived not far from us in Mount Vernon.

On Sundays they always joined us for dinner, recreating a small piece of Venticano life. A few weeks after Molloy fired us, Claudio settled into his Sunday pasta with more than his usual appetite.

"I bought another building," he announced, "down on Fourth. There's a store on the ground floor. The old lady who ran it died last month. Her sons don't want it—it's full of buttons and thread and dress patterns. What do they know about dressmaking?"

He turned to Tilly and Pip and me.

"It's yours. Since you girls can't seem to work for somebody else, work for yourselves. I don't want to hear another Molloy complaining to me. And I don't want you crying to me if you fail. This is the last job I'm gonna dig up for you. Don't let the vendors charge you too much or convince you to buy anything you don't need. Don't give your customers too much credit. Work hard. I'll check the books once a month."

He threw the keys on the table, finished his wine and left for the Palace.

Tilly, Pip and I looked at one another. We were proprietors now, over thread and yarn and buttons and lace. We were respectable. Our mother would be proud.

CHAPTER 14

"Divina e Bella"

Paolo wrote poems. His little nephew, Nino, brought one to me.

I saw Nino almost every day, on the Avenue when I went down to do the marketing. He was so funny. A skinny little fellow, full of energy, always running, playing. His mother, Paolo's sister Flora, kept him very clean, his clothes always well mended. The first time he saw me, he called out, *"Bellissima!"* and clutched his heart and fell in a swoon at my feet. He won me over. I couldn't resist him. After that, he followed me around from shop to shop, carrying my basket, offering his advice on the quality of the vegetables, babbling about his American teacher at the No. 10 School. He was learning English. He showed off his new words like a new toy. I often bought him a peppermint at Artuso's.

"I'll tell Zio Paolo I saw you today," he said whenever we parted on the corner—Flora didn't allow him to leave the block. "He'll be jealous. He'll wish he could be me, walking by your side and making you laugh."

I always laughed in spite of myself and shooed him back to his games. He started to bring me little presents. A flower plucked from the vacant lot across from the school; a drawing he'd sketched on the back of an envelope; a piece of his mother's coconut cake neatly wrapped in a cloth. Then one day, he greeted me with a carefully folded sheet of blue notepaper.

All this time, he'd been as if an emissary from his uncle. "Zio Paolo did this, and Zio Paolo did that…" Paolo's name and deeds were never far from Nino's lips.

I didn't have time on the street to read what Nino had given me, so I took it home and opened it in the kitchen. On the blue notepaper were words written in Paolo's strong and elegant hand. I recognized the handwriting from the papers Claudio sometimes brought home. It was a poem, entitled *"Divina e Bella."*

I was so lost in thought this morning.
I could not take another step but
Found myself rooted, waiting,
Hoping that Giulia would pass by
And bestow upon me
The dazzling beam of her smile.
But my Beauty does not show herself!
Thoughts of her crowd out all else,
Throng around me with doubts.
Perhaps she feels nothing of what
I feel for her?
I swear, if I do not see her
My heart will shatter.

I folded the note and placed it inside my blouse. I didn't tell my sisters, and I didn't tease Paolo. I was afraid Nino had stolen the poem. Paolo certainly hadn't asked him to give it to me. The next day, when I saw Nino, I gave it back, scolding him that he must replace it in Paolo's papers undisturbed, that he had no right to let me have it.

Paolo's poem set off such confusion in my head. I was flattered by the intensity of his feelings for me. But I was unused to men who hid their emotions behind words written in silence and locked away in a drawer. I preferred to be whirled around a dance floor, to feel Roberto's desire for me in the press of his hand on my back. But I was beginning to see that, except for those moments on the dance floor, Roberto and I had little else to share with each other.

I returned the blue notepaper to Nino, but I didn't forget the poem. I kept the words enclosed in my heart.

CHAPTER 15

The Christening

On a Sunday in February, my friend Antonietta christened her firstborn, a little boy she had named Natale. Half the neighborhood turned out for the celebration. Her husband, Giacomo DiDonato, was well known in Mount Vernon. People didn't ignore his invitations. Not even the police ignored this event, although it was hard to believe they'd been invited by Giacomo. But they were there, standing outside Our Lady of Victory during the Mass and later, more of them, down the block near the hall. Somebody must have warned them that there might be trouble, that there were those in both Giacomo's and Antonietta's families who would've preferred that such a cause for celebration never come to pass.

People were lined up outside the hall waiting to get in,

clutching their envelopes, their medals, their blessings for the baby boy. The priest had done his work in the church, but now the old women with powers were ready to add their voices, murmur their spells that would protect the boy in ways the Irish priest couldn't even imagine.

It had snowed on Thursday and it was frigid, but still people waited, small bursts of conversation or the brittle tinkling of gold charms dangling from gloved fingers piercing the February air. The police had built a fire in an ash can on the corner of Fifth and Prospect to warm themselves, scowling over the flames at the bad luck of drawing such a duty.

Antonietta's brothers were also outside—having a smoke, watching the line of well-wishers, watching the police. My Roberto was there—the one they called the Scarecrow, the one with whom I'd been keeping company.

What happened next was unclear, full of the scum of rumor, self-deception, self-aggrandizement. The newspapers, based on police reports, gave one account. Eyewitnesses—the aunts and cousins, the countrymen on both sides who were standing in the line—gave other versions, each containing some elements that coincided, some of their own embroidery. Antonietta's family remained silent.

There was one element that recurred in all accounts—that the origin of the afternoon's events was a conversation in the line questioning the paternity of the child. It was Antonietta's brothers who overheard the provocative comments. And it was Roberto, as oldest, who led them to avenge the besmirched honor of their sister.

Fists let loose. Women screamed. Crucifixes and medals of Saint Anthony were hurled into the snow. The throng surged as if caught in a maelstrom. The police, roused from their resentful apathy, descended with truncheons at the ready. Words, shouts, the quickening ripple of danger, like an animal beating its hoof on the ground to warn its herd, reached those inside. People rushed out into the snow, to defend, to witness. Antonietta, faltering and confused, clutched the baby, paralyzed by what had happened to her celebration until her mother grabbed them both—as well as the white satin bag filled with the gifts of well-wishers—and led them to a small room that led onto the alley. I myself stood in the doorway as people rushed in one direction or another.

The Scarecrow was at the center of the confrontation, his towering height an easy target for the cops, who were making their way toward him. And then it happened. A uniformed arm reached around from behind, encircling Roberto's neck. The cop's other hand then covered Roberto's face, trying to pull him back. Suddenly, the hand flew away, blood pumping, spewing all those surrounding Roberto. The arm around Roberto's neck released its hold as the cop sought to stem his own blood. Roberto ducked and disappeared. But not before he turned his head—his mouth a twisted, carmine slash—and spit out a finger.

The smell of blood sent another tremor through the crowd. As abruptly as they had converged upon the fight—the men compelled to defend the honor of one family or another, the young boys driven simply to partake in the frenzy, the old women bound by ancient oaths to fling their curses—they now scattered, flying from the fringes in all directions.

An ambulance and police wagons began to arrive, bells furiously sending out yet another warning to those still engaged in the melee, police reinforcements pouring out of the wagons onto the street to subdue the violence of the mob with a violence of their own.

In contrast to the fury and confusion outside, a hollow and desolate silence had seeped into the hall. Without an audience, the musicians had long since ceased their rondos and ballads.

The floor, only minutes before filled with knots of chatting neighbors and romping children, was now strewn with remnants of food half-eaten, coats forgotten in the madness to join the brawl, a shoe lost in the press of the curious. The last of the mothers had shepherded her children out the same door through which Antonietta had been led to safety. My own family had all left before the fight, but I'd stayed behind to enjoy the waning moments of the party, to listen to the music, hoping to dance one last time with Roberto.

Earlier in the day, I'd darted about from one group to the next, a playful sprite. First dancing with the children, then whispering playfully into the ear of Roberto. I had felt as if a scherzo played in my head.

But the liveliness and joy that had animated me were drained from my body. I was alone; I was not safe. I backed away from the front door, feeling stricken. I thought the hall was empty. Then I heard the sound of footsteps racing down the stairs two at a time and a voice calling my name. My head jerked toward the voice, my eyes charged with terror. It was Paolo. I felt a fleeting relief wash over me, but then my attention was immediately drawn back to the door by renewed wailing and screams. In a few seconds, the cops would be inside.

Paolo reached me and reached out for me, taking my trembling body into his arms and guiding me toward the alley door. I knew only that I had to get out of there, away from the fighting, away from the cops. I was terrified of what would happen if someone told them I was Roberto's girl.

The alley was still clear, and Paolo hurried us over the hard-packed snow, throwing his coat over my shoulders because we hadn't had time to search for mine. It wasn't far to Claudio's house—just a couple of blocks over on Sixth. But the way was rutted and slippery, slowing our silent progress.

Halfway there, I stopped, twisting my body away from his side. I grabbed the rough bark of a tree for support, bent into the road and began to retch.

Paolo held me from behind, brushing away the stray curls that had fallen into my face. At first, I resisted his help, pushing his hand away; but then, overwhelmed by my heaving, I submitted. I even allowed him to wipe my mouth when, spent and exhausted, I lifted my head and leaned against the tree, eyes closed against the demons I'd seen that afternoon.

We had barely spoken since he'd called out my name. What words could I utter? How could I describe to him what I'd seen? But he did not ask me for words. He put his arm around me again, taking more of my weight than before. Paolo knew I was still unsafe out there on the street. We could still hear the strident call of the wagons and the shouts of those chasing and being chased.

I had been depleted by the vomiting, in my will to reach safety as well as my physical strength to do so. But Paolo made us keep moving.

Up ahead, a man approached us. It was Claudio. Word had reached him of the fight and he'd come to find me.

"You should've gone home with the rest of us," he barked. He raised his hand to strike me. Instead of flinching, my response was merely a sullen and wan silence. "Get in the house!" He gestured dismissively with the raised hand. I trudged up the stairs and slammed the door behind me, but not before I saw a look of disbelief and disapproval on Paolo's face. He seemed to be assessing my brother in a different way that afternoon, judging him not as a business partner, but as a man who might mistreat a woman.

Claudio and Paolo remained outside in the snow. Paolo described the chaos and offered to return to the hall to retrieve my things, but Claudio decided to go back with him.

When they arrived, the last police wagon was pulling away. One of Antonietta's aunts emerged from the alley and began gathering the medals and charms that lay scattered in the snow. She would have to purify them and bless them again. Any of the magic they'd once possessed was now lost—especially if they'd been trampled or splashed by the blood whose traces lay everywhere.

On Monday afternoon when Paolo opened the Palace, the place vibrated with the drone of hushed, excited voices. The newspapers had reported that morning that the finger had not been found; neither had Roberto. He had vanished, protected by the silence of his family. There was talk of nothing except the christening and the ferocity of Roberto. If the rumors hovering above the whiskey glasses and distracted card games were true, Roberto was on his way to Italy.

CHAPTER 16

The Iron

Another loss wrenched from me, this time in the other direction. Back to Italy, they all said. Disappeared, hidden, flown. The blood wiped from his mouth, the memories of eyewitnesses wiped clean. Did I want that mouth on my mouth again? Did I want to taste that blood over and over again in my dreams?

I felt so alone. The feelings I thought I had for Roberto seemed no more than a foolish girl's daydreams. The thrill of being held by him in a dance was now overshadowed by the realization that there'd been nothing of substance—only heat—between us.

The days since he'd been gone were my undoing. The warmth with which our connection had surrounded me was unraveling like a poorly knit sweater. I dragged myself to the store every day and pretended to some industry, but I was weighted down by my worries, by the fatigue that overtook me until I could not lift my body one more time in any kind of movement. I collapsed onto the bench in the waning afternoon sunlight and leaned my head against the wall.

Claudio came almost every day to inspect, to check up, to spy. He had not forgiven me for the taint I carried by my connection to Roberto. The cops even came to question *him,* big Claudio, with all his friends in the right places. People had been whispering to Claudio, people who thought they knew things, who thought they could gain Claudio's favor with their revelations. After that visit from the cops, he raged into the store. Tilly was in the back sorting spools of thread; I was up front, doing the tallies from the previous day, waiting for customers. He drew his hand across the countertop, leaving a track in the dust, and began to rant about how filthy I was, how lazy. I suspected this had nothing to do with my housekeeping, but I didn't keep my thoughts to myself. I yelled back. Big Claudio! Trying to keep his sister in line! That's it, isn't it? The neighborhood's saying, Look who he lets her get mixed up with.

So Claudio didn't want to hear any more. He wanted me to shut up. He grabbed the first thing his hand touched, which was one of the irons we sold. Not the buttons or the packets of needles in five different sizes or the bolts of rickrack or satin ribbons. An iron. We kept about five of them out on the shelf. He did it so quickly, I didn't have time to duck, didn't have time to protect myself. The iron met the side of my head.

He didn't even turn to see the damage he'd done, the blood, *my* blood, not some cop's blood, seeping through the fingers I had clutched to my scalp. He raged out the same way he'd raged in, my life a personal affront to his dignity. Tilly, who'd been cowering, hiding in the back room, crept out to help me.

But I didn't want help. I ran out onto the sidewalk, screaming at my brother, screaming at the mess my life had become.

Claudio strode away from me, putting the winter city landscape—of slushy paths and buttoned-up people, hurrying with their heads down—between us. When I reached the corner, shivering and hoarse, he was already two blocks ahead of me. Whatever had fueled me was used up and I felt the cold, the throbbing in my head, the sticky matting of my hair.

Broken, I turned back—again—to the sudden, solid presence of Paolo.

CHAPTER 17

Tears and Blood

Paolo took me to his sister Flora's house. She drew a basin of warm water and sponged away the blood from my face and hair.

"Ai, you poor child," she consoled me as she ministered to me. I could not see the wound, but I'd felt it with my fingers, felt the flesh ripped jaggedly apart exposing something soft and wet. My head throbbed, my throat ached. I wanted to lie down and pull the covers over my face.

Flora did not have the skill of Giuseppina, but she had a gentle touch and a kindness I hadn't experienced since setting foot in America. She turned to Paolo.

"What Claudio has done to this child is a sin! You find him

and tell him that! And tell him you're not bringing her back to his house."

I wasn't afraid to go back to Claudio's. But to defy Claudio, to fling his anger back in his face by not returning home, was an idea that seized me.

Paolo was silent. Did he agree with Flora? Would he shield me from Claudio, even though he was Claudio's best friend?

I looked at his face, so familiar to me. The neighborhood saw my brother Claudio with respect—for his success, his powerful friends. But for Paolo they had a kind of deference—for his intelligence and his learning. It was Claudio they came to when they needed a favor, but it was Paolo they turned to when they couldn't understand something—a paper from the government, a letter from home they couldn't read or respond to. It set him apart, put him a little on the outside of the everyday life we were all caught up in. It made him lonely, in spite of his connection with Claudio.

I had for so long purposely ignored Paolo's presence in my day-to-day life or, at least, treated him lightly. A friendly voice, a smile, a hand with my packages, a handkerchief for my tears, an arm to support me over the rutted ice. I had only seen these small parts of him, offered with such restraint and graciousness, because I had not wanted to see the passion and the will restraining that passion. I had not been willing to see the whole man.

Flora's baby started to wail in her crib. Flora put aside the cloth and went down the hallway to tend to her. The blood was still trickling down my forehead, mingling with my tears. I grappled for the cloth and held it against the wound.

"Here, let me help you," Paolo whispered. He eased the cloth from my hand and tentatively dabbed. "I don't want to hurt you. Let me know if I do." He was hesitant. Almost afraid to touch me—not because of the blood but for other reasons.

Paolo stood before me, his head and heart filled with words that he did not utter out loud to me, and his hand—in a gesture that felt, at that moment, closer than an embrace—stained with my blood.

The intense pain of the last hour, the gnawing emptiness of the last weeks, even the longing for my home and family in Italy that I thought I'd put behind me after all these months, suddenly filled my vision. I began to cry, wildly, unrestrained, huge tears spilling down my face.

I felt Paolo's hand lift from my forehead in a moment of confusion. "Am I pressing too hard?" I shook my head, not knowing how to express my own confusion—sadness, despair, loneliness, gratitude, hope. How could I be feeling so many different, conflicting emotions? I did not know myself. I had always been so *sure*, the roots of my self so well-planted and nourished by Giuseppina's teaching. Perhaps in this cold and lightless city I had lost my bearings. I did not know which way to turn toward the sun and so I revolved as if on the carousel that came to Venticano every August, dragged in pieces in a wagon pulled by four massive horses and assembled in the piazza before us eager and curious children. It spun us around and around until we were dizzy with glee and abandon and the delicious fear that if we let go of our painted horses we'd be thrown off over the edge of the cliff to which the piazza clung. That was how I felt at that moment with Paolo—dizzy with the fear that I was about to be hurled into the unknown.

And just as I was about to fly out of control, engulfed by my pain, Paolo caught me. He reached out his arms—his confusion and hesitancy wiped away in an instant of recognition and understanding—and pulled me toward him. My tears and my blood mingled on his starched white shirtfront.

There, within the circle of his arms, I stayed.

CHAPTER 18

Yolanda's House

"You've done a good job in my absence, Paolo," Flora said when she returned to the kitchen with the baby in her arms. "Not only has the bleeding slowed down, you've actually brought a smile to Giulia's face."

Paolo and I abruptly pulled away from each other, away from warmth, from the sound of his heart beating beneath my ear, from the threshold we had apparently just crossed. I looked into his eyes and saw my own reflection.

"I think I can bandage that now, Giulia." She handed the baby to Paolo, who nuzzled her belly and then balanced her on his knee while Flora wrapped a strip of torn toweling around my forehead. When she was satisfied with her work, she knelt in front of me, took my hands in hers, and spoke to me intently.

"Giulia, I told you when Paolo brought you here that I would not willingly let you return to Claudio's tonight. I mean that. But I don't think it's wise for you to spend the night here. I am not your family. Perhaps they'll understand if you don't go back, but I know they won't understand if you stay here. They won't trust me if they suspect even a fraction of what I saw a minute ago between you and Paolo. They'll think I'm offering you a haven for lovemaking.

"I'm sorry if this is embarrassing you. But you both know that's what they'll think. And Claudio could come storming up here demanding you back. We must find another place for you, safe, with family. Is there anyone we can turn to?"

Who in my family would shelter me against Claudio? Tilly had hidden herself in the back room. Pip, when she heard what had happened, would purse her lips in a thin line and think I got what I deserved for being Roberto's girl. My cousin Peppino, who did Claudio's errands, fetched him his morning coffee? His father Tony, Papa's younger brother? Maybe. He admired Claudio's shrewdness, his success in making a life for himself in America. That was why Uncle Tony came here in the first place, awakened by Claudio's success, tempted to create his own out from under Papa's shadow. But Claudio had become another Papa. Peppino worked for Claudio, not for his father. Perhaps Uncle Tony was the right choice, in fact, my *only* choice.

Flora bundled up the baby, and she and I set off for Tony's apartment. Paolo left with us but then turned off to his own pursuits. It was best that he not be with us, that he not be the one standing between my brother and me.

Zi'Yolanda opened the door with a shriek.

"Giulia! Giulia! What has happened to you? Did you fall in the street? Come in, come in. And who is this with you? Ah, yes, Flora. God bless you for bringing our Giulia…but isn't

Angelina at home? Why didn't you go home, sweetheart? Wasn't Tilly with you? Oh, my God, oh, my God. Something terrible has happened, hasn't it? Shall I send for Claudio?"

Zi'Yolanda twisted her hands in mounting confusion and concern as she asked her questions without stopping for answers, racing from one possibility to another, a crescendo of disaster and the incomprehensible rising in her voice.

"Tell me, tell me everything. *Someone,* not something, has done this to you, am I right? I knew it—I knew it as soon as I saw your face. Here, here. I just made a pot of coffee. Have a piece of anisette bread—it's all I have in the house. I don't bake until Friday. Uncle Tony likes his ricotta pie fresh for the weekend. No, you're not hungry? Of course not. But tell me. Oh, wait till Claudio finds out! Was it one of those DiDonatos looking for information about Roberto? As if you knew anything—"

"Zi'Yolanda, be still for a minute. Listen to me."

"I'm trying, sweetheart, I'm trying. Do you want a glass of brandy?"

"Zi'Yolanda! Come away from the cabinet for a minute. Put the glass down. Claudio did this to me, Zi'Yolanda."

She dropped the glass.

Flora's baby started to cry.

Zi'Yolanda, finally, was speechless.

"I need a place to stay, Zi'Yolanda. I don't want to go back to Claudio's house tonight. May I sleep here?"

Zi'Yolanda knelt down to pick up the glass shards.

"Claudio? Claudio? In all my days, I would never have thought… Your father is a loud man, he pounded his fist on the table now and then, but something like *this,* never, never. Uncle Tony, too. He barks a lot, but raise his hand to me—I swear to you on my mother's grave—never. Where does this come from? How does Claudio think he can do this? Of course you can stay tonight. And if I know your uncle Tony, he'll go get your things out of Claudio's house and move you in here permanently."

She got out her dustpan and broom and swept up the splinters. She looked up at Flora with the baby on her shoulder.

"You're a good friend to Giulia?" She wasn't sure, I could hear it in her voice, see it in the narrowing of her eyes.

Flora nodded as she patted her daughter's back.

"Then you'll keep your mouth shut about this? This kind of thing, it shouldn't go outside the family." To me, she said, "Why didn't you come here first, sweetheart? Didn't you trust Uncle Tony and me to take care of you? You had to go to a stranger?"

I started to explain that it wasn't my choice. I was going to tell her that Paolo had brought me to his sister, but Flora interrupted me.

"Signora Fiorillo, Giulia meant no disrespect. There was a lot of blood at first. I live close to the store—that's where it happened. I think Giulia realized how much attention she'd attract if she came all the way here with a bloody head. So I cleaned her up a little before bringing her to you. I don't know much more about what happened. I'm a good friend to Giulia, Signora. And I'm not a gossip."

Yolanda emptied the glass bits into the bin. She seemed satisfied with Flora's answer, but I could see she wanted to hear more about what had happened and didn't want to ask me in Flora's presence, especially if Flora knew as little as she professed to know.

"No, no. Please don't be offended, my dear. I'm grateful to you for taking care of her and for bringing her here, you with the baby, too. Your first? No? So, you must have a lot to do at home, supper to prepare, the baby to put down. I won't keep you. Giulia is quite safe with us."

After Flora left, Zi'Yolanda stopped her fussing with the broom.

"So, you wanna lie down, sweetheart? I'll make up Pepe's bed nice and clean for you. Or you wanna talk about it?"

"I think I'll lie down, Zi'Yolanda. There's not much to say. Claudio came into the store. He got mad. He picked up an iron and threw it at me."

"He ever hit you before this?"

"No, never."

"I don't understand it. Well, when Uncle Tony gets home, you can bet he'll have a word or two to say to your brother."

I shrugged. Claudio listened to nobody, not even Uncle Tony. Any words Uncle Tony might shout or scold would be ignored, just like Claudio used to ignore Papa.

"Maybe I'll have that glass of brandy before I lie down."

When I woke up it was dark. My head throbbed but the bandage wasn't leaking. The bleeding had stopped. Peppino's bed was in a corner of the dining room, and Zi'Yolanda was setting the table. I smelled soup.

"You feeling a little better, angel? I made some 'scarole and meatballs. Uncle Tony's washing up in the kitchen. You wanna sit up and eat something with us?"

When Uncle Tony came to the table he took one look at my head and started to curse.

"That son of a bitch. He should be my son. If he were, I'd teach him once and for all not to lay a hand on his own sister. God Almighty! That's who he thinks he is. I'll tell you one thing. I'm not letting you go back to his house. Not tonight, not any night.

"He can bang on my door all night long. Wake up the whole damn neighborhood, for all I care. You hear that, Pepe?" He turned to my cousin.

"You tell your boss this is where his sister is and this is where she's going to stay."

After supper, Peppino went out. He had barely looked at

me during the meal. I had never seen Uncle Tony so angry or so determined. Something had happened to our whole family that afternoon when Claudio had hit me and I had accepted refuge from Flora and Paolo. Something like this would not—could not—have happened in Venticano. So much damage in one afternoon…so little protection for me…so little solidarity in the family. I saw at supper that this was going to rend us apart. Already Tony and Peppino had chosen sides—one to stand by me, the other to follow Claudio.

This frightened me more than the blow from Claudio. What would my sisters do, sheltered under Claudio's roof? What would my parents say when they were informed? Why weren't they here now, to protect me, to prevent the catastrophe I feared when Claudio came storming up the stairs to fetch me home?

Or would he not come at all? Would he leave me here with Tony and Yolanda, cutting himself off?

Another home for me. I was no longer welcome in the house of my brother, nor my grandmother, nor my mother and father.

How I longed for a home that I could call mine.

CHAPTER 19

The First Letter

I waited into the night for Claudio to come raging into Yolanda and Tony's the way he'd raged into the store that afternoon.

Yolanda jumped at every slammed door, every footfall on the stairs, pricking herself with her darning needle more than once during the evening as she sat at the cleared dining table with a pile of Peppino's and Tony's shirts and socks.

My head hurt too much to sit up with her after we ate. I didn't even help her wash the dishes. She had shooed me back into the bed.

"I'll take care of this tonight, sweetheart. You go and lie down."

I turned my body to the wall, grateful not to have to listen to Yolanda's worries, Yolanda's gossip, Yolanda's aches and pains. Even Yolanda's criticism of the absent Peppino didn't interest me. Peppino had been my least favorite cousin when we were children. He was a tease who'd once brought me a rose he'd doused with pepper. I had sneezed and coughed for almost an hour. But what had hurt the most was his ridicule. I had thought he liked me, was offering me a special gift with the rose. When I held it up to my nose to admire it and began to sneeze so hard that tears welled up in my eyes, he whooped and hooted with laughter, and his friends leaped out from their hiding places to laugh and taunt with him. I threw the rose down and stomped on it with my foot and kicked Peppino before I turned my back on him and walked home with as much dignity as I could.

Now I was lying in his bed, huddled against the wall, waiting for my brother to show himself.

But he never came. No pounding on the door, no shouted curses, no scenes between the blustering Claudio in charge of everything and the outraged Tony, protector of his niece.

I began to drift off to sleep, floating in and out of dreams, when I heard a respectful knock at the door and then muffled voices. It was late, the room already dark, Yolanda and her darning basket gone.

I heard Uncle Tony speaking quietly and without excitement to whoever had come to the door. It could not be Claudio. The voices were too reasonable. The way one talks to strangers, not to family.

Zi'Yolanda's voice pierced the calm. "Tony, Tony? Who's there? What is it? What does he want?"

"It's all right, Yolly. It's Paolo Serafini. Go back to bed. Everything's okay."

Peppino's bed was positioned so that I couldn't see through the archway between the dining room and the front room, where Uncle Tony stood talking to Paolo. Paolo, here. A few feet away across a darkened room. I sat up, straining to hear his voice, wishing I could go out to him but not trusting myself, afraid that I'd throw myself into his arms, sure that if I did so he'd return the embrace. And there would stand Uncle Tony, mouth agape, not believing his eyes for a few seconds, then jumping from the scene before him to my brother's rage. Tony would explode, feeling betrayed. Yolanda would come running in her nightclothes and grasp whatever fragments she could to feed the clothesline crowd in the morning.

No, I had to remain in bed, show indifference, feign sleep. Anything to prevent them from recognizing the wildness beating in my heart, the agitation I felt knowing he was just beyond reach.

"Tony, I stopped by Claudio's house early this evening to tell Angelina and the girls that Giulia is safe with you. Claudio I haven't seen. He hasn't shown up at the Palace yet. Angelina said he had a meeting in New York and she wasn't expecting him home till late, so I don't think you'll see him here tonight. Unless he runs into somebody like Pepe, he's not even going to know where Giulia is. So rest easy. Maybe by tomorrow he'll have cooled off." He paused. "How's Giulia doing? The girls were upset, wanted her home with them, but I said leave her alone, let her rest out of Claudio's way."

"Thanks, Paolo. That son-of-a-bitch nephew better not show his face around here for a few days. His father should only be here. He'd kill him for touching a hair on his sister's head. I may do it for him.

"I understand your sister fixed her up. God bless her. Giulia's indebted to her and to you."

"Flora would've done nothing less. It's how she is. Look, I'll try to talk to Claudio as soon as I see him. He listens to me…sometimes. Anyway, I just wanted you to know. I've got to get back to the Palace."

"Keep an eye on my son. He hasn't learned to control himself yet. Thinks the night should never end, you know what I mean?"

I heard the door latch, the lumbering of Tony's feet back to bed with Yolanda, the brisk tap of Paolo's shoes on the stairs that ran along the outside wall next to my bed.

I moved from the bed to the front window, reaching it in time to see him stride from the building. I pressed my palms against the glass, wishing he'd turn around and glance up. But he walked off into the night, his head down against the cold wind, his hands thrust into his pockets.

A blue envelope arrived at eight the next morning, delivered by Nino. He was on his way to school and had run to Yolanda and Tony's in order not to be late.

He knocked on the door in a rapid, impatient-little-boy way. "Giulia? Giulia? I'm looking for Giulia Fiorillo. Is she here?"

I heard his voice on the landing, breathless, loud, for all the building to hear.

Peppino opened the door in his undershirt, sullen from being roused at too early an hour, from having to sleep on the sofa when he came in at four in the morning, since Zi'Yolanda had put me in his bed.

"Yeah, what do you want?"

"Is Giulia here?"

"Yeah. Why?"

"This is for her. Give it to her, please." Nino tossed the envelope to Peppino and flew down the stairs.

Peppino took the envelope and studied it as closely as his sleep-heavy, wine-blurred eyes allowed. He turned it over in his hand, studied the inscription, checked to see if the envelope had been sealed. I watched from the archway of the dining room as he slid his grimy thumbnail under the flap.

"Is that for me, Peppino?" I crossed the room in two swift steps and put my hand on the envelope, my thumb pressing down on the flap Peppino had begun to peel open.

He kept his hand on the blue paper, not releasing it to me.

"Whose brat was that? And who's sending you letters through him?"

"I won't know that until I open the letter, Peppino."

"Is this the reason Claudio hit you?" His hand tugged against mine.

"It's none of your business. You're not my brother. And neither one of you is Papa. Give me the letter."

He still wouldn't let go. The struggle over this piece of paper was waking him up.

"Something's not right," Peppino challenged me. "Some stranger early in the morning. What is it, a love letter? Why so urgent? And how did he know you were here?"

"Peppino, I told you. I have no idea who wrote this because you won't let me open it. And even if I did, I wouldn't tell you."

But I did know, of course. I knew the blue paper. I knew the flourish of the pen. I knew Nino. I was desperate to read the words, but kept my longing to myself. I didn't need to give Peppino, with his nosy questions and his big mouth and his loyalty to Claudio, the opportunity to learn such a secret about me. The secret was still so new that I'd lain awake all night, bewildered. What was I to do with this knowledge? This man who'd been a steady, silent presence in my life had now spoken, had now taken me into his arms. How could my understanding of him, my feelings for him, change so much in just one day? People around me thought my world had turned upside down because Claudio had hurt me so savagely. But they were wrong. I was not going to let my life fall apart because my brother couldn't hold himself in check. He had made me angry but he had not made me afraid. What made me afraid right then were my feelings for Paolo. I was not looking for this; I had not asked for it in my prayers or even my dreams.

I had been thrown off balance by Paolo. I had no warning, no months of preparation and anticipation for the way I felt.

This brought so much unease to my heart. I felt out of control, bobbing and diving among turbulent waves that washed over me with ever-increasing height. Volumes of emotion. Voices within my head expressing doubt, telling me this shouldn't be. I shouldn't feel this way—so suddenly, so differently. I was too confused. I needed to understand more. I needed to anchor myself, to keep myself tethered to something real....

I needed the letter, becoming tattered and smudged in Peppino's hands and mine. We were scrabbling like two children over a chestnut. One taunting, the other clutching.

"Pepe, what are you doing up so early?" Zi'Yolanda shoved her head out the kitchen door. "You wanna cup of coffee? Who was that at the door?"

Her hair was still down in a graying braid behind her back, her cotton housedress protected by a flowered apron. My own mother, her hair still black, never appeared even for morning coffee without her hair smoothly pinned in place.

"What's that? You two look like you're fighting over the last piece of cake. Did someone bring a message? From Claudio?"

"It's for me, Zi'Yolanda. But I don't know who it's from because your son won't let me have it."

"If it's from someone in the family, why didn't they come in person?" Peppino jumped in. "And if it's from a stranger, it's not right...."

"Since when did you become a judge of what's proper and what's not? You with your American girlfriend who stays out with you half the night like a *putana?*" Zi'Yolanda was warming to my side.

"Look, why don't you give me the letter and I'll open it right here in front of your mother and you."

Zi'Yolanda gestured to Peppino to let go of the letter. She was as curious as he, but for more benevolent reasons—romance, gossip.

"Maybe it's about Roberto," she ventured with a mixture of hope and fascination.

Peppino reluctantly loosened his fingers and I slipped the envelope out of his grasp. I opened it calmly, careful not to tear the paper, not to betray my mounting agitation.

Inside the blue envelope lay a folded sheet of blue paper, covered on all four sides with writing. I didn't want to read the entire letter in front of Peppino and Yolanda. Even if I read silently, I was afraid that the emotions expressed on paper would spill over into my eyes, my face, betraying me to those I was least willing to reveal myself to.

"Oh, look, it's from Flora! How sweet!"

Peppino and Yolanda nodded in satisfaction. Yolanda couldn't read a word beyond her own name. Peppino thought he could read, but I'd seen him struggle with simple words. They probably wouldn't know, had they taken the sheet from me and pored over it, heads together, whether it was a grocery list or a death threat.

A friendly note of concern, asking whether I'd spent the night comfortably, hoping the bandages had served me well. That's what I told Yolanda and Peppino. And that was, in part, what the letter said. Except that it had been written by Paolo and not Flora. The rest of the note I resolved to read in private, so I refolded it, replaced it in the envelope and tucked the envelope inside the sleeve of my blouse.

Peppino, deprived of the opportunity for outrage, sulked into the kitchen, Zi'Yolanda padding behind him to serve him a cup of coffee.

Later in the morning, on her way back from doing the marketing, Yolanda decided to stop by Angelina and Claudio's to get me some fresh clothes. Uncle Tony didn't want me out of the house yet. He didn't want me running into Claudio alone before someone—preferably Uncle Tony—had had a chance to talk to him.

Zi'Yolanda was gone a long time. Long enough, I'm sure, to have a cup of coffee with Angelina and fill her in on all she, Yolanda, was privileged to know. Angelina must have been relieved to learn that she'd lost one of her boarders, even if only temporarily. But after a few days without my cooking and entertaining her sons, she might come to appreciate me. God knows, she hadn't yet.

I wondered if Angelina was surprised. Had Claudio ever hit her? I'd never seen or heard anything in all the time I lived with them. A lot of gruff words, shouting matches at the table, Angelina petulant and whining and ultimately punishing Claudio by leaving him to brood alone while she went upstairs to be by herself. Leaving us with the dishes and the sweeping and picking up the broken pieces of whatever Claudio had flung from the table. Not so different from my parents' house.

But I never saw him hit her. And I never came home from work to find her with a swollen lip or a bruised face. Not that she would've confided in me if he *had* hit her—in some place covered up, hidden by her skirt or blouse. But I don't believe he ever did.

Claudio had a violent temper, but until that day he had exercised it with his voice, his words, his smashing of objects that had sentimental worth to Angelina, like the china fruit bowl she'd kept on the sideboard, carried with her from Abbruzzi, wrapped in layer upon layer of bedding. It had survived the land journey to Napoli, the ocean crossing, the trolley to Mount Vernon. But it had sat there by the dining table for three years, ever ready, ever in Claudio's view, within reach when he was provoked to new heights of anger. Who knows? Claudio was so adamant about his disdain for Italy. He believed he'd escaped a place of fools and losers. He had no good memories, no lingering doubts about his decision to leave. So maybe Angelina's bowl had sat there all those years shouting *Italy* to him. And when the moment had come—some disappointment, some failure he could throw off onto the deficiencies of our homeland—he'd picked up this symbol of Italy accorded a place of honor in his own house and thrown it out the window. Which fortunately had been open, so we didn't have to replace the glass. But the bowl had fallen to the stone terrace behind the house, smashed among the begonias withering in clay pots and the toys belonging to his sons.

Angelina hadn't spoken to him for two weeks. Had Claudio possessed an object of equal emotional importance to him, I'm sure she would have smashed it with a furious pleasure. But what was important to Claudio? His horses? They were his livelihood, but I don't remember him speaking affectionately about a single one of them. He called them "the bay," "the chestnut," "the gray." He didn't even give them names.

What mattered to Claudio were his deals—getting something worth more than he'd had to pay for it. But Claudio treasure something, preserve it, keep it? I didn't think so. He would tell you that he was always facing forward. He didn't look back—not to the business he would've joined with Papa, not to the early days here in America with no horses, no money.

"I keep my eye on tomorrow," he said. "I keep my eye on the other guy. Where's he going, how's he going to make his mistake."

But this time, it was Claudio who'd made the mistake.

Maybe I should've sat at Yolanda's table considering my own mistake as I shelled the peas Yolanda had left for me. Maybe I should've whimpered for Claudio to forgive me for being lazy. Wasn't that what he'd said in the store, tracing his finger through the dust on the counter? Or maybe for dancing with Roberto? Couldn't I see he'd be the kind to get mixed up with the law in a way that brought too much attention upon himself, upon me, and then upon Claudio? Or maybe, like Angelina's china bowl, for just being around in Claudio's life.

Standing there in the store, provoking him to rage simply because he had to look at me every day and be reminded of something he couldn't control.

I didn't think so. I didn't think it was my mistake. If Claudio opened my head with a flat iron, it was Claudio who had done something wrong. And who was going to tell him that? Uncle Tony was full of big words, calling Claudio a son of a bitch, but not to his face. Paolo? As much as he loved me, was he ready to choose between Claudio and me? Or did he think he could be the go-between? The man of honor who restored peace to our family?

I didn't want peace right then. I wanted people to look at the horror on my forehead and feel the anger that I felt. But who could I count on for that?

Even Yolanda, concerned as she was and unable to understand how this could happen, was afraid of Claudio. I could hear it in her voice when Paolo came to the door. The tremor, the crack, the waiting in anxiety for hell to break loose or break down the door. Tilly was also afraid. From the first moment, when Claudio had heaved into the store, she'd hidden in the back, making herself small. When we were children and Papa was yelling at the dinner table, Tilly and I had closed our eyes fiercely tight, believing that if we couldn't see him, he couldn't see us and make us his next target.

Everyone here still seemed to believe the same magic. They closed their eyes to Claudio.

But I looked my brother in the eye.

CHAPTER 20

Paolo's Words

The gash Claudio put in my head put a rift between him and Paolo. After Claudio hit me, Paolo's friendship with him became strained. He spent less and less time with Claudio. In the past, they'd often stayed late together at the Palace, closing up the place with a few glasses of grappa and a card game after they'd counted up the till. But after, it was all business between them. Paolo continued to keep an eye on the place in the evenings from the piano and he did the books, but he left as soon as the money was counted for the night. If Claudio wanted to smoke a cigar and play a few rounds, he did it with Peppino and his ruffian friends.

Paolo removed himself from Claudio's presence because otherwise he would have attacked him for what he'd done to me.

He wrote to me that he could not control the anger that rose in him when he remembered finding me that day on the street. It blinded him, the thought of my blood and my pain. The only reason he didn't go after Claudio was to protect our secret, to keep our love from those who would try to drive us apart.

Each morning a letter had come for me since that first one I'd wrested from Peppino's filthy hand. But even though I'd received a letter every day, I had not seen Paolo since I watched from the window that first night at Yolanda and Tony's as he'd walked away into the darkness.

He had attempted to keep what was happening between us as private as possible. He did not want to cloud the situation between Claudio and me—did not want to give Claudio more ammunition. It wouldn't take much for Claudio to accuse me of being a whore. God knows, I had demonstrated neither the propriety of Pip nor the innocence of Tilly in my history with men.

Only Flora had Paolo's confidence. After the first day, he did not send Nino with the letters. Flora brought the others, stopping by for a brief daily visit, passing the blue envelope to me when Yolanda's attention was occupied elsewhere, taking the white envelope that enclosed what I had written in secret in response to Paolo's letter of the day before.

Flora brought me Paolo's letters with such discretion that Yolanda never suspected. I don't think she could even imagine that a man would court a woman in such a way. It was not within her experience of life.

I don't think I imagined it myself before I began to read Paolo's words and was engulfed by them. Signore Ventuolo had taught me the power of words on a page—but those were words written for many eyes. Paolo's words were written only for me.

My mother wrote letters. I remember, on the days the post came, how Mama's face would light up at the stack of envelopes—from her friends in Benevento, her own mother and later, from Signore Ventuolo. She would retreat to her room and only emerge when all the letters had been read and answered. She might say twenty words to Papa all week, but she filled pages in her letters. The envelopes going out in the next day's post were always thick, heavy with whatever it was she found the need to say.

Paolo's letters spoke for him as my mother's did for her.

In them, I began to discover the complex man who had been hidden from me. In them, he began to reveal himself. I learned of his passions—for me, for his work, for his music.

He wrote to me that he'd never loved another woman with such intensity, that my beauty and gentleness brought him so much happiness—happiness that he wanted only to give back to me. He told me that I owned his heart.

He wrote to me about his work with the union. Other unions, like the Knights of Labor and the AFL, kept the Italians out. But the Wobblies, the International Workers of the World, had opened its doors to men like Paolo, and he went barreling through that door brandishing his pen like a sword and pouring his outrage at the injustices suffered by laborers into speeches and strikes. He was the secretary of the union. It sounds so quiet, so innocuous—recording the minutes of meetings and writing the broadsides that were handed out to workers and sent to newspapers. But I knew that the words Paolo was writing were not so quiet.

He wrote to me about what he did late at night at the Palace. When things quieted down and everybody had a drink, he stole a few minutes at the piano, composing a song he wanted Caruso to sing. As he composed, he heard the notes sung in Caruso's inimitable voice and knew that only Caruso could bring the music to life. Paolo carried a sheaf of creased staff paper in his coat pocket, folded up at the end of the night after he locked the Palace. Each evening, he retrieved it, unfolded it and placed it on the top of the piano. He studied the marks he'd made, replaying their pattern lightly on the worn keys and then fingering the next measure. Around him were murmurs or shouts, the splash of whiskey in glass, the scrape of heavy boot on oak floor. Still, he listened and called up the voice he'd only heard once but held in his memory like a mother recognizing the cry of her newborn infant. And then he wrote, furiously, passionately, his hand moving as if guided by Caruso himself.

These were Paolo's words; this was Paolo's world.

If I had not had his letters, I would have felt abandoned. But I knew that he kept away, sending the letters as his substitute, to protect me from prying eyes and damaging rumors and to protect us in this fragile state of early love from the interfering words and innuendo that can pull lovers apart.

CHAPTER 21

Back to Work

I went back to the store after two weeks. Pip had been ill and Tilly had her hands full managing alone. She'd always been the back-room person, content to count spools and organize piles of merchandise. She liked to climb up on her stepladder and restore order to a shelf I'd been haphazardly emptying and refilling. She found satisfaction in those tasks. But as soon as a customer entered the shop, the little bell over the door tinkling, Tilly ducked her head, descended from the ladder, and retreated to the back of the store to fetch me and then hide. She was desperately shy, barely able to whisper a greeting.

I was good in the front of the shop. I chatted with customers, discovered what was going on in their lives, found ways to encourage them to buy things they hadn't thought of when they'd arrived at the store.

After two weeks of confinement in Yolanda's house, I saw the store as an opportunity. I wanted Paolo to walk through the door. There was no Yolanda to rush off to Angelina's with a report. Tilly would be mildly perplexed by his visit, but would not be able to hear what was unsaid.

I spent the first day back alternating between reverie and commerce, longing for Paolo to appear but often too busy to notice that he wasn't there. I was a dreamer, but not when doing business. The last customer of the day was indecisive. I took down half our supplies before she made up her mind. She chose six buttons and complained about their price, their quality. When she finally left, I had a pile of boxes on the counter to replace and a throbbing headache. I wanted to leave the mess for Tilly but when I turned to ask her for help she was already putting on her hat and primping in front of the mirror. Shy Tilly had a suitor—Gaetano Novelli. He was as round as she was and his cheeks and nose were chafed a permanent red in the bitter chill of that winter. He had invited her to coffee.

She was gay with anticipation, and I hadn't the heart to make her stay and help me clean up. As soon as she left, I pulled the shades and started putting away boxes. I was on the stepladder, shoving the last carton onto its shelf and imagining myself walking, not back to Yolanda and Tony's that night, but to the Palace to find Paolo, when the bell sounded. I thought I'd locked the door!

"I'm sorry, but we're closed…" I swiveled on the ladder to face the door. It was Peppino.

"Pop sent me down to walk you home. Don't expect this every night. I've got more important things to do than be your nursemaid."

"You don't even have to do it tonight, Pepe. I can get myself to your house just fine."

"Yeah, and if I show up without you, I'll have to listen to my old man rag on me about family responsibility and I'll have to pick my mother up off the kitchen floor where she'll have fallen in a faint, screaming, 'I knew it! I knew we shouldn't have trusted him.' No, cousin. Spare the family at least one night of hysteria. Come home like a good girl, keep Tony and Yolanda happy and out of Pepe's hair, and Pepe will stay out of your business in return."

"I have no business for you to keep out of, Peppino."

"Right. That's why you're in so much trouble with Claudio, why you have to come running to your uncle Tony to protect you. You've got some business, girl. Seems to me this family spends too much time straightening out Giulia's escapades, protecting the almighty Fiorillo name and reputation."

"It's your name, too, and I don't see you doing all that much to keep it untarnished. How much money do you owe, Pepe, to keep playing cards at the Palace every night? Does my brother pay your debts for you? I'll bet it's not your father. Does he even know about the gambling? Or does Yolanda protect you?"

"You have a big mouth, Giulia. But I can hurt you more. Pop would get angry about the gambling, but in the end he'd have to give up, say, 'Boys will be boys,' and 'Let him ruin his own life.' But a daughter with a reputation, that's another story. Nobody wants a whore in the family, Giulia. Least of all the Fiorillos. So get your coat and lock up. My mother's got dinner waiting."

I slammed the last box onto the shelf. Pepe and I trudged home in silence.

CHAPTER 22

Unwelcome

After a month, my welcome at Yolanda and Tony's was growing thin. Uncle Tony had not confronted Claudio, and Claudio, of course, did not come to Uncle Tony. If Claudio was upset that I hadn't come back to his house, he didn't show it. Instead of yelling and hitting, he acted as if I didn't exist. He had wiped me away, like some fly on one of his horses' flanks. Like the dust he'd dragged his finger through on the counter just before he'd hit me.

Good riddance! I'm sure he thought. One less mouth to feed, one less mouth to listen to in his household of women.

Tony avoided my face when he came home at night. His gaze no longer took in the fading bruise on my forehead. He scrubbed the dirt from his hands but he was never able to get all of it out. His palms seemed permanently crazed with thin black lines of embedded grit from his work as a laborer on a road construction crew. He also could not wash from his face the years of exposure to sun and wind, and here in America, bitter cold. After he washed, he sat at the table, already set by me. Yolanda's things weren't as fine as my mother's. Cotton tablecloth, not damask. But starched and ironed. Heavy, plain stoneware dishes, not painted bone china. Yolanda served Tony immediately, the steam rising off the mounded food on his plate. He ate his macaroni in silence, drank his two glasses of wine and fell asleep in the chair in the front room.

Pepe watched me from across the table. Glowering with re-sentment, searching for secrets. Pepe was annoyed by my presence in his house, so he made himself as annoying to me as possible. He scratched his bare chest in my face, his pale skin soaked in sweat. He threw to the floor the few clothes Yolanda had fetched for me when he was looking for something that he claimed I'd misplaced. I took all of Paolo's letters with me when I went to the store. I was afraid that Pepe would find them if I left them at Yolanda's—not accidentally, but deliberately. I didn't trust him. He was a violator. Careless of himself, careless of his mother's devotion to him, her only son. He mocked her behind her back. Ignored her pleas that he make something of his life. Took her money—that she slipped to him when Tony wasn't around—to pay off the debts he never seemed to be free of.

I knew that Pepe had begun to complain to Yolanda about my presence. I had taken his bed, I knew his games, I heard his lies. I didn't hear him talking to Yolanda, but I heard his words coming out of Yolanda's mouth. After Claudio had left them alone, she'd begun to convince herself that his silence was reconciliation. If Claudio wasn't breaking the door down, then everything must be okay. She didn't see his refusal to talk to Tony or me as the smoldering fire it could very well be. A few more weeks of my defiance and Claudio's refusal to acknowledge it, and we could've had a conflagration, a fireball that would probably have been seen back in Venticano.

But Yolanda, fed by Pepe, chose to see the fire banked, muffled, maybe even extinguished by the other, more important concerns in Claudio's powerful life. I was a speck. Blown away by the wind, washed out of Claudio's eye, brushed off by a preoccupied hand. Yolanda saw what she wanted to see. Life goes on. Everybody make nice like nothing happened. See, the bruises are fading, the cut is healing. In a few weeks you won't even know anything happened.

"So, sweetheart, you miss your sisters?" she asked me one morning, a month into my stay. "You wish you could be back with them? Maybe we should have a family dinner. I'll invite them all, make a nice *antipast'*. A little minestrone, some *manicott'*. Mercurio's got some good breast of veal this week. I could stuff it with *alici* and hard-boiled eggs. What do you say? We'll fill their bellies, raise a few glasses of Uncle Tony's Chianti, clear all of this up. Then you could go home."

"Claudio's house is not my home anymore. I don't want to share a roof with a man who acts like he did, even if he *is* my brother."

"What do you want to do, spend the rest of your life not talking to your brother? Look at your uncle Tony and your papa. How many civil words have they said to each other in ten years? They can't even live in the same country. Uncle Tony would never admit it, but believe me, it eats away at him. And over what? Some slight, some insult that I bet neither one of them remembers. It shouldn't be like that, it shouldn't. Not when it's family."

CHAPTER 23

Anna Directs from Afar

But no dinner of Yolanda's was going to move my brother. Only my mother could do that. She wrote to Claudio, as she wrote to all of us, every month. When she learned of what Claudio had done, she picked up her pen with a vengeance, and she sent me a copy.

Figlio mio,
Your last letter has arrived safely and the money has been put to good use, paying for Aldo and Frankie's next semester of study with the Franciscans. Frankie, as I've written you before, is an especially apt pupil. Father Bruno says he will be ready for the university in two years. If only I had been able to offer you the same opportunity! I look at Frankie and I see you at that age—

the same intelligence, the same ambition. But you have put your sharp mind to good use nevertheless, as I never doubted. I shall always be grateful to you, Claudio, for what you now make possible for your brothers, and for the safety you have provided your sisters.

You know I have always trusted you, had faith in you. And you have never disappointed me. I could always hold my head high—with your father, with his sisters, with the gossips in this village—whenever your name was mentioned. I have been proud to say, "That is Claudio Alfonso Fiorillo, my firstborn. A man of honor, of respect, of success." Even when you left here, stubborn and embittered, I knew in my heart that you were doing the right thing, the thing I had raised you to do. Who, after all, found you the money to leave? Whose jewelry was pressed into your hand to buy you passage to your dreams?

That is why I cannot believe what I have learned in a letter from Tilly that arrived the same day as your money. Why I cannot accept that my faith in you has been rewarded by behavior I would expect of a lowlife like your cousin Peppino, but not of my own son.

Tell me that the event Tilly described to me did not take place. I would rather have her be a liar than know that a son of mine has laid a hand on his sister. The man who has done this is a stranger to me, cannot have my blood in his veins.

But if it is true, and you wish me to acknowledge you as my son, then go to your sister and beg her forgiveness. Give her back the safety and protection of her family. God knows what will become of her if you do not. Far worse than the laziness of which you accused her. And far worse than any pride you have to swallow to go to her. Do not bring any further public disgrace upon this family by abandoning your sister to a life on her own. You know as well as I do that she will not stay with Tony and Yolanda. Where will she go? To some American boarding house where no one knows

*who she is or cares when she comes or goes? Do you want your
sister to be seen as no better than the village whore?*

Has America done this?

*I shall wait to hear that both my daughter and my son have
been restored to me.*

Your loving mother,

Anna

CHAPTER 24

The Apology

I was helping Yolanda dry the dishes after supper. Uncle Tony had gone down the street to his neighbor Fat Eddie's to play cards and Pepe had told his mother he was going to work at the Palace. We were alone.

The knock on the door startled Yolanda, and the pot she was scrubbing slipped from her soapy hands and clattered into the sink.

"Who, at this hour?"

"I'll go, Zi'Yolanda," I told her, wiping my hands on my apron. Before she could hold me back I was in the front room.

"Who's there?" I asked through the door.

"Claudio."

My hand flew to my head, to the slight ridge of the scar

that had formed at my hairline, pressing the memory of that blow, that day, into my fingertips.

"Open up, Giulia. I've come with a message from Mama."

I straightened my back, willing myself to be strong, to withstand the power on the other side of the door. I lifted my chin, seeing in my mind's eye the stubborn tilt of my mother's face defying the sun, defying the murmurs in her own house as well as in the village on the day Claudio left for America. My hand came down from my head and touched Giuseppina's amulet that I wore under my blouse.

Then I opened the door.

Claudio filled the room, taking possession of it without looking at me.

Zi'Yolanda was frozen in the kitchen doorway, twisting her hands.

"Claudio, Claudio. You've come. If I'd known, I would've had something ready. You hungry? I got some *broccoli rabe* and beans from supper. No? You want a drink? Some anisette? Uncle Tony, he's not here. You want me to go get him? He's just down the street...."

"I came to talk to Giulia."

I was still standing by the door, my arms now folded across my breast, holding myself together. I waited.

"Mama has written. She says you belong at home with your sisters. With me. You're my responsibility. No offense, Zi'Yolanda, but Giulia has a home with us. The boys, they ask for you every day. Angelina has her hands full without you. Pip doesn't know what to do with a runny nose and Tilly spends all her time at the store counting straight pins as far as I can tell.

"People are starting to talk, to say you don't live with us anymore. They think you're on your own, with nobody watching out for you. No sister of mine should be the subject of such gossip. It reflects on the family. On me."

"*I've* given them nothing to gossip about. I go to work. I take care of business, I come home and help Zi'Yolanda in the house. If people are whispering, Claudio, it's not because of anything *I've* done."

"This has gone on long enough. You've made your point. I lost my temper. I throw things all the time when I get angry enough. And that day you made me plenty angry and you happened to be in the way when I let go.

"But I've calmed down. I can live with a little dirt in the store. But I won't put up with your stubbornness about not coming back to my house. I've come to take you home."

I looked at Claudio. All the time he'd been talking, his eyes had been somewhere else, not meeting mine.

"Mama wrote to me, too," I said. This time he looked at me.

"She told me that when you came to me asking forgiveness, I should be ready to give it."

"So, I've come."

I shook my head. "She didn't say I should forgive you when you *came* to me. She said I should forgive you when you *asked* me to forgive you."

Zi'Yolanda gasped.

I knew from the copy of the letter she'd sent me that my mother had told Claudio to ask me for forgiveness. Did she do this for me? Or to restore the image of Claudio that she burnished every day, held up to the light of my father's disdain and my aunts' clucking. Claudio her star, her salvation, her reward. It didn't matter to me why. She had done it. Had been the only one in the family with the will to confront him and the wits to corner him.

I forced myself to move away from Claudio. I turned my back to him and crossed the room to sit in Uncle Tony's chair. I struggled to still my voice, to still my trembling hands. I had always been the chatterbox in our family. The one who always had something to say—a joke or a riddle in the chapel at Santa Margareta when I should have been whispering the rosary, or my insistent interruptions at the dinner table at my parents' house, my chattering stories.

But this was not the time to distract my audience. I bit my tongue, nearly drawing blood, as I waited for Claudio—to erupt, to leave, or to listen.

He began to mutter dismissive curses, throwing his hand in the air, gesturing at no one except perhaps our distant mother.

The trolley clattered by on the street below.

Zi'Yolanda retreated to the kitchen—in fear, in confusion, or perhaps hoping to find some morsel she could offer Claudio to appease him. When Claudio realized we were alone, he looked at me, not with the eyes of a cornered animal, but with those of a shrewd one. He hissed the words at me, in a barely audible voice.

"I'm sorry."

His tone wasn't one of defeat, but of dismissal. As if the apology wasn't important to him. As if he could afford to be magnanimous, generous. But he had said the words.

I stood up.

"I accept your apology," I said.

CHAPTER 25

In Hiding

I went back to live at Claudio's house after he apologized. It meant that I was under more scrutiny at home as well as at the store. But as our love deepened, Paolo and I began to take more risks. We continued to write to each other every day and found ways to meet, sometimes openly on the street, engaging in a few minutes of polite conversation while we stared hungrily into each other's eyes, sometimes secretly in the back of the store.

One Sunday afternoon when I'd gone down to the store by myself to unpack a shipment of fabric, Paolo surprised me. He had brought a small cake for us from Artuso's bakery. He told me he wished he could have brought the piano from the Palace, too, because he had a song he wanted to play for me. I asked him to sing it. At first, he protested. He was a piano player, not a singer. But I coaxed him—how else would I ever hear it? I asked. Claudio certainly wasn't about to let me come to the Palace some night. So Paolo relented and began to sing for me. As he did, I lifted my arms and began to dance around him. Then he reached out for me and took me in his arms. We continued to dance around the storeroom, his lips close to my ear, filling it with song.

Flora lived right across the street from the store, and Paolo allowed Nino to carry the letters when Flora couldn't get over. Everybody knew he was my special boy, my little sweetheart. It was natural for him to dash into the store on his way to school to grab a peppermint. That he also slipped me a blue envelope with a wink and a grin—well, I took care to call him to the back of the store for our exchange.

But Paolo's life at that time was becoming one of *nascondiglio,* concealment. Not only were we hiding our love from my family, but he was also hiding his other life from the police. He was often gone, to New York City or upstate, as his work with the union consumed more and more of his life and put him in more and more danger.

The newspaper of the Italian immigrant community—*Il Progresso Italo-Americano*—was filled with stories about the horrors in sweatshops and the brutality of the police and the bosses against workers who only wanted to put food on the table. The IWW was in the middle of the unrest, and the politicians and American newspapers were furious.

I held my breath every time Paolo left Mount Vernon. I never knew if he was just going to a meeting or if the police had stopped him somewhere and found his papers with their incendiary words. It made him ill sometimes, the passion he poured into expressing his ideas about justice; and it frightened me. The risks he was taking, the enemies he was making.

Claudio thought he was an idealistic fool, a Don Quixote jousting at windmills. But Claudio had no sympathy for workers. Claudio had never sat behind a sewing machine in a factory or worked in the Pennsylvania coalmines. His time with a pick and shovel in New York had been short. He prided himself on figuring it out—using his brains as well as his brawn. He saw quickly that he wasn't going to reach his dream digging ditches for someone else. My mother's jewelry had paid for more than his passage to America. He bought his first team and wagon with money from her. She put the reins in his hands.

Paolo had no gems from his mother. But he had a degree from the University of Napoli and had worked on an Italian labor newspaper before he'd arrived in America. It was that experience and the people he knew from *Il Germe* that brought him into the IWW. Paolo was a man of ideas who threw himself into action.

If I thought his feelings for me would slow him down, hold him back from doing something rash, I was wrong. Trouble was brewing in Schenectady at the General Electric plant and *Il Progresso* printed a story about the involvement of some of the men from the IWW. A knot grew in my heart with every word I read.

One afternoon, Tilly and Pip had gone to do errands. It was lunchtime, a quiet lull when I could steal a few minutes with Paolo, face to face in the back of the store. With half an ear I listened for the bell on the front door. The heavy curtain between the front of the shop and the storeroom was closed.

"Here, I have something for you," he whispered, as he emptied his pocket onto the counter to retrieve a new poem for me. He took my face in his hands as he kissed me and then began to read the poem. But out of the corner of my eye, I saw on the counter a train ticket to Schenectady.

I let him finish his poem and kissed him again, but my mind and my heart were pulled in the direction of that ticket.

"What takes you to Schenectady?"

"Business. Don't worry. It's not another girl."

"I don't worry about other girls. But I worry about business. Are you going because of General Electric?"

"What do you know about GE?"

"What I read in *Il Progresso*. Tell me you're going for some other reason, not for the union. Tell me it's just a coincidence that you're going to Schenectady."

He looked away from my gaze and put the ticket and other loose papers back in his pocket. I pulled him toward me again and pounded my fists against his chest.

"Don't go! I can't bear the thought of you in the midst of that trouble. You'll be hurt. You'll be arrested. I won't sleep knowing you're in danger. Don't go!"

He pushed my hands away.

"I have to go. You don't understand. It's who I am."

The bell jangled in the front. He kissed me once again, hard, and went out the back door.

The next day, he went to Schenectady.

I couldn't tell anyone of my worries. Instead, I retrieved Claudio's crumpled copy of *Il Progresso* every night from the table where he tossed it after dinner. I took it to my bed and smoothed it out, looking for dispatches about the strike. I pored over the pages, hoping to catch a glimpse of Paolo's face in the grainy photographs, but of course the workers were inside the plant, in the first sit-down strike in American history, and the newspaper only ran a photo of the building surrounded by police and soldiers. I didn't know if Paolo was inside, giving courage to the strikers, or outside, making trouble for the authorities. I searched for any fragment of news that might reveal to me that Paolo was safe. I found nothing, only reports of brutality and fury.

Every morning I returned to the store, hoping this would be the day I would see Paolo again. Finally he returned. I saw him walking down the hill toward the Palace, looking as if he'd seen a ghost. A thin scab extended across his forehead and he was limping. His steps were measured and careful, not the usual swagger and energy that was so characteristic of him. I wondered about the bruises I couldn't see.

He did not come to the store that day or the next, and Nino did not appear with a message from him. Knowing he was back and not hearing from him was in some ways worse than when I had no knowledge of him at all. I didn't know why he was ignoring me. I was afraid of what had happened to him in Schenectady.

I attacked the dust on the floor as if my broom were a weapon. At home, I slaughtered onions with my knife, furiously chopping them into hundreds of pieces while the tears streamed down my cheeks. I swallowed my loneliness, unable to tell anyone of my fears. I cried myself to sleep thinking he had no more words for me.

Finally, one morning at the store as I was sorting through the bills that had arrived in the post, I found a letter addressed to me and postmarked Schenectady. I tore it open, heedless of my sisters. I read the letter quickly, scanning it for the familiar words of passion and longing. I found those words, with relief. But then I read on.

Forgive the smudges on the page, my beloved. My hand is bleeding from a scrape suffered when the police shoved me against the pavement and I haven't had time to tend to it. I have seen too much today that I cannot describe to you—desperate men, impoverished but determined, making history here, but at great cost. I am tortured by what I am witnessing. This is everything I work for and believe in, but I fear I am asking too much of you to share in it. I have realized today that the life I have chosen is incompatible with loving a woman.

I stifled a cry and shoved the letter into my pocket. I knew I had to see him, had to talk to him. But I also needed to understand in my heart what it would mean for me to stand by him, to know that the man I loved could face imprisonment or worse.

I watched for Nino that afternoon as he returned home from school and slipped him a note for Paolo, along with a piece of chocolate. In the note, I begged Paolo to meet with me in the store at closing time. I waited anxiously as the day darkened, knowing that I could not delay my arrival home without arousing suspicion. Just as I was about to give up hope that he would come, I heard a light tapping on the back door.

I let him in and turned out the light so no one could see us. I reached out for him, afraid he might not return my embrace, afraid I might hurt his battered body. But he took me in his arms, gently and tenderly.

"I've missed you so much!"

"I've missed you, too. Did you get my letter from Schenectady?"

"This morning."

"It was agonizing to write. I adore you, Giulia. But I cannot ask you to love me in return when the path I am on is so precarious, so dangerous."

"I've thought about your words all day today, preparing myself for this conversation. I searched my soul to know if I could accept this part of you. Paolo, I do not want to lose you. I know now that this is your life, that I can't make you turn away from it because of my fears. I will stand by you, Paolo. I will never stand in your way or hold you back from your calling."

"Are you sure? I can never give you the kind of security Claudio provides for Angelina, or that your sisters expect."

"I have never wanted what my sisters want. What I want is you. All of you."

He kissed me lightly on the lips. "You have me."

The city-hall clock tolled faintly in the distance.

"I have to get home or they'll send someone to look for me."

"*Addio*. I'll write you tomorrow."

He slipped out the back door and I locked it behind him. I left by the front door and made my way back to Claudio's, my heart both light and solemn.

CHAPTER 26

Secrets

Secrets are hard to bear, hard to conceal, when one is in love. We had continued to hide our feelings because my family, led by Claudio, had decided that my recklessness with men—first Vito in Venticano, now Roberto in Mount Vernon—had to stop. I had behaved once too often in a way that flouted the proprieties my family expected of its women. But despite Paolo's and my efforts at discretion, my sisters began to suspect that something was going on and were furious with me. My emotions were written all over my face. If I hadn't seen Paolo on the street early in the morning on my way to the store, or if Nino hadn't come by on his way to school with a letter for me, I was desolate. I went through the motions of restocking the shelves or waiting on customers, but my mind was on the emptiness, the aching, the longing to hear Paolo's voice or feel his lips on mine.

We were like crazy people, addicted to each other. We continued to meet in the back of the store. A few moments behind the curtain, his arms around me, pulling me close, covering my face with kisses, pressing his body against mine. I was breathless; I was excruciatingly happy to be near him. I didn't care what people thought.

But my sisters cared. One morning, Pip noticed my flushed face and the disarray of my hair as I hastily smoothed back the loose strands when she called me from the front of the store. There were half a dozen customers waiting to be served.

"What are you doing back there, Giulia? Daydreaming? Didn't you hear the bell jangle five times?"

She looked at me sharply when she saw two of our customers eyeing me up and down as if I'd walked out in my underwear.

"She's been unloading boxes all morning. We should've gotten my cousin Peppino to do it, but you know, the boys are never around when you want them for any heavy work." Pip made up the story hastily to deflect the gossips.

I took my place behind the counter and helped Josephina Simonetti find the fabric she needed to reline her husband's coat, trying not to get lost in the memory of Paolo's lips grazing my neck as he eased himself out the door to the alley.

When the store was quiet again, Pip let me have it.

"I don't know what you were doing back there, but I pray to Jesus, Mary and Joseph that you were alone. If something's going on behind our backs, Giulia, don't think you can hide it forever. I guarantee you that within fifteen minutes of leaving here, that Simonetti woman was telling whoever would listen that you came out of the back looking as if you'd just gotten out of bed."

"I don't care what Josephina Simonetti thinks of me."

"Well, *I* care, and Tilly and Claudio and Uncle Tony and Zi'Yolanda. People talk. This is America, with no mother and father to protect you, to show you how to behave. We don't want people in the streets whispering about you, saying no one controls you."

Before I could respond, she went on.

"If someone's visiting you in the back, God forbid, it's got to stop. Sooner or later somebody will see him and sure as hell won't think it's a delivery boy."

She grabbed a box overflowing with trim.

"Stay up front and straighten this out."

Later that day I wrote to Paolo about Pip's suspicions and her watchfulness. Every time I went to the back room, she moved in that direction, too, her ear cocked to catch the sound of the door opening or another voice. I felt like a caged bird, flitting from one end of its prison to the other without hope of finding a way out. By the time I got home, I was distraught, frantic at the thought that Paolo and I had no safe place to meet. I knew we could defy Pip, but that increased our risk of being discovered. And then what? Would my family forbid me to see him?

Paolo saw the toll our secret was taking on me, how unhappy I was when I couldn't see him, how worn down I was by the berating of my sister, her demand that I not bring shame to the family but act with propriety. My freedom to come and go was restricted. Pip or Tilly did the marketing in the early morning before we opened the store. Paolo and I had counted on those morning excursions as an opportunity, however brief and wordless, to feast our eyes on each other as we passed on the street. He had swallowed me with the piercing blue of his deep-set eyes. My pulse quickened as we passed within a few feet, the air between us stirring and our hunger for each other leaping across the chasm of the sidewalk. It was enough, that glance that took in all of me, embraced me with the pleasure and appreciation of his whole being. It got me through the day.

But my family put a stop to even that. They didn't know who was admiring me, but they believed if they kept me out of sight, whatever fire I had kindled would die down, cooled by my disappearance.

But the longing only increased, the fire raging even stronger because we were denied one another. Somehow, despite our loss of those precious moments of public contact, we managed to sustain the private exchange of words. The letters continued, written in secret on my part, passed with a packet of fine-gauge cotton to Flora or left under a rock behind the store for Nino to retrieve and bring to his uncle.

We filled the letters with our dreams and our tears. He wrote to me:

> *I cannot explain in words how my heart beats for you. I dream of you all the time....When I write, I am so happy because I have your image in front of me. I'm crazy about you, Giulia. You are home cleaning the house, but I feel you next to me. I was suffering terribly earlier today when I had to go to work and didn't see you. I needed to tell you I love you. How much longer do we have to wait? Our hearts are suffering, and for me, it's painful to stay away from you.*

The torture of separation was too much. Paolo watched the store whenever he could get away from work early and waited for my sisters to leave. One day Pip went to New York to shop for new stock. I offered to close the store at the end of the day so Tilly could go home and start supper. I was sweeping up when I heard a tap on the back door.

I thought it might be Claudio or Peppino checking up on me again, but when I looked through the glass and saw that it was Paolo, I dropped the broom and leaped into his arms. Tears filled my eyes as he held me.

"Listen to me, Giulia. I've made a decision. Flora has convinced me that this secret we carry in our hearts is dangerous. To go on hiding like this could end in disaster with your family if they find out. I've decided to speak to Claudio, to tell him I want to marry you." He stepped away from me for a moment to see my face and watch my reaction. I saw a flicker of doubt in his eyes. He was questioning whether I'd heard him clearly, whether I believed him, whether I would accept him in front of my family.

"You would tell Claudio that? I am bursting with joy, Paolo. But what if he says no? What will we do?"

"Believe me, Giulia. It's the best way. We act honorably. We can be honest about how we feel in front of the world instead of this concealment. I will present myself as a respectable man, calling on you at your home instead of hidden in back rooms. As much as I desire you, it shames me that I have to treat you like this, sneaking behind your family's back, risking your reputation. No, I'm determined to do the right thing. I'll convince Claudio that I respect him and your family. I'm not a stranger. Let me do this for us."

He promised to come to my house the next night to speak to Claudio. I was agitated the whole day, jumping every time the bell rang over the door, dropping a whole tray filled with spools of thread and having to get down on my hands and knees to retrieve them. When I got home that night, I washed up and combed my hair after supper.

"Who are you primping for?" Pip wanted to know. "What's going on? Don't think you're leaving the house at this hour of the night."

"I'm not going anywhere. I'm expecting a visitor who's coming to talk to Claudio."

It was Pip's turn to be agitated. I picked up a stack of shirts that needed darning and calmed myself by threading a needle and starting to stitch while I waited for the doorbell to ring.

At eight o'clock, I heard a familiar voice at the door, and Angelina called out from the hall.

"Claudio, Paolo Serafini is here. If you want a cup of coffee, ask one of your sisters to make it. I'm still putting the children to bed."

Pip looked at me. "I don't believe it! Not him. No. No. No! What a mistake. This must be a joke or a bad dream. He's nothing but trouble, him and his union. You'd be better off in a convent than keeping company with him."

Pip fretted in the kitchen, banging pots on shelves and furiously scrubbing the sink, muttering some kind of litany under her breath while she anxiously eyed the closed door to the parlor, where Paolo and Claudio were drinking their coffee. I strained to hear their words over the angry din Pip was making. Finally, Angelina yelled from upstairs that she couldn't get the kids to sleep because of the noise. The baby started wailing. I kept my head down over the mending, trying not to prick my finger.

I worried that Paolo's plan to be open was a mistake. As difficult as it had been to hide from my family, to write my letters in secret, to sneak an embrace in the back room, at least I hadn't been forced to confront their anger. What if Claudio said no? What if that provoked my sisters to an even stricter watch over me? I might not be allowed out of the house at all, not even to go to the store.

My mind began to race ahead, to scenes of disobedience and defiance. I had climbed out of windows before; I knew I'd do it again to be with Paolo, not just to dance for an evening in the moonlight, but to run away with him. A recklessness rose up inside me as I contemplated the aftermath of Paolo's conversation with Claudio. I was ready to walk out of the house with him that evening if my family forbade me to see him.

The door to the parlor opened and a haze of cigar smoke wafted into the kitchen. Pip stopped her scrubbing and turned around, her hands dripping and red. I stood up from the table.

Paolo came out first and turned toward me, with a gentle smile and a nod. He reached for my hand and brought it to his lips.

Pip threw her dishrag in the sink.

"Are you crazy?" She directed her wrath at Claudio. "What do you think Papa would've said? Do you think he would have allowed this?"

"This is my house. My America. I make the rules here. If she goes back to Italy, Papa can tell her what to do, but for now, it's my decision. Better for her to see someone I know than a stranger. Better that Paolo come to me honestly than to have her hiding."

Claudio and Pip acted as if Paolo and I weren't there. Let them battle with each other rather than with me, I thought. Pip's mistake had been to call up Papa's name.

I walked Paolo to the door, ignoring my brother and sister. He took my face in his hands and kissed me publicly for the first time. It was another turning point for us, this acknowledgment in front of others. But the recklessness I had felt while waiting for Claudio and Paolo to finish their conversation fled in the face of Pip's animosity. I was no longer sure how wise it would be, even with Claudio's permission, to flaunt our love.

The doubts I felt that night were accurate. The women in the family almost immediately began an assault on my relationship with Paolo. They shook their heads; they whispered knowingly to one another, mouth to ear, eyes cast quickly back at me; they clucked in disapproval or pursed their lips.

"He's so wrong for you, Giulia. Think of what Mama will say, what she expects. A good partner for Claudio, yes, he's good with the books. But he'd be nothing, *have* nothing, without

Claudio carrying him along. What does he do with himself, when he isn't doing Claudio's business, except moon over that piano fingering tunes? It's nice to have him around on a Saturday night, but what about the rest of the week when you need to put food on the table?"

"What kind of life can you expect from an agitator like Paolo? Somebody in the neighborhood with a cousin upstate told me Paolo was involved in that GE strike. With the life he leads, he could be thrown in prison any minute. And *then* where would you be?"

"You think you can eat those letters after you marry him, or use them to put clothes on the backs of your children? Do you expect Claudio to keep you, like he does now, after you marry?"

"You had a much better prospect in Roberto, Giulia. His family has a good business. He's got the same instincts as Claudio. You'll see. Roberto will be back, ready to step into his father's place. I heard that the old man's sick. Roberto's just waiting for the right moment, a quiet moment when the cops are occupied with someone else. Then he'll show up, looking for you. And where will you be? In some tenement with two bawling kids and not enough to feed them, with your body sagging, your fingers rough, and your husband playing the piano every night, or worse, in jail. Wait for Roberto, Giulia."

"Paolo's so funny-looking with that red hair. Remember how you used to swoon over Roberto's looks? Remember how elegant he was, how everyone noticed him at the dances? All the other girls envied you, wishing he had chosen them."

"You need to *think,* Giulia, instead of peeking out the curtains every five minutes. Who needs it, I ask you? It's like you're sick. A sickness in the head. You act like you'll die without his love poems every day. Pretty words on a page. I can live without those, thank you very much."

CHAPTER 27

Funeral

Roberto Scarpa's father finally died after all the murmuring speculation that he was mortally ill. Some people said he died of a broken heart; others that it was from anger over Roberto's rash stupidity. Some, the police included, thought Roberto might come back to bury his father. The family held off putting him in the ground for a few days and the rumors that the Scarpas were waiting for Roberto could not be contained.

No fragment, no matter how absurd, escaped my sisters or Yolanda, who sat every afternoon with the grieving widow. In the evenings at dinner, each scrap of information was dutifully brought to our table for discussion and, of course, for my continued indoctrination in the wisdom of waiting for Roberto and abandoning Paolo.

"Zi'Yolanda says she and Signora Scarpa are saying the rosary twice every afternoon at four o'clock. Once for the soul of the father, that he'll make a good journey home to God, and once for the heart of the son, that he'll make a good journey home to his mother who needs him," Tilly reported earnestly.

"I heard that one of the brothers sent a telegram to Italy even before they had the priest in to hear their father's last confession," said Pip.

Even Angelina had news. "One of the boys said the cops have been watching the house ever since the old man died. They got a tip that Roberto was already on his way."

Everyone had an opinion, a theory. How quickly had Roberto's family gotten word to him? When was the next ship leaving Napoli? How would Roberto disguise himself to thwart the police?

Zi'Yolanda's prayers were as fervent as those of the distraught Signora Scarpa, abandoned by her husband in death and by her oldest son in his flight from the law. Zi'Yolanda held out hope of Roberto's return, convinced that I would leave Paolo and fly willingly into Roberto's arms over the coffin of his father.

What did they feed each other, Signora Scarpa and my aunt, as they bent and muttered over their clacking beads? Two crazy old women concocting a frothy zabaglione of despair and fantasy that was all air—no eggs.

And my sisters? How they ate it up every evening when Yolanda made her daily report. They concocted fantasies themselves, remembered swirling dances and whispered intimacies in the parlor of the Hillcrest Hotel. They weren't there at the christening. They didn't have the memories I did, of swirling snow flecked with blood and screamed obscenities. They heard the music of the piano on Saturday nights. I heard the silence in the hall on Sunday afternoon: a suddenly emptied room encircled by sirens, shouts, the crack of baton upon head. A suddenly emptied life, adrift and cut off from the dreams and illusions that had fled through the crack forced open by my lover's brutality.

They all prodded me, wondering if—hoping that—I had doubts about my fledgling love for Paolo, faced with the prospect of Roberto's return.

I went to the Scarpa funeral. Antonietta was my friend, after all, before her brother had become my dance partner. She was pregnant again. Natale was a robust little baby despite the difficult omens at his christening, and he appeared to resemble his father more and more with every passing day, putting to rest—or at least putting behind closed doors—whatever wild accusations had ignited the events at the christening.

Antonietta did not look well. I think it was more than burying her father and holding up her desolate mother. She was not the girl who'd giggled and daydreamed with me behind John Molloy's back. But then, neither was I.

The Scarpas had waited a week before asking the priest to say the Mass of the Dead. Not enough time for Roberto to travel from Italy. Roberto's younger brothers, convinced of the futility of waiting, finally extracted permission from their grief-crazed mother to lay their father to rest without Roberto as witness. Antonietta, who seemed so weakened by her situation in life, missed Roberto terribly and blamed herself for his forced disappearance. She'd probably been right there with Signora Scarpa and Yolanda praying for Roberto's secret return.

During all the heated speculation before the funeral, Paolo said nothing to me. If he burned with the same question as my sisters—"If Roberto comes back, Giulia, whom will you choose?"—he kept those fires to himself. Paolo did not go to the funeral. He made some excuse about needing to be in the city that morning, leaving me to go with my sisters. Leaving me to make my choice, if I had to, without his presence.

The Mass at Our Lady of Mount Carmel was full, and I took a seat toward the back with Zi'Yolanda and my sisters. Claudio had paid his respects at the house. He spent as little time inside a church as possible.

The priest droned, banks of candles blazed—all lit by the obsessive grief of Signora Scarpa—and a pungent incense wafted from the nave, attempting to mask the odor of the decaying body.

More than once, Antonietta and her brothers searched the congregation, only to whisper with shaking heads to their bent and wailing mother, "No, Mama. He's not here."

At the final blessing, the five boys took their positions at their father's casket, leaving an empty place where Roberto should have stood to shoulder the weight. At the sight of her sons, Signora Scarpa accelerated her keening, and Antonietta, awkward and heavy, struggled to support her mother as they followed the casket out of the church. Zi'Yolanda cast a meaningful glance at me as the brothers marched past us, but I focused on the eyes of my friend and offered her my blessing.

Zi'Yolanda was determined to accompany the body to its final resting place, not out of respect for the ritual but in anticipation of the drama that would still, she was convinced, play itself out. She had talked Claudio into providing us with a carriage for the trip to the cemetery in Riverdale, so we joined the cortege threading its way through the Bronx.

By the time we arrived at the gravesite, the tension that had filled the church had lessened. Only a small group of family and friends had made the trip, and if the police were watching, they were well hidden. The grave was a short walk uphill from the drive where we left the carriages. The flowers had arrived ahead of us and were piled around the recently dug hole. Mountains of flowers, wreaths, hearts, sprays of lilies and carnations, ribbons printed with endearments or prayers, a profusion of familial grief and community solidarity. Somewhere in the masses of blooms was one with the Fiorillo name attached. Up close, one could see that the edges of the flowers were already tinged with brown.

We clustered around the grave. The Scarpa boys, their father's coffin safely positioned at the side of the hole, gathered around their mother. My sisters and I and Yolanda were opposite them and to the rear.

The priest intoned the Latin prayers for the dead. Then the gravediggers, who had been standing at the periphery, leaning on their shovels, moved forward, slipped two canvas straps under the coffin and lowered it. Michele, the second-oldest son, held his mother back as she attempted to throw herself across the polished wood of her husband's coffin. The gravediggers, used to the hysteria of widows, continued methodically. Shovelful by shovelful, they began to fill the grave. The rest of us began the final procession, grabbing a handful of dirt and tossing it into the hole. As I reached the edge, I looked across at one of the gravediggers, at his long, muscled forearms and powerful hands gripping the wooden shaft of his shovel. I held my breath as I raised my eyes to his face, obscured by beard and visored cap pulled well over his brow. For an instant, he lifted his head and looked directly into my eyes without breaking the rhythm of his shoveling. In his gaze was recognition and defiance, pride, cunning, warning.

I saw new lines around familiar eyes, pressed into flesh that had become reacquainted with the sun. I saw, still smoldering, the glint of desire that had once pulled me into feverish dances and intimate conversations. I saw the man I had lost, not only to Italy but also to violence. I knelt to fill my hand with earth, my lungs with air. The movement brought me close enough to see the hairs on his long fingers bleached even lighter now; close enough to remember my hand enclosed within those fingers. This was no apparition. No figment conjured up by the crude chants of my aunt. No dim memory that I could conveniently wipe away or easily put aside with false assuredness.

This was flesh and bone and breath, inches away from mine. Defying me to reveal him, daring me to leap across his father's grave, full of a man's confidence that I would do as he demanded—stay or come, be silent or profess my desire.

I stood again to steady myself, to hear my own thoughts instead of his. And as I slowly sprinkled the earth over his father's coffin, I let him slip through my fingers as well, brushing the last bits of dust from my palms.

CHAPTER 28

Flora's House

Flora came to the store to ask me a favor. She had become a friend to me, offering me welcome and kindness. I found myself so lonely at home, no one taking my side, no one wishing me well. I was so exhausted by the voices battering at me every day—my aunt and my sisters, harpies who conducted my life like an orchestra leader with his baton; the neighbors, who watched every step I took, whether alone or accompanied. My own voice, that used to sing, chant, cast simple spells, spin funny stories, was now stilled, dumbstruck, seeking words that did not want to be found.

So Flora was a relief—like a sensible, solid hearth. She baked me delicious coconut cakes and listened to me. It was automatic for me to agree to the favor. She and her husband had to go to New York City, something legal they had to attend to. She wanted me to come and stay with the baby. Nino was in school most of the day, so it was only the baby who needed tending. I told Tilly and Pip I wouldn't be in the store and steeled myself against their complaints.

"She has no sister to help her," I told them. "If you want, I'll take the accounts with me and work on them while the baby sleeps."

I got to Flora's apartment early enough to catch a smile from Nino as he left for school. I slipped him the sour ball I had waiting for him in my pocket. I winked as he shoved it into his mouth, shifting it with his tongue to hide it from his mother as she kissed him goodbye.

"God bless you for doing this, Giulia. There isn't anyone else I'd trust with Rosina. Is there anything I should explain to you?"

"I don't think so, Flora. I've taken care of my share of babies, from my little brothers to Claudio's boys. I don't expect any surprises. And Rosina knows me. She'll be fine. Go, go. Look after your business and don't worry about us. That's my girl!"

I took Rosina into my arms and sang her one of our childhood rhymes. Then I swept her into the kitchen for her porridge while Flora and her husband quietly left.

Rosina scooped up tiny fistfuls of oatmeal and licked it from her fingers as I assisted her with a slender silver spoon— a christening gift from Paolo, Flora had told me. She was hungry and abandoned herself to the milky pleasure, humming softly as she sucked on her fingers, leaning eagerly forward every time I approached her with the spoon. She laughed and opened her mouth.

When she was full, she turned her head in distraction toward the window, the light and shadow, the sounds of the street below: the screech of the trolley, the clatter of horse and wagon, the urgency of voices greeting, bargaining, arguing. Food no longer held her interest. The life all around was calling to her.

I took my cue, and wiped up the remnants of her oatmeal, playing the finger games Giuseppina had sung to me. Then I lifted her from her chair and carried her over to the window so that she could see what had so attracted her.

Rosina slapped her hand against the glass, making her own music, trying to get the attention of those in the street below. The avenue was just coming to life. Mercurio the butcher was rolling out the awning over his shop window to shade the rabbits hanging from metal hooks, the tripe mounded in bowls over ice. Ferruzzi the greengrocer was filling his sidewalk bins with potatoes and onions. Tilly was removing her key from her bag and about to open the door of the shop.

Rosina was growing tired of the display of sunlight and street life at the window and began to tug on my right earring. I carried her to the corner where Flora had a small box of amusements for the children—a rag doll and a cigar box filled with wooden blocks. I sat cross-legged and stacked the blocks for her to tumble with a gleeful swipe—a game I'd seen her play with Nino more than once. But Nino had far more patience than I, far more playfulness. In time, however, Rosina knocked over her last column of blocks, crawled to her doll and, clutching it, climbed into my lap with drooping eyes.

I crooned no more than a few minutes before her head fell heavy against my breast. I sat still, accepting the stillness, enjoying the moment of doing absolutely nothing except feeling this baby sleep contentedly in my arms.

As I sat, I heard a knock, a man's voice, Flora's name called from the other side of the apartment door.

I rose carefully, shifted Rosina's weight to my shoulder and went to answer the door.

"Who is it?" Flora had not told me to expect anyone. What man would visit her during the day?

"It's Paolo."

I opened the door immediately.

"Giulia! I didn't see you this morning on your way to the store and I thought that I'd missed you—that I'd been too lazy to get up as early as you and was being punished for my laziness. But here you are! What brings you here? Is Flora ill? Is that why you're holding the baby?"

"Oh, Paolo. What a surprise! A wonderful surprise! No, no. Flora's not ill. She and Giorgio had an appointment in the city. She asked me to take care of Rosina for a few hours and I knew Tilly and Pip could spare me at the store for a day."

Paolo took off his hat and entered the apartment, giving me a tentative and awkward kiss on the cheek as he reached around the sleeping Rosina. It was not our usual embrace.

"I was just about to put Rosina down. I'll be right back. Do you have time for a cup of coffee, or are you on your way somewhere?"

"It can wait." He unbuttoned his jacket as I moved down the hallway to Rosina's bed. She stirred and fumbled for her doll as I laid her as softly as I could upon her mattress. I did not want her to wake up at this moment.

Paolo and I had experienced great intimacy in these few short months. But it had been mostly an intimacy of words. When we'd been together—our encounters on the street, his stealing into the back of the store—we had never been truly alone. Bodies, voices—noisy and inquiring or merely haphazardly aware of us—all encroached upon us, obstructed us from that final intimacy.

I knew so much about Paolo. How he thought, how he felt,

how he spent his days and nights. But I did not know the warmth of his bare chest, the shape of his back, the weight of his body molded to fit the hollows and curves of my own.

I walked back down the hall to Paolo after assuring myself that Rosina slept. I walked slowly, soundlessly. I did not want to wake her; I did not want to reveal myself to any listeners lurking beyond the walls and windows. I wanted to be silent, invisible. I did not want to exist at that moment to anyone except Paolo.

CHAPTER 29

Stillness

Paolo lifted his head as I approached. He had bolted the door to the landing, drawn the curtains in the front room. Done what he could to shield us.

I saw the flicker of longing in his eyes. A smile on his lips, opening his heart to me. A stillness. No words. No gestures. Not even that nervous habit he had of pushing his hat back, running his fingers through his hair. No movement at all. It was just Paolo and Giulia facing each other in a dim room. The space between us was a gulf, an Atlantic Ocean of the unknown, the uncertain. Potential destruction or potential happiness. We did not move toward each other. We did not turn away, breaking the stillness with a gesture or a word.

Part of me was ready to jump into my silly chatter—to be

the girl peeling eggplants so long ago who took a man's hand-kerchief so unknowingly, who gave it back saturated with unspoken and unrecognized promise.

I felt no certainty in that moment. I looked across the space between Paolo and me and saw my future, my pain, my salvation, my honor, my desire, my dreams. I felt the blood begin to surge into the vein on my neck, swelling it to a knot. My hand fluttered, then rose to cover the vein as if it were my private parts, some shame that I must hide. Did Paolo feel the same hesitancy? The same sense that stepping forward was stepping off the edge of the world?

I looked into the blueness of his eyes. So transparent, so clear. I felt that I could look through them. Not like Claudio's almost black eyes—guarded, hidden, a mask. Paolo wore no mask, at least not with me.

What did I see during that silence between us? Heartache. Hope. A questioning. Not a demand, not an order, not an expectation. He was asking, "Do you want me? Will you have me? Are you willing to step to my side, separate yourself from your family?"

And I asked myself, *am I?* Do I move into the circle of Paolo's arms and leave the grasp and clamor of my sisters and aunts, the rules of my mother, the protection of Claudio? Can Paolo protect me? Can he place his body between the world and me? In his arms, in his bed, will I find a refuge? Will I find a life? Not only food on my table and in the mouths of our children, but also nourishment for my loneliness and weariness. Will he be able to feed me with his words, his music? Will he sing to me in our bed? He had told me that I came to him in his dreams. So real that he thought I was already there, in his arms, in his bed. He woke up sweating, breathless, spent, as if I had embraced him. He woke up, he said, filled with my light.

I moved toward him.

"This is unbelievable to me. To have you here." I drew briefly back. "Did anyone see you come in? Does anyone know that you're here?" My face constricted in fear of this last obstacle.

"No one knows where I am. And Flora wasn't expecting me. I stopped by on a whim, without a plan. Just a good morning to my sister was all I had on my mind. Now, of course, there's much more…." He smiled and pulled me back into his embrace.

We held each other in silence and at length. There was, for the first time, no urgency, no anxious listening for the approach of others, no bittersweet sense that this joy would be cut off long before we wished it to be. We had *time*.

I didn't know when he was expected elsewhere. He did not inquire when Flora and Giorgio were returning. Neither one of us tried to calculate how long Rosina might doze.

I think we both imagined that by not asking, by not recognizing time, we could, for once, ignore it. The sheer luxury of holding him without the ever-present knowledge that we might have to break away at a second's notice was exhilarating.

I felt every inch of him: the rough wool of his jacket, the starched cotton of his shirt; his arms around my waist, not poised to release but still, firm, a brace against everything that battered at me and pulled me away from him. I was aware, as well, of the firmness between his legs.

I was no longer afraid. I welcomed this moment and what it promised. We made love slowly, not in a crazed and frenzied way, although that was how I had felt all the times before, when we'd been able to capture only fragments of our passion for each other. He undressed me one button at a time, a kiss placed on each inch of flesh revealed with each succeeding button.

When he took off his own shirt I saw and felt the curling red-blond hair and pressed my face into his chest. We lay on the floor, stretched out upon a patterned red carpet filled with flowers of many colors twisting and entwining themselves. We faced each other, belly against belly, hands clasped, in relief, in disbelief.

For the first time since I'd known him, Paolo was wordless. Instead of creating eloquence with pen on paper, he wrote that morning on me, his fingers describing his love on my skin. When he stopped I took the hand and kissed each of his fingertips, lingering on the third, the ink-stained sign of his writing life.

"Your lips will turn blue," he murmured.

"My family will simply believe that I'm crazier than ever for you, kissing the letters that you write to me, trying to swallow your words."

Down the hall, Rosina's voice mewled plaintively.

I kissed Paolo one more time and then gathered my clothes together.

CHAPTER 30

Anna's Advice

It was my mother's intervention that finally stilled the voices of my family and dismissed Yolanda's objections to Paolo as if they were the mutterings of a fool. Even from a great distance, her voice and her decisions carried weight. She wrote to me as soon as she knew what was going on.

Figlia Mia,
I have just received a letter from Zi'Yolanda concerning your recent attachment to Claudio's business partner, Serafini. She wrote—or rather, your sister Pip has written for her, because poor Yolanda didn't have the advantages you girls have had—that everyone, your uncle Antonio and herself, your sisters and your cousins—disapproves of your rushing into Paolo's arms.

Zi'Yolanda entreated me to write to you as a mother. How else would I have, except as a mother? Whether you will heed me as a daughter is another question entirely. As I said, Zi'Yolanda claimed to have the support of the entire family. She said you have been foolishly swayed by Paolo's courtship, besieged daily by his love poems. You listen to no one, apparently, stomping from the kitchen with hands over your ears, seeking refuge in the home of his sister Flora instead of among your own sisters. You have always been the defiant one, never linking yourself, even as a little girl, to any of the others. Perhaps I shouldn't have let Giuseppina take you when she did, or keep you so long. But what was I to do at the time, forced to my bed to prevent the twins from coming too soon, and then losing Giovanni when he and Frankie were only three months old. My worry for him and my helplessness and grief when he died were overwhelming. Mark my words: you cannot know greater pain as a woman than to have a child die before you do. May you never experience it.

May you also never experience the pain of a daughter who thinks she can find her own way, unheeding the advice and wisdom of family in the matter of men. May you not know the ingratitude and shame of a daughter who whirls from one man to the next, not knowing what she seeks.

However, as disappointed as I am in your flightiness, I am extremely reluctant to rely upon the judgment of Yolanda. She is a fool, and you will be more of a fool if you heed the yammering around you. In this Papa and I concur—one of the few times in twenty years that we have agreed on something.

I do trust Claudio. He obviously has great respect for Paolo. It would certainly be good for the partnership to bring Paolo into the family.

We have heard through Claudio that Paolo has asked for your hand. Papa and I are prepared to accept.

I shall write to Yolanda myself. Be a good girl. Write to me. Your loving and concerned mother

CHAPTER 31

The Veil

Standing in front of the altar at Our Lady of Mount Carmel, I saw a flash of light, as if there were a halo around my head. Tilly, at my side, screamed. And then Paolo's hands were upon me, ripping the veil from my hair, my face. I breathed a choking smoke. My eyes filled with water and a searing pain. I gagged on the smell—acrid, bitter. Then I heard the wailing behind me, the mutterings of the old women. I had been too close to the candles.

I turned to where Paolo had flung the veil, where he was stamping out the flames on the marble steps by the Madonna's altar. It was a blackened tangle of strands, like an old cobweb hanging from the rafters of a barn. Ashes. I felt the color, the life, seep out of my face, slowly dripping into a puddle of fear at my feet. Paolo saw me, took two strides to my side and caught me as I began to sink, to crumple. He cradled me, surrounded me, whispered into my ear, kissed the singed ends of my curls. I noticed the black smudges on his fingertips, the fine, powdery soot on his white shirt cuffs.

Tilly was whimpering. The priest was fumbling with his spectacles and his prayer book. He had just risen to his feet after checking the damage to the carpet.

Paolo coughed, still holding me tightly, and said quietly to the priest, "Father, I think we can continue now."

The words droned past me without any meaning. I felt Paolo squeeze me gently when I was supposed to answer. Tilly composed herself enough to help me take off my glove and Paolo caressed the ring onto my trembling finger.

I could not think. I could not rejoice. I heard only the terrified gasp reverberating through the church, the hum of prayers trying to dispel the evil omens hovering amid the candles. I saw only the consuming flash that followed the thousand glimmering filaments embracing my head. I smelled only candle wax, burning silk, charred hair. I buried my face in the white roses and lilies that I carried, but their fragrance was denied to me, overpowered by this memory that I also carried out of the church, into my life.

Somehow, Paolo propelled me away from the priest, down the aisle, out into the fresh air. At the foot of the steps waited the carriage. Two white horses. Paolo had ordered them especially for today, with flowers entwined in their harness. Paolo lifted me into the carriage and kissed my ankle as he settled me against the cushions. He climbed up next to me, and in this moment of repose, removed his handkerchief from his jacket to wipe first my forehead and then his own fingers. He signaled the driver to start. Behind us were the carriages of our families, other people on foot. It wasn't far to the grand salon of the Hill-crest Hotel, just across the railroad bridge on Gramatan Avenue.

We moved forward slowly. I hid my head in Paolo's shoulder. I had no desire to rise up, to display myself to the family behind us, to the strangers who lined the road, to the children waving. Because my head was down I did not see the speeding truck that suddenly startled the horses. I only heard the frantic neighing of first one and then the other animal, the rough, angry shout of the driver, the grating of the wheels, the lurching and twisting of the carriage and then a frenzy of movement, a loss of control, the carriage hurtling, the clatter of the wooden bridge under us, the carriage lifting, straining, shouts, wood splintering. Paolo's body was tense, once again surrounding me, protecting me.

Suddenly, we came to a jolting, thudding stillness. There were more shouts, the shuddering, heaving sound of the horses panting. In one swift, unwavering movement, Paolo lifted me from the carriage and into the urgent arms of Claudio, who had rushed up from the carriage behind us.

Paolo stepped down and together the two men flanked me, walked me around the carriage to the other side of the bridge. I turned and looked back. The bridge was beginning to swarm with people—the families who had followed us, the onlook-ers along the road. The driver unhitched the horses. The carriage was tilted against the shattered railing of the bridge, halted in its plunge by a single metal post.

I turned away from this vision of what might have been, from the erupting hysteria of my sisters and aunt, from the horror of my uncle. Up ahead, through the windows of the Hillcrest Hotel, wafted the music of a piano.

My wedding day.

From the very first days of our marriage, Paolo brought us out of the shadows where we had been hiding our love for one another. On Sunday afternoons I'd put on my red dress and take his arm as we walked down the hill to Hartley Park, retracing our steps on that Sunday long before when he had escorted Pip and Tilly and me to the band concert for the first time.

Paolo usually couldn't wait to get to the park, his exuberance infectious and childlike. He'd clipped the concert schedule out of the *Daily Argus* and always knew exactly what band would be playing. Often, as we walked, he'd be whistling songs he knew to be on the program, entertaining us with a prelude before we even arrived at the park gate. One Sunday he told me he had a surprise for me, a discovery he'd made. I was eager to know what it was and cajoled and pleaded with him all the way down the hill, but he insisted that I had to wait until we were inside the park. Once there, instead of heading toward the band shell, he led me away toward a grove of arborvitae growing in a semicircle. Within the grove he stopped and put his finger to his lips as I started to question him.

"Wait and listen," he said.

Within a few minutes, I heard the tap of the bandleader's baton on the wooden podium and then the opening notes of the tune Paolo had been whistling. The music was as clear as if we had been sitting in front of the bandstand. But instead of being in the midst of a hundred others, we were alone in the grove.

He bowed deeply and said to me, "Signora Serafini, may I have this dance?"

And then he took me in his arms and swept me over the grass in time with the music. I felt his arm around my waist, his hand caressing the small of my back and sometimes wandering lower. His other hand was tightly entwined with mine, as if he never wanted to let go of me.

We danced that Sunday through the entire concert, until we

were breathless and a little dizzy from the warmth generated between us. For the rest of the summer we danced to the concerts from within the grove, alone with each other and the music.

CHAPTER 32

The Strike

Above the Palace were two apartments. Claudio gave Paolo and me one as a wedding gift. We had three rooms—a kitchen in the middle with a room in front that we used as a parlor and one in back that was our bedroom. The toilet was out in the hall between the two apartments. Paolo and I had fixed up the rooms since we'd been there, but they were narrow and dark. I could not see any trees when I looked out the windows. In the summer, I put some pots of begonias on the fire escape.

One morning, I had just returned from the market, my basket heavy with onions and broccoli rabe and peppers, when I found Paolo in the kitchen. We were four months married, my breasts already tender, my belly slightly swelled with the baby that had taken hold inside me that first time, at Flora's.

I remembered the morning he'd come to Flora's, seeking his sister but finding me, my longing, my readiness. Was this the reason for his unexpected appearance—was he looking for the same thing now? I put my basket down and went to him. He was seated at the kitchen table, a cigarette in one hand, his pen in the other, a loose sheaf of papers spread across the tablecloth—columns of figures, cryptic words. No poetry this morning.

I put my arms around him, kissing the part of his neck that was exposed above his collar.

"Buon giorno, Signore Serafini. Come sta?"

He patted my hand and kissed it absentmindedly. This was not a man hungry for his wife's body. His face was pinched and furrowed, and I could detect the signs of an oncoming headache. He crushed the cigarette in a coffee saucer, threw down the pen and pushed back his chair. The pen scattered drops of blue ink across the cloth. I picked up the saucer and brought it to the sink. He knew I hated the stench and the dirt when he brought cigarettes into the apartment.

He paced the floor, moving from the kitchen to the front room and back. He stopped at the windows that overlooked the street, but stood to the side, by the curtains, so that someone looking up couldn't see him.

I rinsed the saucer and pulled the tablecloth off the table, first gathering his papers together in a pile.

He jumped at me. "What are you doing? Don't touch them. It's business." He grabbed the loose papers from my hand. "They are none of your concern." He stuffed the papers into his pocket.

Tears stung my eyes and I pressed them back with the palm of my hand. His words had been like a slap across my face.

"I'm a businesswoman. I understand business. How can you not talk to me about business, especially if it affects you? Don't you trust me to understand?"

I saw the pains shoot across his face, the color drain from his skin. Even his copper hair looked dull, leaden.

"Are you in trouble? Do you owe someone? Tell me. Tell me."

I went to him, held his face in my hands. I wanted to scream at him. I wanted to caress him. Take away his pain. Take away his false pride. If I could help him, he had to let me.

He took my hands and pulled them away.

"I shouldn't have come home. I'm going out."

He left the apartment. But when he left the building, he didn't use the street entrance. Instead, he went through the Palace and out through the alley.

He didn't come home for supper that evening. I put a covered plate in the icebox and climbed into bed with one of the books my mother had sent. Around ten, I heard the piano downstairs in the Palace and knew it was Paolo. I was able then to sleep, listening to his melancholy music.

Sometime around three, I heard him on the stairs and then in the kitchen. He ate the *pasta e fagioli* I had made for him, cold and in the dark, his spoon grazing the bottom of the bowl with every stroke. When he was finished, he put his dishes in the sink and left his shoes by the door.

I waited, my back turned away from him, my breathing steady. I wanted no more words that night. He undressed slowly, placing his watch and cuff links in their box on the dresser, hanging his shirt and trousers methodically. When he lifted the covers to climb into bed, I could smell the wine, the homemade Chianti he and Claudio sold by the gallon downstairs. His body, normally so taut and strong, was slack and heavy as he settled beside me. He muttered my name as he buried his face in my hair. Within minutes, he was asleep. He slept fitfully, calling out unintelligible sounds and moving his legs uncontrollably. At five, as a gray light filtered over our bed, I could see that he was soaked in sweat, his face the same color as the early morning sky.

I got up and took a soft towel from my linen cupboard. I filled the washbasin with water and brought it to his bedside. I washed his body. Although he stirred at first in protest, he subsided and submitted, finally drifting into a less troubled sleep.

I dressed and made a pot of coffee. In the pocket of his jacket, hanging on the kitchen hook, I could see the papers, still there, crammed as they had been earlier.

My mother would've taken those papers, studied them, deciphered them. She would have confronted Papa and then presented a solution. She was often furious with Papa, but they were always united. More than once, she'd accused him of generating disasters and then reached into her reserves of cunning and intelligence and will to rebuild from the ashes of my father's failures.

What failure was Paolo hiding? What loss could he not share with his wife? I believed he still saw me as a spoiled child, a privileged daughter, unused to financial uncertainty. I was determined to show him I was not fragile. That I could shoulder his pain, not just wipe the sweat from his troubled face.

I could hear his breathing in the next room, the sounds of the street coming alive below us, the factory whistles starting their round, the trains heading for New York with New Rochelle businessmen aboard on their way to banks and shipping firms and law offices.

I left the papers in his jacket. I didn't need to spy to know it had to do with money. Money he didn't have—that we didn't have. I got dressed, not in my marketing clothes, but in my shop clothes. Clothes I hadn't worn since my marriage and the family's decision to sell the store. Pip had left to marry and move to New York, and Tilly's husband, Gaetano, whom she had married a month after my wedding, made enough to relieve her as well. Whatever profit Claudio had realized when the final papers had been signed he had kept for himself.

Between Paolo's salary from the union and his share of the profits from the Palace, we had thought there would be enough for us. But now I understood from Paolo's fear that there wasn't.

I went downstairs and left word at the Palace that I wanted to speak with Claudio. Then I walked over to his stables and found him in his office. We spoke. I made my offer; he accepted.

The next day, the Palace would begin serving lunch and dinner. I was to give Claudio twenty-five percent of the profits and keep the rest for my family.

It had been easier to talk to Claudio than to Paolo. By the time I'd gotten back from the stables, Paolo was already gone, the bed a damp and rumpled pile of sheets. I changed out of my street clothes and stripped and scrubbed the bedding. Better to begin the evening with fresh linens, a fresh heart. I hung the sheets on the line above the alley, ironed the tablecloth that I'd soaked in bleach the day before. The ink spots had disappeared as if they had never marred it.

In the afternoon, I made lists of provisions I would need for the Palace, rolled up the sleeves of my housedress and began to scrub the unused kitchen behind the bar. When Paolo stayed away again at dinnertime, I put his plate in the icebox and sat at the kitchen table writing menu cards in the hand the nuns had taught me at Santa Margareta.

I heard no piano playing downstairs that night, so I was startled when the doorknob turned shortly after ten. I'd just spread the cards out to dry.

"What's this?" He thrust his chin at the table.

"My answer," I replied.

"To what question?"

"My own. How can I be a good wife, a woman, not a child? I don't want to be your burden."

"You're not a burden."

"I made you angry yesterday with my fears."

"I was angry with myself, not you."

"Do you think I can't understand your problems?"

"You shouldn't have to."

"You admire Flora, don't you?"

"I love her. She's my sister."

"But you approve of her, how she handles herself, her affairs?"

"Yes, always. I have great respect for Flora."

"I want you to have respect for me as well."

"I adore you, Giulia. That's why I anger myself. That I can't provide for you, for the baby—what you deserve. There. I've said it. I can't provide."

He sat with his head in his hands.

"The union is going out on strike again. We only organized the workers a few months ago, and the leadership is calling for a strike at the clockworks. What little steady income I brought in from the IWW will be wiped out."

"Paolo, look at me. Take your hands away from your eyes. Look at me. I am no precious china doll, with feet good only for dancing and hands made only for holding sweets. These feet are planted firmly on the ground. These hips have balanced laundry baskets and bolts of fabric and Claudio's sons—and, soon, God willing, our own. These hands have harvested my grandmother's garden and counted the till at the shop at the end of the day and kept the books. We're going to survive, Paolo. Strike or no strike. The women in my family don't sit fanning themselves while their men sweat.

"Do you think I married you because of your job? Do you think I defied all the curses and the advice of my sisters and my aunts because of money? Do you think I gave you my heart and my soul because you bring home a steady paycheck?

"You provide, Paolo. You provide nourishment for my soul. You provide music that makes me soar. You provide a joy in my life I did not know existed. Never, never tell me again that you can't provide. *We* provide. For each other."

I was kneeling in front of him, holding his face in my hands. Praying silently to every saint I could remember to help me rescue him, rescue us. And I called upon my mother for her strength of purpose. Her stubbornness. Her unwillingness to accept defeat.

That night I felt a shift take place between Paolo and me. For the first time, I understood what it meant to be a woman. It had nothing to do with the power I had discovered as a young girl in Italy—the hunger I could elicit in Vito's eyes with a bared shoulder or a quickening castanet. Nor was it the satisfaction I had gained in Paolo's arms, from those first precious moments on Flora's carpet of many flowers to our own marriage bed. It was not even my changing body as the child inside me grew and took shape.

It was something entirely apart from my physical self. It was a recognition of my own *serieta*—my solidity, my strength, when confronted with the doubt-ridden soul whose face I held in my hands, whose future rested in my arms. Up until that moment, it was Paolo who'd been strong—Paolo who had caught me in my fall from my own family, Paolo who had snatched the burning veil from my head, Paolo who had lifted me from the carriage run amok. But Paolo's courage—the courage of men—seemed limited to the physical dangers of the world. Soldiers in war, hunters, builders of bridges and tunnels. The courage of women is much more subtle. Builders of the home, protectors of the man's image of himself. Feed the family without destroying his pride. Be resourceful without undermining his own faith in himself. Be the beating heart that fuels his hope.

I told Paolo the next morning that I was growing bored without the store. Claudio had mentioned how hungry the men were who came to the Palace—how he could keep them longer, attract more to the bar if he could offer a meal now and then. Sonny behind the bar knew how to pour a drink, but couldn't even light the stove. It would give me something to do during the day, if I cooked for the Palace customers. Claudio was willing to let me try. We'd see if these Americans would eat my sausage and peppers.

I slipped into the kitchen as the watchmakers began their strike. It kept my mind off the fury surrounding the clockworks, the picket lines, the shouting, the cops. Paolo came home at night exhausted from shuttling back and forth between the owners and the workers, between the local and the national union. One time, he arrived with a bloody head, a bruised arm.

He was too tired, too preoccupied, to notice the money filling the jewelry box in my top drawer. He was simply grateful for the warm meal I put in front of him and the warm body I welcomed him with every night.

CHAPTER 33

Carmine

When the pains started one afternoon I dismissed them, ignored them, went on with preparing the evening meal for the Palace. But the pains didn't stop, didn't fade away as they had in the past. I managed to serve dinner to the men who'd come to depend on my cooking, who had helped my business flourish in only a few short months. But when Paolo arrived to play the piano, I told him it was time to fetch Flora and Tilly. He had rushed, white-faced, to bring them to me.

I had tried to appear calm when I'd told Paolo, but I was so frightened. I wasn't ready. It was too soon. This baby was not due for two more months.

I should have remembered. Somewhere in me should have been Giuseppina's wisdom, her healing, her hands on my belly.

But nothing. I searched frantically, calling her name, wandering through the past as if through the rooms of her house. Where was she?

Oh—another one…too long…no rest.

I was cold, my body was shaking, the sweat ran down my cheeks, my neck. I heard the voices of Tilly and Flora.

"She's so tiny. How will she ever manage?" someone whispered, thinking I couldn't hear.

If Giuseppina had been there, she would have shown me, guided me. Why couldn't I remember? Why hadn't I paid attention?

How long had this been going on? I couldn't remember. I couldn't take another minute, another pain. The light—I saw the light through the window—was it morning already? Why didn't it stop? Why didn't the baby come?

"The head, here's the head." A voice, agitated. A flurry of activity around me.

"Just a few more minutes, Giulia. It's time to push." Tilly bent close to my ear.

I couldn't bear this pain for a few more minutes. It was tearing me apart. Giuseppina!

A darkness, a silence. It was over.

I turned my head to Tilly; my hands reached out, beseeching, for the life that had just struggled and ripped its way through me.

But Tilly came toward me empty-handed, empty-eyed.

I released a wail that came from no place I had known before, not even in those lost moments of pain from the last hours. In that agony had at least been hope, life.

There was no other sound except mine—blood-soaked, emptying, the howling of a she-wolf in the mountains above our village.

Someone tried to hold me, to comfort me with chamomile

tea and a cool cloth pressed to my forehead—as if the pain were in my belly or my head, as if there were some simple remedy to restore me.

But I was broken, shattered as though I'd been hurled from a bridge onto stones below. My body lay curled in on itself, hollow.

In the corner I saw Tilly fumbling with a match and a red glass. She lit the votive candle and set it down on the dresser. I heard her droning prayers to saints I no longer remembered, to a God who had, in this moment, turned away from me.

I turned away, as well, from Tilly's piety. In the other corner I saw Flora at the table with a basin. She was washing the baby's body with great tenderness.

I did not even know if it was a girl or a boy. I begged Flora for the child. She faced me. Without hesitation, with understanding, she carried the swaddled corpse over to me.

I raised myself up, felt the blood leaving my body, leaned back against the pillows. I took the silent, still-warm body into my arms and unwrapped it.

A son. Paolo's son. "Carmine," I said.

His skin was a purple-blue. His eyelids were nearly transparent. His hair was the color of a sunset. He had all his parts—nothing missing, nothing damaged. The only thing missing was breath.

It was my turn to bathe him now. My tears came, huge drops that fell from my eyes to his fragile chest. I felt as if I would lose my own breath, my grief came so fast, so relentlessly. I clutched at Carmine, unable to accept that in these last seven months I had been unable to give him life.

He had kicked me two nights before. So resounding, so full of himself that Paolo had felt it, too, lying next to me. Paolo had cradled my belly in his hands, then, pressing his ear to it, listened for his child. I had always felt cherished by Paolo, but this pregnancy had turned me into an object of such adoration and desire it had been almost impossible to fathom the depth of his feeling for me. Whenever my mother was pregnant, I remember my father's eye wandering farther and farther away the bigger her belly grew. But Paolo had been drawn closer and closer with each passing month. He found me so beautiful.

Paolo...Paolo. Where was he? Had someone told him? Or had they all been so preoccupied here with me, with death?

Flora came and gently took the baby away from my grasp.

"I'm going to dress him now, Giulia, before he—" She stopped, not wanting to say what would happen, what would take him farther away from the living child I thought I'd be holding now. He would grow cold. He would stiffen. He would rot.

I released him to her. The clothes I'd made for him lay wrapped in tissue paper in the top drawer of the dresser. A jacket, a gown, booties, a hat. Crocheted with a 00 hook and the finest gauge cotton. My aunts had written with suggestions for more useful things, without ornamentation, that would stand up well to repeated washings. Practical quilted kimonos and plain muslin gowns. I had made those, too, dutifully.

The stitches on the baby's jacket were tight and smooth. When I brushed it along the side of my cheek, it glided like silk. There were no mistakes, no dropped stitches or uneven edges. If I had discovered a problem as I was working, I ripped out what I'd done and redid it. It was perfect.

But it was too big. He would never grow into it.

There was a small cross and a medal to pin to his shirt, in the wooden box next to Tilly's candle. "Say a prayer when you put them on him," I told Tilly. "I can't".

Tilly did not know my emptiness. She fussed, she prayed, she changed the sheets.

Paolo wasn't there in those early morning hours to hear my screams and then the baby's silence. Flora had sent him away during the night to sleep at her apartment when she'd realized how much farther I'd had to go in my labor. He returned home around eight in the morning to a desolate quiet. Tilly had already gone; Flora had put on a pot of coffee and was sitting at the kitchen table. I could see her through the door as Paolo walked in. No words passed between them. A question in Paolo's eyes was answered by the mute shaking of Flora's head. Then a sound emerged from Paolo's throat, a sound of such despair and abandonment that I wanted only to rise from my own pain to comfort him.

"Giulia! Giulia! How could God have taken her from me!"

He'd mistakenly thought from Flora's gesture that he had lost *me*.

Flora quickly got up from the table and put her arm around her brother, directing him toward the bedroom. "No! No! Giulia's here, Paolo. Weak, but alive. It's your son we've lost."

Paolo stumbled into the bedroom and knelt at the side of the bed, resting his head on my empty belly. He put his arms around me and I found the strength to return his embrace, feeling his relief and gratitude that I had survived. For all the comfort and solicitous care I'd received from Flora and Tilly in the last few hours, they hadn't shared my grief the way Paolo now did. We mourned our dead son together, holding one another until our tears subsided.

CHAPTER 34

Milk

Carmella Colavita across the alley had no milk. Flora told me this the morning after Carmine's birth and death, when she came over to help me do the wash. She was elbow-deep in soapy water scrubbing the bloody sheets Tilly had set to soak in bleach the day before.

I waited. Was this neighborly concern or an attempt to demonstrate to me that others, within sight of my own windows, had their problems, too? But Flora did not seem to be concerned about my sinking into misery. She looked at me directly, matter-of-factly.

"So will you help?"

I looked down at my breasts, heavy and aching. I had put hot compresses on them the night before to ease the tenderness. How many days before the milk dried up, unused, unneeded, and my body forgot the last seven months?

I remembered the women in Venticano who appeared like angels at the bedside of a mother who had died giving birth, offering nourishment to a wailing, hungry child. Or who came to the aid of women like my mother, bedridden for months carrying twins, unable to feed both adequately. Who were these women, with their generous breasts, their open arms? My brother Frankie, the twin who survived, could always find refuge in the skirts of Lucia Russo. As a boy of five he'd been chased by some bullies and our older brothers had been nowhere to be found. He'd raced frantically to Lucia's cottage and she'd protected him, chasing the other boys away with her cast-iron pan as she'd cursed them for daring to threaten Frankie.

As a little girl, I hadn't given a second thought to the women like Lucia. She used to come with Frankie and sit by Giuseppina's fire in the winter. She'd felt more welcome there than in my mother's house.

Giuseppina had her remedies, her teas and herbs, for the women whose milk was scarce or thin, but in the end, Lucia was her ally, her final choice, in the battle to keep her grandson alive and growing.

I had no need of Giuseppina's medicines. My blouse was already wet, two round circles of dampness spreading across the front. I folded my arms across my chest to stem the surge of milk. What a waste, I thought.

"Of course I'll help," I told Flora, who nodded.

"She'll be so relieved. She's been frantic with worry. 'It's not like the village at home,' she told me, 'where someone would be on your doorstep in an instant to feed an undernourished baby.' The poor girl has no one here. She came as a bride with her husband. All her own family is still back home."

Carmella brought me the baby that afternoon. Flora had

already hung the sheets on the line out the kitchen window. The day was windless but brilliantly sunny and the sheets fell straight and still as if this were August in my mother's court-yard on Pasqualina's wash day. The sheets betrayed no sign of the struggle. They were restored to their original whiteness.

Flora left a soup for Paolo's dinner before going home to cook for her own family.

Carmella's little girl appeared sickly. She was very fretful, did not know what to do with a nipple. Moved her little face from side to side, screaming.

Carmella could not keep her hands still as she watched her daughter against my unfamiliar body. Her hands were rough, worn, not at all the hands of a woman younger than I was. She grasped the cloth of her skirt and bunched it in her fist, then released it, repeating the gesture as she muttered some words— prayers, a lullaby? I tried to coax the baby to turn toward my breast but she did not stop screaming. She was so hungry.

When she opened her tiny mouth to scream, I slid in my finger. She stopped abruptly and sucked my finger. With my finger still in her mouth I eased her to my breast. She contin-ued to suck. Her mother took a deep breath. My milk surged into my breasts, so painfully that I gasped. The baby's blue-veined eyelids fluttered and then closed. Her agitated, frantic body slowed its kicking and grasping. Little noises of content-ment filtered up. I watched her face; I watched her mother's face. The baby finally fell asleep at my breast, and the tiny fists that had been pummeling the air were splayed across my lap.

I sat staring at her for several more minutes while her mother's tears fell quietly. I did not want to let go of her. I wanted to feel that weight leaning into me, to hear and measure that breathing, to smell that mixture of soap and milk.

But then I handed her back to her mother.

"*Grazie*, Signora Giulia," she whispered.

"Bring her back later when she wakes up."

When she left, I placed my hands on my breasts. They felt lighter. A gift, I thought. For me, for this baby, for this mother.

I turned and lit the stove under the soup and began to set the table for Paolo. I knew that he expected me to be still resting, not up and about, and I wanted to surprise him.

I no longer felt tired.

CHAPTER 35

Bread and Roses

After Carmine died, I got pregnant again, and again carried the baby for seven months. It was such a tiny thing, tinier than Carmine. A little girl. Emilia, I named her. I can say her name now, in a soft voice, but the memories of those dead babies haunt me still. My mother was right. There is no other pain, not even the pain of bearing those children, of giving birth to them, that is greater than the pain of losing them. Take my arm, my eye, cut me up piece by piece. That is what it's like to have a child snatched from life.

The winter after I lost Emilia was bitterly cold. It drove us all inside, including the customers of the Palace. The bar was full every evening and I kept warm over the stove in the kitchen, burying my grief by filling large pots with meatballs and sausage.

Paolo's grief was as raw as mine, but his pain was compounded by guilt and fear. Guilt that it was his passion, his desire for me that had caused us these losses; and fear that the next time he would lose me as well as his child. A man does not know how to behave at these times. When he should have been able to walk down the street with his son riding on his shoulders and screaming with delight, "*Babbo, Babbo,* look at the sky," he had only an empty cradle and an empty wife.

It is no wonder to me that he turned outside, taking refuge in his work with the union in the same way I had hidden in the Palace's kitchen. I didn't have the will to hold him back or even question him, as his days and then his nights became consumed.

One night in January when he'd returned from New York City, I came up the stairs from the Palace to give him his dinner. I found him packing, throwing shirts, socks, his notebook and pen into an open bag on our bed.

I watched, my already pale face and slumping body losing whatever was left that had held me together over the last few months. I felt myself sink to my knees and leaned against the door frame for support.

"What's this all about, Paolo? Where are you going?"

"Lawrence, in Massachusetts. Twenty thousand workers have walked out of the woolen mills. Many of them are women and children, mostly Italians. In the last two days they've stopped production in thirty-four mills. New York got a telegram this morning. This isn't something that the cops or the state militia are going to quash in a couple of days. The workers need help, a strike committee, organized relief. Joe Ettor and Arturo Giovanitti are going, and I'm going with them. I know the leaders—I worked with them when I was up there last year. They need me."

He was almost feverish as he moved around the room grabbing clothes from a drawer, sweeping his books from the night table into a pile that he thrust into the bag. He was no longer the shell of a man who'd only been going through the motions of life in the last two months. He had reignited the fire within himself and it was smoldering in our bedroom. His face was flushed and his eyes glistened as he ticked off a mental list of what to take.

"When are you leaving?"

"Tonight. I'm meeting Joe and Arturo at the train station."

He was a man of action that night, a man with a destination and a purpose. He was also a man who did not see me trying to cling to something solid and permanent as I was about to lose him to history yet again. I remembered Schenectady, and how little power I had to hold him back.

"Why now? Why the urgency? Why do they need you if the others are going?"

"Because this is momentous. Twenty thousand people, Giulia. It's what we've been waiting for. They believe in us, they hear what we've been trying to tell them for years—that their power is in their collective voice."

I pulled myself to my feet. My face felt as flushed as Paolo's. I was jealous. Jealous of the passion he was feeling, not for me, but for a cause, for twenty thousand human beings struggling to put a loaf of bread on the table and clothes on the backs of their families. And I admired him, too, for the role he was about to play.

But watching him prepare to leave was killing me. My hands were shaking and I could feel the tears stinging my eyes. Other women, my sisters and mother included, had to endure the callousness and betrayal of husbands whose eyes and hands wandered, who thought nothing of keeping a mistress on the side. I knew I was the only woman Paolo loved. I had no doubts about his faithfulness. Even when he was gone to the city overnight. Even though I knew there were women involved in the union movement—American women who saw marriage as a convention of constraint. Even when Pip or Zi'Yolanda would insert the knife of their own discontent tipped with the poison of rumor and conjecture.

Pip, especially, who lived in New York and who believed herself to be the authority on everything that happened there.

"How can you continue to tolerate his involvement? It's bad enough that the Wobblies are preaching anarchy and would kill us all if they could. But *that woman,* Elizabeth Gurley Flynn, that intellectual up on the platform with them—how many of the men do you suppose *she's* slept with? How do you know she hasn't invited Paolo into her bed when he's working late on one of those speeches that get him into trouble with the police? I warned you, Giulia, when you were first seeing him, what a mistake it would be."

Pip's words were seeds she tried to plant, hoping they'd force their way into my heart the way weeds here break through the cracks in the sidewalk. But I had no cracks. My love for Paolo, my faith in him, was as strong as on our wedding day. I didn't believe her. I didn't believe the muck and the dirt she tried to drag into my home.

But I knew that although I was the only woman in Paolo's heart, I had to share space in there with his work. It wasn't some American girl who was my rival, but an ideal. How do you overcome that? How could my kisses, my warm and pliant body, the safety and repose he found in my arms, measure up to the excitement and sense of being on a fast-moving train hurtling toward his goal?

Standing there, holding back my tears, I saw that I could not be a substitute for that. I went to the laundry basket where I'd stacked the ironing I'd done the night before. I plucked three neatly folded handkerchiefs from the pile.

"Here, you'll need these."

He took them from me, placed them on top of his other things and closed the bag. He looked at me, at the weariness staring out at him from my dark-circled eyes, but he also saw my acceptance and resignation. He realized that I would not try to hold him back, and I imagine he was grateful for that. He took me in his arms and held me, wordless.

"I'll write. I don't know how long it will take."

I broke the embrace first. I did not want to remember him pulling away from me.

"Stay safe," I said as he turned and walked down the stairs. *Come back,* I thought, *because I'm pregnant again and I don't want to raise this child alone.*

CHAPTER 36

Letters from Lawrence
January 18, 1912

My dearest Giulia,
I am writing this on Thursday night from the rooming house
where our group from New York has found lodging. In only a
week, Joe Ettor has organized a strike committee and our leaflets
have blanketed the town. On Monday morning, afraid of the
message that is reaching the workers, the mayor ordered in the
local militia. They are patrolling the streets—college boys from
Harvard who have no idea what it means to lose the money in
your paycheck that paid for three loaves of bread each week. That
is what drove the workers from their looms—a reduction of two
hours' pay because of new, faster machines.

Already, the spirit in the streets is alive, crackling. Thousands

of workers are marching and picketing, a surge of humanity that is like one organism. Even when repulsed, like storm waves hitting the beach, they surge again. This afternoon, at a demonstration in front of the A&P Mills, the company goons drenched us with fire hoses. The temperature was so cold that the water turned quickly to ice on the streets, freezing into icicles on the men's beards and the women's eyebrows. But instead of being pushed back and dispersed, the crowd retaliated. The younger ones picked up chunks of dirty, ice-hardened snow along the road and flung it back at the goons. The police, who'd been on the periphery of the crowd, waiting for them to give up in fear, saw that something different was happening. Something defiant, something unified. They moved in and began arresting people, throwing them into wagons. Don't worry. I managed to elude them. They only got a few people— thirty at most—and there are twenty thousand of us still in the streets. They cannot arrest us all. They cannot ignore us.
Per la vita,
Paolo

January 29, 1912

My darling Giulia,
Another cold and dark night in Lawrence. This afternoon, Joe Ettor spoke to a mass meeting on the Lawrence Common. He is a voice of calm and reason. He has managed to bring together so many nationalities—Italians, Poles, Germans, French, Syrians—with the power of his ideas. No one else could do it— no other union even wanted these poor, unskilled, uneducated ragged folk. I heard him up there on the platform we had built out of scrap wood, a man inspired by the faces in front of him, raw from the cold and the days of picketing, but warmed by the fire of his words. I stood behind him, scribbling down phrases as he spoke them, my fingers clutching my pen as I tried to

capture what he was saying. Then he jumped down into the crowd and led them on a march downtown.

While Ettor has been leading the strike, Arturo Giovanitti put together the relief committees. Soup kitchens, food distribution, doctors—the striking families are being cared for so that no one feels compelled to go back to work out of desperation.

I cannot express to you how proud I am to be a part of this, to see my people stand up against the tyranny of the mill owners and the complicity and enmity of the government. The governor ordered in the state militia and the state police. They are afraid—of women and children with no weapons except their own sense of justice.

I want you to know how much I miss your loving arms around me. I have only these words that I write to you to warm my soul.
Per sempre,
Paolo

February 1, 1912

Dearest Giulia,
As you have no doubt read, Ettor and Giovanitti have been arrested, falsely accused of a murder that occurred miles away from where they were. The government believes it can disrupt the strike by imprisoning them. Already, martial law has been imposed. Public meetings have been declared illegal, and even more militiamen are patrolling the streets. Everywhere you turn stands a soldier with a gun.

But we are not alone. At the behest of the strike committee, I telegrammed the IWW in New York. More organizers are on their way to Lawrence, including my compadre, Claudio Tresca, from Naples.
All is not lost.
Paolo

February 5, 1912

Dearest Giulia,
It was thrilling. I can still hear the strains of the "Internation-ale" sung in nine languages by twenty-five thousand workers. Bill Haywood, one of the leaders of the IWW, arrived on the train this afternoon and fifteen thousand of us met him and carried him to the Common to speak to the others gathered there. Haywood is full of tactics for passive resistance. We picket the mills constantly, our white armbands proclaiming our unity.

My beloved, I know I have asked so much of you already by leaving you alone while I fight this battle. But I have one more request.

Because the strike shows no sign of waning, we think it best to find a safe place for the children, away from the danger here. The Italian Socialist Federation is organizing safe homes for them. I beg you, take one or two of these children into our home. I know you will care for them as the loving mother you will one day become to our own children. Let these children experience your warmth while I am away from you.
Yours forever,
Paolo

CHAPTER 37

The Children's Exodus

Because he asked me, I said yes. My family, of course, was outraged. Claudio was already irritated that Paolo had gone to Lawrence. He was less concerned about Paolo's leaving me alone than the fact that he had no one he trusted managing the Palace. It meant that Claudio's activities were constrained; that he had to spend more time at the Palace. Claudio didn't like the monotony and restrictions of shopkeeping, of maintaining the day-to-day life of a business. Instead, he preferred to be out in the world, sniffing out the next deal. His presence every night was a burden for me, as well. It provided too many opportunities for him to watch me and criticize me. When he heard about the children from my sisters, he came storming into the Palace's kitchen.

"What's this I hear from Tilly—that you're going to take in some brats from Lawrence? You don't have time to help Angelina with our kids anymore, but you can be a foster mother to strangers?"

Pip's concern, on the other hand, was not my unavailability to be a nanny to Claudio's brood, but the hygiene of the children. "Do you have any idea how filthy they are? They live like animals in the tenements. They'll be full of lice and disease. How can you bring them into your home? And how do you know they won't rob you of what little you have?"

But I would not be swayed. Paolo had begged me to do this, and besides, my heart went out to the mothers trying to care for their children in the midst of all the unrest. In my eyes, these women, as poor and illiterate as they were, were trying to do right by their families. The least I could do was ease their burden somewhat by putting a roof over their children's heads.

I got Claudio to drive me into Manhattan the day the children were to arrive by train. Always looking for ways to appear as prosperous as the American bankers who disdained his success, he had bought one of Henry Ford's Model T town cars the year before and was happy to show it off in Manhattan.

I had packed a basket with some bread filled with peppers and eggs, and I'd collected some warm clothing—coats and mittens and socks—that Flora's children had outgrown. I was unprepared for the spectacle that greeted us. Thousands of socialists from the Italian Federation had gathered to welcome the children. Bands played, banners were flying. I worried about finding the children in the confusion. But somehow, despite the presence of so many supporters, I found them, thanks to the good planning of the women who'd conceived of and organized the children's exodus.

As we drove back to Mount Vernon, they sat in the back seat of the car, wrapped in the too-big coats and devouring my sandwiches. A brother and sister, Tino and Evelina, their pale but clean faces took everything in—Claudio's car, the city outside the windows, the strange lady in the front seat speaking their language.

When we got to Mount Vernon, Claudio left us at the Palace. I led them upstairs to the apartment, where I'd made beds for them in the front room. They had nothing with them, not even a paper bag with a nightshirt or a hairbrush.

The first thing I did was draw them a hot bath in the tub in the kitchen. Their bodies were so scrawny, so undernourished. I put them in two of Paolo's old nightshirts, gave them each a hot bowl of minestrone and put them to bed. The younger one, Evelina, was only five. She sucked her thumb and barely spoke, but she was trembling and close to tears. I took her in my lap in the rocking chair Paolo had bought me to rock our own children in and that I hadn't been able to bring myself to use. I sang her every children's song I could think of. She finally fell asleep, her head heavy and damp against my breast. The baby inside me had not yet begun to flutter and kick. Instead, I held this silent little girl and dreamed that one day I'd hold my own daughter like this.

Tino and Evelina stayed for a month, until the strike was settled. It was sending the children away that had turned the tide. There was so much public sympathy for them that the mayor of Lawrence ordered a halt to the trips. The next time a group attempted to leave, the police attacked the mothers and children, beating them back from the train station. It was a horrific scene, captured by newspapers all over America.

After that, the workers of Lawrence were not alone. Protests and outrage spread around the country, and the mill owners had no alternative but to settle.

The children of Lawrence went home as Paolo returned. They were well fed. I had stitched each of them some warm clothing. I'd learned how to keep a child still long enough to braid her hair and had taught them both the letters of the alphabet and how to write their names.

By the time Paolo walked in the door again, my belly was rounded with our own child.

CHAPTER 38

Waiting

There was no hiding that I was pregnant again. But this time, no other woman carrying a child would look at me for fear that her own baby would follow mine into death. If they had to pass me on the street they'd walk to the other side. Old women offered me advice. Eat this. Don't drink that. Don't climb. Don't bend. Don't carry. Pray to Saint Anne. Pray to Saint Jude.

Paolo walked around in a haze of guilt.

"Giulia will die next time!" Pip screamed at him the night we let them all know another was on the way.

He was afraid to touch me, convinced that his passion for me, undiminished after more than three years of marriage, was to blame for the babies' not surviving. We slept separately—I alone in our bed, crying myself softly to sleep, Paolo on the sofa in the front room, tossing fitfully. It was a lonely time. Most nights, he stayed downstairs at the Palace till early in the morning, playing cards with my cousin or writing music to keep from facing sleep alone. I had no such refuge. I fell into bed exhausted from the routines of the day, from the growing heaviness of my body, from the fears of what still lay before me. I listened for the sound of life within me. I measured the vigor of a kick.

Worry filled my nights. The racket of clattering wagons from the street outside, the tinkling of glass and murmured voices downstairs, the shouting from the Colavitas' apartment across the alley—all kept me awake and thinking. This wasn't good for the baby, I thought, lying on my pillow, tears trickling in rivulets down my neck.

During the day, the other women tried to make little of my experience.

"You're not the first to lose a baby, Giulia. Look at Maria Fanelli, at Rosa Spina. Every time they're pregnant they miscarry. Face it. It happens. What are you going to do, stop making love to Paolo? It's life."

"You can't dwell on these things, it'll make you crazy, like Jenny DeVito, remember her? That girl never carried a baby past three months. Started talking to herself, cut off all her hair. They say her husband got some *putana* in Napoli pregnant because he wanted a son and was convinced Jenny would never give him one. At least you're holding on to them, Giulia. They grow with all their parts. You'll get there. And if you don't, you don't. It's what God gives you."

I tried to keep in my head what it had been like in Venticano with Giuseppina. I knew that not all the babies she birthed actually lived. I knew this was a part of a woman's life. But the fear that I'd *never* be able to bear a living child consumed me. I listened to the way other women talked about childless neighbors. How pitiful! God spare me from the fate of my own sister Letitia—eight years married and never even pregnant, praying novenas and making pilgrimages to bless her with a child.

Sometimes I thought that if Giuseppina had been here she'd know what to do. She knew how to help my mother. My mother bore nine children, all living, breathing, whole. Frankie's twin was three months old when he died, so it wasn't like dying at birth. What had Giuseppina done? What secrets? What herbs? I didn't remember anymore. The older women here, women like my Zi'Yolanda, I did not trust. They didn't have the secrets, the *knowing* that Giuseppina did. They offered a mishmash of household remedies. The nurses from the Social Service came and tried to teach them about germs and hygiene and they half listened. Partly they didn't understand, especially when the nurses shouted at them in baby English and made pantomimes with their hands. After the nurses left, the women laughed at their naiveté, their modern ideas. But sometimes, in spite of their disdain for American ideas, those ideas crept into what they did and they started to forget the old ways. Or they never learned the old ways in the first place.

Yolanda wasn't very smart. She "dropped" her babies, she said, without a thought, without a worry. She could not understand my sleeplessness.

My mother wrote me with advice.

"Get into bed," she cautioned, when she learned of my third pregnancy. "Let the others do for you."

She seemed unaware of what my life here was like. I had no employees in the Palace kitchen to help me prepare and serve fifty meals a day. I had no widowed, childless sisters-in-law as she did, to run my household. I had no mother-in-law to whisk away responsibilities and take them under

her own roof while I languished, propped up on linen pillowcases. Flora, God bless her, did what she could to allow
me some rest from day to day. Pip, in Manhattan with her
husband, was a stranger to us. She had finally achieved her
dream of a life as a lady. When she came to visit with her
husband, Ernesto, she wore an elegant coat trimmed with
fur. Her fingers, which a few short years ago had struggled
with bobbins and pin and thread, were warmed in a
matching fur-lined muff. Her hat, velvet, with a sweeping
brim and a feather that arched down across her brow and
grazed her left ear, reminded me of the hat my mother used
to wear. Pip had a dressmaker to whom she gave meticulous
instructions. Like Letitia, she was childless. But she made no
pilgrimages. She and Ernesto traveled to Atlantic City. They
went to the opera.

Tilly lived only one street over, but she already had two
daughters—Annunziata and Dora—and was pregnant as well
when my time came.

As distant as I'd been from my mother, I wanted to write
to her, "Mama, come now to me, as Giuseppina came to you
when you were in need."

But I didn't. She still had Papa and my three brothers at home.
I don't think she was prepared to come to America, to leave her
life of ease and comfort, her annual sojourns to the sulfur baths
at Ischia, her shopping expeditions to Napoli, her correspon-
dence with great minds at the university. What kind of life
would she have found here? When she encouraged me to have
others do for me, no, I don't think she had herself in mind.

I had made no preparations for this baby. Antonietta said the
American girls had a party when someone was pregnant,
bringing gifts for the baby before it was born. I shivered when
she told me. Such bad luck! I had no cradle, no shirts, no gowns.
Nothing to pack away again or stare at lying flat and empty in

a corner. I tempted the fates with the white jacket I'd crocheted for Carmine and I got to use it as a shroud. Emilia I buried in a dress Tilly gave me from one of her little girls.

I didn't have time to sew anyway.

In the mornings, I did the marketing and then went downstairs to the Palace kitchen and prepared whatever meal we served customers that day—lasagna, chicken *salmi,* sausage and peppers. I often sat outside the back door to peel the vegetables. The cats came around for scraps and sometimes the girls who worked for Signora Bifaro at the hotel behind us were out on the steps. They smoked; they played cards; they were out there in their lingerie as if they didn't care who saw them. They didn't look after themselves very well, those girls. Their peignoirs were dirty, the hems trailing in the dirt on the steps. Their feet and their necks weren't clean, and they wore makeup to hide their sallow skin— bright patches of rouge on their cheeks and smeared kohl around their eyes.

Paolo and Claudio pretended I didn't see the men who, after a round of drinks at the Palace, slipped out the back door, past the crate where I sat with my garlic and onions, and climbed the stairs with one of the girls. The girls leaned against the railing and looked the men up and down. But they didn't look them in the eye. And when they were chosen, they tossed their cigarettes over the railing. The cigarettes usually landed at my feet, still smoldering, stinking, a slash of dark red lipstick at one end.

Sometimes, when it was slow and the girls were bored with their card games, they joked with me.

"Hey, Giulia, you're so pretty. You should be up here with us instead of down there chopping onions and peppers."

"Giulia doesn't need to be up here. She's got that handsome husband to take care of her. And from the looks of her belly, Paolo takes very good care of her. Isn't that so, Giulia?"

The girls laughed when I blushed.

One day Claudio came into the kitchen while I was frying some meatballs. I was busy over the stove, but he wanted to talk.

"I don't like you sitting out back. It looks bad."

"What, you think somebody's going to mistake me for one of Bifaro's girls?" I turned so that my belly was unmistakable.

"You know what I mean." Claudio thought I should've learned that time he threw the iron at me not to talk fresh to him. But I didn't let Claudio tell me what to do. He was not my father.

"You mean, when I sit there it makes the men uncomfortable. I know who they are. I know their wives. And if they feel too uncomfortable, maybe they're not going to go through the door and up the stairs. Maybe they're not going to spend their money with Bifaro. And if they don't spend their money with Bifaro, then you don't get your cut."

I turned over the meatballs. What did he think, I was some little girl who didn't know what those women did? Did he really believe that I didn't see a connection between him and Bifaro's convenient location?

"You insult me, and you insult Signora Bifaro with your suspicions. Do your cooking in the kitchen, Giulia. You look like some goddamn *cafona* out back with your knife, feeding the cats. Act respectable. Don't give people a reason to talk."

"The only ones who talk, Claudio, are the whores."

My daughter Caterina was born in early November. The late-afternoon light was reaching over the rooftops and through the lace curtains in the bedroom, stretching across the floor and onto the bed. I heard the tiny wail, the first gasp of air and life. Flora lifted her into my arms and I felt the slippery warmth, the fluttering movements that signaled she was alive.

Paolo had retreated downstairs to the Palace, pacing, waiting, not even playing the piano for fear it would disturb me. But when he heard Caterina cry he came bounding up the stairs, a man bursting with hope and pride.

CHAPTER 39

Z'Amalia's Inheritance

A few weeks before Caterina's birth, Papa decided to visit New York. He took the mountain road from Venticano, just as he had the predawn morning he drove Pip and Tilly and me to our destinies. Just as he had, since then, carried more and more of our countrymen away from the village and toward America.

At Avellino, he joined the regional road that leads through the valley to Napoli. At the outskirts of the city, he wove his way through streets, past market stalls and pink-walled tenements, until he reached the wide expanse of the Via Caracciolo. When he arrived at the harbor, however, he did not discharge his passengers and return to the mountains.

He boarded the ship himself.

"I'm coming for a few months," he said. "I do not intend to stay. I come only to decide if Claudio's business warrants the money Claudio, swallowing his pride, has asked me to invest."

Papa had money to invest because Z'Amalia, Giuseppina's wealthy sister, had finally succumbed to her many ailments, her loneliness and her arrogance. She had left everything—her villa on the perimeter of the Parco di Capodimonte in Napoli, her paintings, her piano, her gold accumulated over years of hoarding—to Papa.

The cousins were furious, but Papa said, "Where were you when I visited her every week? Who sat with her in her rooms smelling like death and listened to her complaints? Did any of you bring her a piece of cake or take her for a walk in the garden?" He ignored their outrage. He bought a new suit and sat in the front row at the funeral.

So Claudio, who as a little boy used to endure with Papa his visits to Z'Amalia, her desiccated fingers pinching his cheeks and offering him stale chocolates that had turned dusty white in their satin box, now thought it was time to expand his business. He wanted to build the roads, not just haul the stone for the builders.

But he needed Papa, Papa's money, to do that. I know what it took Claudio to put aside his own bitterness to ask. Greed. Ambition.

And it was my mother who had interceded. A business opportunity, she told Papa. Make the money grow, don't hide it under the bed the way your aunt did. You're no old woman. You're an astute businessman. You said yourself your bones are getting too old to travel these roads day after day. And, even if it's Aldo at the reins, he carries fewer and fewer passengers, except to take them to the ships.

So go see if this is the right business. Decide for yourself. And take the boys with you. They're old enough now, and will give me no peace if you go without them. I can manage here myself while you make up your mind about Claudio's business. Somehow, perhaps appealing to Papa's own greed, she had convinced him.

They were more alike than they cared to admit, Papa and Claudio. Even though they'd parted ten years before without a word between them since.

On the morning of Caterina's birth, Papa arrived in America. He brought with him Z'Amalia's money, my brothers Aldo and Frankie and Sandro—no longer willing to be left behind—and a gift from Giuseppina for the baby she was sure would be born alive.

Their arrival stunned me, emphasizing the passage of time since my own departure. The boys were all tall and strong, their faces the faces of men. Aldo, almost twenty-four, had cultivated his imitation of Papa so well that, from a distance and in dim light, one could be excused for mistaking the two. He had even put on weight and affected the three-piece suits that Papa's tailor in Napoli must have fashioned for him. Our altar boy, Frankie, not even shaving when I'd left, now turned his sixteen-year-old face to me with a finely trimmed mustache. Not the voluminous, waxed statements of Papa and Aldo and all the other men of my family, but an outline, like the charcoal sketch made by a da Vinci before creating a masterpiece in full color. Sandro, at fourteen not yet taking a razor to his face, was nonetheless taller than all of them, his little-boy energy transformed into muscle and bone.

They tumbled into Claudio and Angelina's house and into our lives, breathing American air, listening to American voices, walking on American pavement as if they were once again in the hills playing the games inspired by Claudio's letters. They had rehearsed this scene before. They knew their lines.

Papa, however, was a stranger in the home of his oldest son.

Angelina did nothing to ease his discomfort, her sense of being put upon evident in the firmness with which she placed every additional plate on the table. After dinner the evening of their arrival, she herded her brood—Alberto, now eight, Armando, six, Vita, four, and Magdalena, two—up to bed...but first she opened the windows of the dining room to air out the smoke from not only her husband's noxious cigar, but now that of her father-in-law as well.

What took place that evening Claudio shared with me many years later, because I was able to listen with the ears of a businesswoman, not the ears of his youngest sister.

Claudio sent the boys down to the Palace that night and turned to an impatient father, waiting at the recently cleared table, fingers taking the measure of the damask tablecloth, comparing it to his own.

Claudio put two glasses and a bottle of grappa on the table, watching Papa's hands. They were calloused and toughened, familiar with handling leather reins, lifting heavy freight, evaluating the muscled flanks of his horses. But they were also manicured, as carefully trimmed and buffed as his mustache. Claudio believed he understood Papa.

"So show me," Papa said. "Show me this dream."

Claudio pulled open a drawer in the sideboard and withdrew a brown folder bound with string. He retrieved several pages from the folder and spread them out on the table. Those pages were his translation of what Papa had defined as a dream—a word Papa used to describe the fairy tales of fools, the deluded fiction of those not rooted in reality.

Claudio had first listed what he'd gleaned from fragments of conversations, minutes of municipal meetings, obscure references in the *Daily Argus*. Land that was to be developed. Roads that would need to be paved. Bridges that would need to be erected. Tunnels that would need to be dug. Next, he'd gathered the names and prices of the equipment required to pave and erect and dig. Then he'd calculated the number of men necessary to run the equipment, hold the shovels, heave the picks. He had factored in his relationship with Paolo, his business partner and brother-in-law. If the construction industry became unionized, he'd use that relationship to influence any deal he might be forced to make with the union. And last, he'd predicted what the city of Mount Vernon and the state of New York—what America—would pay to extend its reach, turn woods and fields into city. A great deal, he said. Far more than it would cost him to build.

"There's something missing in your costs," Papa said, looking up over his spectacles from the numbers he'd examined, "unless business is done so differently here that you don't need it."

Claudio removed another sheet from the folder.

"I didn't forget."

He pressed his lips together in a smile of victory. The price of influence was carefully noted on the last sheet, with cryptic initials and amounts, annotations as to what might be required: liquor, women, a cash donation to a campaign chest, a funeral wreath at a mother's untimely passing.

"I'll take the numbers up to bed with me to study, and then sleep on it. How much are you asking me for to underwrite this venture? What are you prepared to give me in return?"

Papa made a few notations in his notebook and took a long draft on his cigar.

Claudio, sure of Papa's interest, but knowing him well enough to understand that he had to come out feeling the victor, made an offer that he was willing to negotiate, but presented as firm. Let Papa mull and calculate and pare and refine. He, Claudio, felt his father's blood in his veins, heard the pace of his breathing in his own breath. After ten years, he had learned that he could not escape his father in himself, and so turned that to his own advantage. That Papa would win something was irrelevant to Claudio because he would win more. An empire. Carried first on his own back, but then on the backs of his sons.

He gathered the papers together and handed them to Papa. He poured them both another shot of grappa and lifted his glass.

"Salut!"

Claudio got more than he bargained for with Papa's investment. They made their deal the next morning after Papa had slept, as he'd promised. In the morning the house was a chaos of small children, hungry and noisy, the two boys being scrubbed and fed and sent off to school, the two girls observing their unfamiliar grandfather across the breakfast table with open mouths. Papa's own sons straggled into the room for coffee after a very late night, groaning with hangovers but eager to hit the sidewalks once again.

Claudio suggested to Papa a walk to the Palace. In the early morning it was deserted, as good a place to conduct business as any. Claudio paused at the front door to pull out his key, savoring the look on Papa's face as he took in the polished oak door, the glass etched with the Fiorillo and Serafini names.

Once inside, Claudio realized how smart he'd been to suggest it as a meeting place. Everything about it spoke of Claudio's success—the marble-topped bar with its brass rail, the mirrors reflecting the shelves of liquor and the light filtering across the expanse of the room, the piano, the chandelier. It *was* a palace.

He pulled out a heavy chair for Papa, offered him a drink, which Papa waved away, and sat down to deal.

Papa would give him the money he'd asked for, but wanted to be more than a silent investor. He wanted to be part of the day-to-day operation. He had intended to sell the business in

Venticano anyway. It bored him. This, on the other hand, was greater than an investment. This was new life. Take it or leave it.

Claudio looked into his father's eyes, and took.

He named his new company after the state of New York, not after the family. No need to cloud his opportunities with the taint of Italy. He wanted the business of America. He wanted to *be* America.

CHAPTER 40

Giuseppina's Goodbye

Giuseppina was dying. Word came in a letter from my mother. She wrote that Giuseppina had suddenly grown tired, forgetful, unable to care for the simplest of her needs. Pasqualina moved into her house to care for her.

Giuseppina lingered in some shrouded corner of her brain. She wandered at night calling out the names of the dead, and when she was quiet sat by the stove unraveling the edge of her shawl. Like her shawl, she was shrinking. She forgot to eat unless Pasqualina fed her *pastina* in *brodo* with a beaten egg. Her eyes were clouded with cataracts. She wet her pants.

My mother was grateful that Pasqualina could nurse Giuseppina, although it left my mother, of course, with more to do in her own house.

I tried to deny these scenes that my mother described. But in my heart, I knew that Giuseppina had begun to die the moment Claudio took his first step off the mountain. My mother herself put the first nails in Giuseppina's coffin when she took me away from her and sent me to America.

That Giuseppina had lived this long was a miracle. My mother attributed it to her stubbornness as well as to her own magic. The order had been reversed. Giuseppina should have been the one to leave first, to say goodbye to us, her blood and bone, as she departed this earth. In truth, Giuseppina stayed alive only to watch each and every one of us leave her.

CHAPTER 41

Homecoming

When Giuseppina died, only a few weeks after beginning her decline, Mama and Pasqualina tied up their hair in kerchiefs, donned their aprons and began to clean out Giuseppina's house of unidentifiable and odiferous objects.

"However did I allow you to live in such squalor?" my mother wrote.

I hadn't remembered it as squalor.

Mama and Pasqualina swept, scrubbed, burned years of accumulated debris, whitewashed walls, and opened to air and light rooms that had been shuttered and forgotten. In all her years as mistress of her own house, I don't think my mother had ever engaged in such vigorous housekeeping. But taking a broom to Giuseppina's hearth seemed to release in her a newfound energy and a desire to sweep away not only the artifacts and shards of Giuseppina's existence, but her own as well.

Why should I stay any longer in Venticano? she wrote my father. Why should you come back? Most of our children are in America. Even Letitia and Rassina have decided to leave Italy. Now that Giuseppina is gone, there is nothing to hold us and everything to release us.

Papa, reluctantly seduced by the opportunities that spilled out of every vacant lot where he could envision a building, every rutted path where he imagined a paved road, made a few loud noises, retired to Claudio's dining table to make calculations in a notebook, and finally sent Mama a telegram directing her to come to America.

Pasqualina, who had waited patiently for Papa's return, reacted with panic to the news that he would not be coming back. She adamantly refused to come to America, a place that for her embodied not dreams but nightmares. She was too old to begin again, she said. And what about Teresia? What if they arrived on American shores only to have the authorities refuse her entry because of her simplemindedness? She had heard stories. She knew these things could happen. That one's future and hope could hang on the whim of some uniformed guard with a chip on his shoulder, looking for any reason to keep someone out. No, she didn't want to risk that humiliation. To be sent back. And to what? The house sold to strangers, the land tilled by someone else? And even if they let Teresia in, how would she survive in such a hostile and unwelcoming place? No. Venticano was where she'd been born, and it was where she, like her mother, would die.

My mother, instead of arguing with her or enlisting my father's authority to order her to join the rest of the family, looked instead for a way that would allow Pasqualina and Teresia to remain in Venticano and my mother to leave.

It was another death that gave her what she needed. Silvana

Tedesco, the mother of seven children, had died of malaria the year before. Vincente Tedesco, her husband, was ready to seek a new wife for his motherless sons and daughters. He wanted no more children, so a woman of childbearing age was of less importance to him than a robust housekeeper who could tame his unruly sons and comfort his lonely daughters. Mama presented the idea to both Pasqualina and Vincente, separately of course, and won their approval. Teresia was welcome, as well, especially since she could be so helpful to Pasqualina in the household.

Mama gave Pasqualina and Vincente a wedding feast. She hired a small band to play in the courtyard and a photographer to record the couple so that those of us in America could imagine our aunt in her new life. In the photograph, Pasqualina is wearing her black silk dress, its starkness relieved by the addition of a crocheted white collar. Pasqualina's face is also relieved. The panic that she'd felt at the prospect of leaving Italy had been replaced by the promise of her familiar routines—cooking, cleaning, laundering and ministering to the needs of someone else's children.

My mother left Venticano the very next day.

When she landed in America, she stood on the deck of the *Principe di Piemonte* exactly as she'd stood on our balcony more than ten years before, when Claudio had left Venticano. A plumed and silken bird, a brilliant explosion of color amid the drabness and weariness of the other travelers. She had traveled alone.

On the day the *Principe di Piemonte* docked, we all went down to meet her. She would have expected nothing less. Angelina, Tilly and I with all the grandchildren she'd never held; Pip with her fine clothes; Claudio with his car for her trunks; Papa and the boys with arms full of flowers and Hershey's chocolates; Paolo with a book of poetry.

I had dressed Caterina in the outfit Mama had sent for her first birthday. Cream-colored linen, smocked, embroidered with tiny ducks marching around the hemline, a delicate border of feathered blue stitches on the collar and the fluttering sleeves. I was up the night before ironing it, my belly—large again, hopeful—pushing against the ironing board. I was tired, but the thought of my mother's judgment kept me awake until the dress was perfectly pressed. How I dressed my daughter, how I cared for the clothes Mama herself had provided, how I showed respect to the woman whose drive and ambition and will were the very reasons we all stood there—this was what she'd be looking for as she scanned our faces. Faces she hadn't seen in years; faces she had never seen.

There wasn't a single one of my brothers and sisters whose life had not in some way been directed from across the enormous distance between New York and Venticano by the diminutive, elegant woman approaching us now.

Her decisions, her advice and her control had been conveyed in thousands of words over the years. How does one person amass so much influence? For my mother, it was her ability to sustain her presence in our lives through her words. Like Paolo, her letters had been an extension of herself. I saw what had happened to me and Giuseppina, separated from our daily contact. When I could no longer see her penetrating eye or the jut of her chin moving me in one direction or another, when I could no longer hear her prayers or her spells, when I could no longer taste her herbs or her fruit, I lost her.

But my mother never allowed us to lose *her*.

This was no stranger on the boat, not even to the grandchildren. Each of them had something extraordinary from her. For the girls, exquisite dolls and expensive dresses; for the boys, sets of painted soldiers or toy sailboats. And the repeated message, "This is from your *Nonna*. Remember your *Nonna*."

My mother was a master of the grand gesture. Whatever she

sent, it always stood out. Made people notice. Just as people noticed her.

While the other passengers looked anxiously for a familiar face in the crowd, or in total exhaustion and bewilderment at the enormous city rising up beyond the pier, my mother's gaze took it all in like a queen surveying her kingdom. Her gloved hand, raised as if in blessing, was her only acknowledgment that she'd seen us.

If she searched the children's faces for some glimmer of Fiorillo, I didn't see it. Had I been her, I think I would've devoured those children with my eyes, surrounding them with the fierce protectiveness of a she-wolf for her blood, her line. If she looked with another kind of hunger at my father, whom she had not seen in over a year, I missed that as well.

But I did see her close her eyes and breathe deeply, as if to swallow the city, her waiting family and the air of the New World.

CHAPTER 42

Paradise

When my son was born, it was my mother who rolled up her sleeves and got me through my labor.

"I'm not Giuseppina, with her potions, and her mumbo jumbo," she said to me when I raised my eyebrows at her suggestion that she stand by me when my time came. "But I bore nine children, Giulia. Each birth different. I think I know how to do this."

So it was she who mopped my brow, who rubbed my back, who made me walk when the pains slowed, who—when I screamed that I could take no more, that this baby would be the one to kill me—insisted that I could and would get through this birth alive. And it was she who, finally, eased the head of her grandson into the light of day and then caught his tiny body in her own hands.

When she handed him up to me, I saw tears in her eyes that she quickly brushed away.

We named the baby Paolino. He was the image of his father. There were times during the day when I sat at my kitchen table, shelling peas or darning Paolo's socks, with the baby beside me in his bassinet, and I was brought to a contemplative stillness. I gazed in awe at his blue eyes absorbed by the play of light upon the wall, his mouth shaping and reshaping nonsense syllables in response to my own, his tiny fingers reaching for the light.

Caterina would climb into my lap and stroke my cheek, pushing past the bowl of peas or the pile of mending, past my own reverie, to find warmth and comfort.

In the evenings, when he returned home from the union office to eat dinner before heading downstairs to the Palace, Paolo surrounded himself with his children. Caterina would squeal with delight when he walked through the door and he always bent to scoop her up. He wrote poems for *her* now, little rhymes that he acted out for her with his fingers racing up her arm or tickling her behind the ear. Paolino heard his voice and began to coo and kick his legs. I was able to finish cooking while he filled the room with the children's laughter.

One Sunday afternoon, Paolo surprised me with an excursion up to Bronxville.

"I want to show you something, *cara mia*. A dream I have, for us, for the children."

It was enough for me to be out in the open air, away from the city. We got off the trolley and he led me a few blocks.

"Only a trolley ride from the city, Giulia, and look—look at this little paradise."

I looked. I saw a pony nibbling on a tuft of grass, its ears pricking up as I approached the fence. I saw more: an apple orchard, a stone house with green shutters, pots of begonias lining the window ledges. On the side of the house was a garden, with row upon row of beans, potatoes, onions, cabbage. In the back, a glimpse of laundry—not strung between tenement windows, but stretched out in fluttering rows like the beans.

Chickens pranced in a small fenced yard next to the pony's shed. A bell hung around the neck of a goat, white bearded, looking to share the grass with the pony.

"Some day I will buy this for you, Giulia. This is my dream—to see on your face every morning the look you have right now. To bring you this land, this happiness."

CHAPTER 43

Litany

They brought Paolo to me in the middle of the night.
Claudio and Peppino carried him up the stairs and laid
him on our bed. The blood was trickling out of his mouth and
staining the front of his white shirt.

I stifled the scream that rose up in my throat. I didn't want
to wake the babies, and I didn't want to rouse the curiosity of
the old crone across the landing, although, God knows, she'd
probably heard enough as Claudio and Peppino had struggled
up the stairwell.

It was 2:00 a.m. Claudio sent Peppino to get Dottore
Solazio, but no one knew where he was; we knew the Amer-
ican doctor wouldn't come in the middle of the night to the
Palace's neighborhood.

Claudio helped me undress him. I washed him, trying to cool down his feverish body. He mumbled and thrashed at first. At one point, wild and out of control, he knocked all his books from the bedside table. Then he quieted.

As long as I had something to keep my hands busy I could keep the fears at bay. Claudio strode back and forth in the front room, his fist aching to pound Paolo's enemy as he used to when they'd defended each other on the streets in the early days. But this time the enemy was unseen. No mean-spirited bully, but an incomprehensible demon eating away at Paolo. For the first time in my life, I saw my brother afraid, powerless.

When he saw me standing in the doorway, he stopped pacing, his face searching mine for some sign of change. I just shook my head quickly and looked down. If I let the fears burning behind his eyes leap across to meet mine, I would shatter like the wineglass my father had smashed the night Claudio had decided to come to America.

"I'll go wake Tilly to come and be with you. You shouldn't be alone. What if the babies wake up?" He, too, needed something to do.

"No! I do not want my sister in this house tonight!" I was adamant. "Go look for the doctor again, if you can't wait with me."

I spit the words out, accusing, raging. There was no one I wanted by my side. I did not know if I could bear their anguish as well as my own.

I listened with my forehead pressed against the ice-cool glass of the door to his footsteps, frenzied and urgent, racing down the stairs as he left me. Then I turned back.

I checked first on the babies. Paolo was slipping out of my arms, out of my life, and my first impulse was to gather his children to me to fill my emptiness. I ached to smell their damp curls, to feel the tenderness of their skin, to crush their mouths in a kiss.

Caterina lay on her back, arms stretched over her head, her body extended to its full length. Every time I saw her like this, I was struck by how much she'd grown, how sturdy and hardy she was. Only eighteen months since I'd pushed her out of my belly, and she was already racing ahead of me, into her own life. I brushed a wet strand of hair from her cheek and watched for a grateful moment, the rhythm of life, the ebb and flow of her dreams.

Paolino, in contrast to his older sister, lay on his belly, restless, his impending hunger about to announce itself in a crescendo that would move from a tentative, mewling murmur to an insistent wail. I scooped him up and brought him with me to the chair by Paolo's bedside. His body, beginning then at six months to fill out, molded itself to my own, yielding his hunger, his loneliness in the night, to the warmth and milk of my breasts.

He fell back to sleep, sated, the last drops of milk sliding from his parted lips down his tiny, exquisite chin. I could not bear to put him down. Instead, I sat with him nestled in the crook of my arm. My other hand I rested lightly on Paolo's chest. I felt the life seeping out of him with every shallow, uneven breath.

I bent my head to his ear and began to whisper a litany. Not the prayers the old women mumbled in the church on Friday evenings—I had no use for their incantations.

The litany I recited to him was the words he'd written to me over the years, the words that had recorded the tumult and passion and anguish and joy of our brief time together. I knew the words by heart. His dreams, his longing, his doubts that I loved him in return. They were all I could think of as I waited with him.

Thoughts of you fill me to overflowing. I swear to you that if I do not see you often enough, I feel my heart breaking. If I had to be away from you for a week, I would go crazy with sorrow.

You are my talisman of enchantment.

I want to amuse you and keep you merry. I want to make you laugh, to hear your beautiful, charming laughter, which both eases and torments me.

I cover your face with my tears, and I wipe them away with my kisses.

I don't know how long I sat there. I don't know if he heard me.

Claudio came back with the doctor at last, but there was little he could do except tell us that it was pneumonia.

At 6:30 in the morning, Paolo died.

I found the shirt later, forgotten in a heap on the floor. I tried to wash out the stains, my back bent over the washboard, my hand clutching the naphtha soap, my arm scrubbing in a rhythm that became frantic as I realized that it was too late. The blood had already dried.

CHAPTER 44

The Band of the Bersaglieri

They were beginning to assemble in front of the Palace, men and women in black waiting in the gray drizzle. My mother watched from the window upstairs, waiting for the sound of a wagon, for the sight of horses with black ribbons on their bridles. Behind her, resting on the table in my front room, was Paolo's coffin.

She put out one of the cigarettes Claudio's oldest son had bought for her and straightened her hat in the mirror I kept by the door. They were simple, those rooms of mine, but well kept. She remembered the first rooms she and Papa had lived in, over the stables, with Giuseppina and Antonio snoring close by. No matter how hard she tried, she had not been able to rid those rooms of the pungent odors of horses and old woman's medicine. My home was tinged with the scent of bleach, day-old flowers, talcum powder and the haze of the cigarettes Papa berated her for smoking. She waved her hand to dispel the evidence of the last one and turned to her girls, now gathering themselves for the descent to the procession forming in the street below.

She appraised them, her fine-looking daughters. Letitia and Philippina carried themselves with pride—long, straight backs; well-made dresses provided by their husbands' money; bodies untouched by childbearing. Tilly was softer, more sweet-faced than our older sisters, not as well dressed and beginning to thicken around her waist after three daughters. My mother made a mental note to suggest a shopping expedition to the corsetiere after the demands of that unsettling week were behind us. I was still in the back room, my face bearing the bruised signs of the last tear-soaked days. At least my hair had been brushed and neatly fastened and my dress had been pressed. Tilly had done that.

My mother plucked a piece of lint from Letitia's shoulder and adjusted the veil on her own hat one more time. She came into the bedroom to fetch me.

I sat in the chair between the bed and Paolino's empty cradle. Claudio's wife, Angelina, was watching all the children over at their house until we got back from the cemetery. My feet were tapping out a pattern on the floor—making the motions of walking, as I would have to do soon, behind the coffin of my husband—but going nowhere. In my hand I clutched Paolo's ring.

"It's time to go, Giulia. They are waiting for you." This was not the first time my mother had said such words to me, sending me off to a new life on each occasion. First as a little girl to Giuseppina's house, then to the convent and, eight years ago, here to America. Each time away, to a life she believed was better for me. What life awaited me now on the other side of this day? My mother had not known widowhood. Papa still sat at the head of our table, grumbling or roaring, but still there.

"Here, put on your veil. I'll help you pin it so it doesn't blow off. And where are your gloves? Do you have a dry handkerchief?" She rattled off her list. These were the things she knew about, could guide me in. She was about to take me, one step at a time, with dignity, through the day.

She got me up out of the chair and linked her arm through mine. She was determined to keep me moving, even though my will to put one foot in front of the other was locked inside that wooden box with the body of my husband.

Claudio came up the stairs then, a man of boundless energy despite the onerous weight that his wagon would carry today, despite the stiff collar cutting into his neck. Behind him, moving more slowly and talking among themselves, followed Paolo's two brothers, who had traveled from Pennsylvania, and my brothers-in-law.

Not one of my sisters' husbands had been friends with Paolo. Rassina, the jeweler; Gaetano, the carpenter; Ernesto, the businessman. My mother looked at them. Not men she would have chosen for herself—but then, she hadn't chosen Papa, either. Gaetano was sleepy. Rassina had no heart. Ernesto was simply ugly. Paolo, however, she knew she would miss. An intelligent man, a man with compassion for a woman who would rather read books than pound dough.

"Mama, Aldo should be turning the corner at North Street with the wagon at any minute. It's time to go down."

The men moved past us to the front room and gathered around the table where the coffin had rested for two days. At Claudio's count they hoisted the box onto their shoulders and edged through the passageway into the kitchen, where my mother waited with my sisters and me.

They stopped for a moment to ready themselves for the

long flight down to the street. My mother kept her grip on me in my silence as the muffled whimpering of my sisters began: the drone of Letitia's whispered prayers, the plaintive questioning of Tilly's little-girl voice. As the coffin crossed the threshold onto the landing, an anguished wail rose above the voices and the tears.

"Oh, my God! Paolo! You're leaving this house for the last time! The last time!"

Pip's screams released the cries of the others, shrieks that followed the men down the stairs. All except me, whose stricken face remained frozen, untouched by the abandoned wailing of my sisters.

My mother was exasperated by the unconfined emotion working its way like an infection, or an insidious malaria, through my sisters. Her heart was aching, too, but Paolo was not her husband, not her lover, not her son. To tear her hair out with grief in public was a display she would not allow herself. My sisters did not have the same self-control.

"Subdue yourselves." She spit out the words in a fury. "It's time to follow the men with some semblance of dignity. You are Fiorillos, every single one of you, no matter what your last names are now."

She moved out first, supporting me as I stumbled and faltered, unable to take even a step without assistance. My condition forced her to turn her attention—reluctantly—from the excesses of her other daughters. They continued their keening as they descended behind us to the street.

The wagon was nowhere in sight, Aldo delayed somehow in the few blocks between Claudio's stable and the Palace. Everyone waited restlessly, the men still shouldering the coffin.

My mother wanted to light another cigarette, but she didn't smoke on the street. She held firmly to my arm. The drizzle had let up, leaving a dampness that curled the edges of my hair, a heaviness that muted the shuffle of impatient feet. My sisters, thank God, quieted themselves, resuming their muttered prayers. I stared numbly at the cobbled pattern of the road.

Directly in front of us—waiting as we all were—stood the Band of the Bersaglieri. At ease in military fashion—feet slightly apart, arms clasped behind their backs, eyes straight ahead—they looked off at some distant point, not at us. Their horns floated in silence, suspended across their chests from a tricolor braided cord slung over their left shoulders. For all their military exactness and their remote bearing, the Bersaglieri were flamboyantly plumed birds.

This was no ragtag jumble of musicians Claudio had collected from some dance hall, with fraying jackets and wrinkled shirts, faces still bearing the traces of too much whiskey. The Bersaglieri were a *fanfara*, the brass band attached to one of the most elite infantry units in Italy. They were touring the east coast and my mother had managed to engage them for the funeral. They wore well-cut black wool suits trimmed with polished brass buttons and red epaulets that seemed about to take wing, starched white shirts and broadly knotted red ties. This costume alone was enough to turn heads during a procession. But atop their heads, tilted sharply over their right eyes, were wide-brimmed black hats. Exploding from the front of the crown was a red feathered plume of such exuberance that it defied the grayness, the enclosed and suffocating air of grief.

There were those in the neighborhood who found this display ostentatious. There were people like them in Venticano as well, people who have nothing better to do than to pick away at their scabs of discontent and jealousy.

Paolo and I had next to nothing, so Papa and my mother paid for this. I don't know what I would have done if they hadn't—I had barely enough to pay the priest for a Mass or the gravediggers who made room for Paolo next to our babies' graves in the Holy Sepulchre Cemetery in New Rochelle.

I had hardly left Paolo's side in the three days since his death. After sitting with him during the night in death watch, I had washed his body and dressed him for burial. During the wake, I had been willing to leave his coffin only to feed Paolino. No one could dissuade me. "Have something to eat, Giulia. Keep your strength up." "Rest, Giulia, put your head down for a few minutes." I had ignored them all, all of their ministrations, their offers of assistance. No one could take my place. So my mother took over what I had no heart for. She put everyone to work to prepare for this day. Hired the band, arranged with the priest and the cemetery, organized the women for the food afterward, explained to Claudio how to set up the bier, ordered the lilies from Barletta's. She knew it was easier when it wasn't your own. Your son-in-law instead of your son.

Her final responsibility came that morning as she stood with me on the stoop of the Palace, keeping me upright, feeling the tremor of fear ripple through me as Claudio's wagon rounded the corner at North Street, clattering over the cobbled pavement.

Ever since my wedding day, I had been petrified of horses. As a child, you couldn't tear me away from them. I was always out in the courtyard with my brothers, brushing away the layers of dust the horses had accumulated in their long hauls over the hills, feeding them broken bits of carrots I had snitched from Pasqualina's kitchen garden. Now, I crossed to the other side of the street or backed up against the wall of the nearest building when I saw a horse. This time, as Aldo maneuvered Carl's best team behind the Bersaglieri, I stiffened and pressed my back against the Palace door, covering the Fiorillo and Serafini, Proprietors etched in the middle of the frosted glass.

The wagon stood directly in front of us, draped in black, covered with pots of lilies. The men hoisted the coffin onto the platform. My mother was proud of her choice—a burnished wood, not cheap-looking. Papa had balked at first at the expense, but then, that was what he always felt he had to do. Complain about the extravagance, the unreasonableness of her request, and then, in a gesture of magnanimous generosity, buy not only what she'd asked for but also some additional item. This was why, after the men had positioned the box, Claudio placed a brass crucifix on top of it. Papa's contribution.

It was time for us to move into position behind the wagon. The men broke up their knots of conversation—rumors about jobs about to open up or shut down, politics, especially news from the old country, about which they all had opinions. They had less to say about what went on here because they didn't understand or care about it. They took off their hats, put out their cigars, found their wives.

Paolo's sister Flora and her husband joined us. Flora, her face covered with a heavy veil, left her husband's side and approached me as I stood, stiff-backed and frozen, on the stoop. She touched her cheek to mine and whispered in my ear. Her fingers clasped black rosary beads, the silver cross dangling. With her free hand she pried open my fingers, still cramped around Paolo's ring, and pressed the beads into my hand. I bent my head and raised the beads to my lips.

I am not a religious woman. Paolo's death hadn't suddenly converted me. I could not imagine that the next day would find me among the ranks of the women who attend Holy Mass every morning at 6:00 a.m., say the Rosary at noon, and wash and iron the altar's linen for the priest every evening, although, God knows, it's the path more than one widow has taken. But for the rest of the morning, I cradled the beads in my hand, along with the ring, at times rubbing a bead between my thumb and index finger. Not in prayer, no, but moving my hand the same way I'd been moving my foot back and forth in the bedroom.

After Flora spoke to me, she rejoined her husband among the family gathering behind the coffin. Paolo's associates from the union had arrived to march, my mother was glad to see. A sign of respect for Paolo, for the family. She nodded her head to their tipped hats, their deferential bows.

Claudio conferred with Aldo at the reins and then turned to check the presence of those in the procession. He was ready to give the signal to the bandleader. He glanced over at my mother, his eyebrows raised in a question. To anyone except my mother, it wouldn't have been a question. It would have been an order. Claudio was used to being the boss, to saying, "Now we start to march because I've decided it's time." He did not see his sister paralyzed against the glass. He saw the restless horses, the band that was to be paid, the policemen waiting along the route, hired to clear a path for the cortege.

But because she was his mother, he waited.

She tightened her grip around my shoulders.

"Let's go, *cara mia*. Let's get through this day."

She urged me down the steps and out into the street, directly behind the bier. The fragrance of the lilies crept around us in the muggy air, surrounding us with the smell I have associated with the dead since I was a little girl.

My body was not under my control. My fingers rubbed the bead, and my eyes beneath the veil stared through the coffin, not at it. As slight as I am, my mother did not think she had the strength to support me all the way to Mount Carmel. She motioned to Papa to join us on the other side of me. He took my right arm, which I gave to him without resistance, in a daze.

Claudio strode to the front, signaled to the bandleader, and the Bersaglieri shifted to attention. In unison they raised their horns to their lips and took their first steps as they blew the first note.

The horses reacted to the music piercing the stillness and

tedium of the wait. I heard Aldo speak sharply to them as the wagon lurched abruptly forward. My head jerked up and I sprang back from the wagon, from the mournful tones of the music. I wasn't completely lost. I had some sense of what was going on around me.

We fell into step behind the bier, and the others took their places behind us. My sisters embraced their wailing once again. I remained silent.

CHAPTER 45

Widow

After the funeral, Pip got ready to go back to New York. "I'll take Caterina," she informed me. "Ernesto and I have plenty of room."

"It's better for you both," chimed in Tilly, with Claudio watching tensely from the other side of the room, waiting, letting my sisters do the work of convincing me. Sharing the burden of their widowed sister and her children, that was what this carefully rehearsed scene, this artifice of concern and generosity, was all about.

Widow. I turned the word over in my mouth, parched, aching with the memory of Paolo's last kiss. I gagged on it. I wanted to spit it out, this sour, suffocating word.

There was a heaviness and an ugliness to this word that had

now attached itself to my life. I saw that ugliness reflected in the eyes of my brother and sisters—eyes that averted, eyes that resented, eyes that blamed. I was weighed down, not only by the fact that Paolo had been ripped from my very being and by fears for my fatherless babies, but also by the anger of my family.

As Tilly and Pip danced with false merriment around the welcome my Caterina would find, a room of her own on Canal Street, I gradually gleaned the true reason she had to be separated from me at all. It was Claudio.

He was forbidding me to remain with the children in the apartment above the Palace. He was forbidding me to continue to work there or to hold Paolo's share of the business.

"It's unseemly. A woman alone. People will talk, make assumptions about you." This from Pip, my most proper of sisters, who had never once set foot in the Palace. She was afraid of even the taint of impropriety. What did she think I would do, bare my breasts as I fried the eggplant? Serve up the macaroni with kisses on the side? Join Signora Bifaro's girls on the back stairs of the hotel?

"You are no longer safe here. You've lost the protection of your husband." I've lost much more than his protection, I wanted to scream at her. But what did she, married to an ignorant, desiccated old man, know of what I'd lost? Did she ever hear such poems as Paolo had whispered to me in the night, lips so close that his very breath was a caress, words so pure, so unrestrained, that their very utterance was something sacred? Did she ever feel such tenderness, such mystery, such surprise as I had felt in his embrace?

Not Pip, not any of them, understood my rage or powerlessness in the face of my empty bed, my empty heart. They only understood their own duty. It was a duty they'd carved out, apportioned among themselves, without asking me. Claudio was taking over my protection. He would house me;

he would feed me. I would return to his house, as I had eight years ago when I'd first arrived from Italy. My parents had no room in their own apartment on Eighth Avenue with the three boys still living there. Papa's investment in Claudio's new business had not yet yielded the profits that would later enable him to build a house on the park. Pip was taking Caterina because Claudio's wife said there wasn't room for "all of them." I could keep only one of my children—the baby—with me.

I was numb. I was weary. I had not slept for three days, since the night Claudio had brought Paolo upstairs, bloody and fevered, to die in my arms. I had buried him that morning. I had nothing left in me, neither the words or the strength, to say to Claudio, "No!"

Tilly helped me pack up Caterina's things—a few dresses, stockings, a pair of shoes and the doll my mother had sent just after she was born. Once elegant, the doll had dainty porcelain hands and feet and a porcelain face with painted eyes as blue as Paolo's, a pouty red mouth faded to a pale rose from Caterina's many kisses, golden hair and a chipped ear. Its dress, smocked and cross-stitched in blue, revealed the expensive hand of my mother's dressmaker. A rag doll would've been more appropriate for an infant, but what did my mother know? And Caterina loved that doll. She wouldn't be separated from it. So into the valise it went, to make the journey downtown.

Claudio drove Pip and Caterina back to New York, while Tilly stayed behind to help me pack up my own things for the move to Claudio and Angelina's house.

CHAPTER 46

Silence

After Paolo died, I stopped living as well. I spoke to no one. When my sisters tried to cajole and coax and finally scold, I didn't answer them. When Zi'Yolanda came by with pots of food or a dress for Caterina, I didn't thank her. When my mother sat with me and made a list of what I must do to help myself and my children, I didn't acknowledge her. Even when Caterina climbed into my lap whenever Pip and Ernesto brought her to visit, I could only rock with her as both arms reached tightly around me.

I didn't hear the murmurs in the kitchen, the prayers recited before votive lights, the rising tune of late-night conversations. "What are we going to do about Giulia?"

My family had always been asking that question. She runs

wild in the hills, she climbs out of windows, she daydreams, she loves the wrong man. We have to do something about her.

So once again they tried to do something, but I didn't let them. It wasn't that I stopped doing *everything*. I still got out of bed in the morning, washed myself, dressed. I knew there were women who, after their husbands died or left, turned into pigs who refused or forgot to care for themselves. Whose hair became matted and caked, whose bodies acquired layer upon layer of dirt and odor. Whose houses became infested with bugs and filth. I wasn't one of them. Every morning, I brushed my hair and secured it at the nape of my neck with two long hairpins. I kept my fingernails clean. I bathed and dressed Paolino in clothes I'd washed and ironed. I swept the floors. I aired the bed linens. I lined Paolo's books up neatly on the night table.

But I did all these things in silence. I had nothing to say to anyone. Most of the time, of course, there was no one there except the children. Claudio was at work and Angelina, leaving me to watch her brood, went off to New York to shop and eat lunch at Schrafft's. What was I to do, talk to myself? Become like Crazy Fabiola in Venticano, who wandered the streets talking to the pigeons?

My words simply disappeared. Words had been life between Paolo and me—the breath, the food that nourished us. Without Paolo, the words stopped.

CHAPTER 47

Rescue

It was my mother who rescued me. My mother—pampered, powdered, constantly in stately motion, her life swirling in constellations far removed from us, the children she'd borne and then handed over to someone else. My mother, more familiar with the drape of silk, the poetry of Boccaccio or the variations of azure in Capri's grotto than she was with the terrors that beset her own children. It was my mother who recognized the dark circles under my eyes, who watched me scrubbing the clothes not only of my own son and my nephews, but Angelina's, too, who observed Angelina returning from one of her shopping expeditions laden with boxes of finery for herself, toys for her sons, and not even a piece of candy for my children.

It was my mother who heard my silence and found a way to end it.

"It's so pathetic," she reported one afternoon when she and Tilly and her girls had stopped by. "The little girl—what's her name? Mariangela, that's it. Mariangela he has tied to a chair in the blacksmith shop while he's working so she won't toddle into danger. It's absolutely harrowing—all those tools, all that dirt. So she sits there with those enormous brown eyes, watching, nobody bothering to wipe her nose. She can't be more than eighteen months old. And the two boys, well, half the time they're running around God knows where. I heard that Barbara Nardozzi cooks for them, but I can assure you, nobody's washing them."

"They need a mother." It was Tilly, nodding solemnly in agreement with my mother, who revealed the purpose of their visit to me today. My mother's depiction of the circumstances of the widower Salvatore D'Orazio and his motherless children was intended to do more than just elicit my sympathetic nods.

My mother, continuing her orchestration of what she hoped would be a convincing portrayal of desperate need, cast an expectant look at me.

Salvatore D'Orazio played the accordion. He brought it with him when he first came to call on a Sunday afternoon. He also brought the children. Someone had given them a bath, starched the boys' shirts, put a bow in Mariangela's wispy curls.

He set the accordion down in the parlor and the boys took up positions on either side of it, like little soldiers or altar boys. Mariangela he held on his lap, smoothing her dress with his left hand, the one he used to stroke the buttons of the accordion that play the harmony.

It was March 19, the feast of Saint Joseph. I served him coffee and cream puffs that I'd made earlier that morning, before anyone else was up. It was the only time I was alone, those moments by a hot stove before dawn. The frantic scurry of early morning life when Tilly and Pip and I were working at the factory so many years ago had given way to a different tempo. We were no longer four women straining to fit our lives under the same roof. It was only Angelina and me, and God knows I didn't have to worry about sharing the kitchen or the laundry with her. The difference was the children. The clamor of hungry bellies, the tug of sticky hands. The restlessness of Paolino at night in his crib next to my bed. The books my mother lent me would have gathered dust at my bedside if I didn't have those private moments in the kitchen.

I waited in the parlor that Sunday afternoon. Waited for Salvatore to still his hand, to clear his throat, to shift the weight of his daughter from one knee to the other. I couldn't keep myself from studying his face.

I must admit that when my mother first told me about him, I'd gone out of my way one afternoon to walk past his black-smith's shop and peer in the half-open door. He didn't see me; he was crouched over the hoof of a tethered horse, intent on prying off a damaged shoe. His face had been streaked with sweat and soot, his hair falling over his forehead and periodically swept away with the back of his hand. In the dim light I couldn't discern with certainty the features of his face—I couldn't tell you if they pleased or repulsed me. But I watched him at his work, saw the strength in his arms, the solidity of his legs, and listened to him calm the horse. I moved from the doorway. Later that day, I let my mother know I would allow him to call on me.

On Sunday, not only the children had been scrubbed. The face opposite me was no longer disguised by his labor. His hair had been slicked away from his forehead, black and wet, the hands now fussing with the baby probably pressed to it a quarter of an hour before, smoothing out whatever unruliness he normally lived with. His mustache, equally black, had been neatly brushed and waxed. It drooped and curved up again. Paolo had always kept his face clean-shaven.

"Don't make comparisons," my mother had said. "You'll never be able to decide if you haul up out of your heart these images that become more beautiful, more precious, the longer you live without him in the flesh."

So I tried not to hold up Paolo's exquisite face as I watched Salvatore in his unfamiliar feast-day clothes. I tried not to hear the poetry that Paolo recited to me as I listened to Salvatore speak of his situation, his prospects, the practical and substantial life he might be willing to offer me. I tried not to remember the piano at the Palace and the strains of Paolo's songs wafting up through the floorboards to our apartment as I studied Salvatore's accordion sitting between his sons and hoped that he would never play it for me.

CHAPTER 48

Ice Flowers

The panes of the windows in Angelina's pantry were thick with frost. If Caterina had been there, she would have carved flowers and stars with her fingernail, scraping away at the papery ice until her fingertips were numb.

But she wasn't there. She was asleep under a crocheted coverlet in Pip's house, her face resting against the porcelain cheek of her doll, her hair neatly braided, her fingers, instead of creating ice fantasies, firmly planted inside her mouth.

I moved the sack of onions on the floor to get at the semolina and the cake flour. I placed eggs into a bowl. I wanted to start the pasta, set the dough to rise for the cream puffs before the boys woke up. It was five in the morning.

There was no daylight yet. I worked by the dim overhead

bulb in the kitchen, but I didn't really need to see. I piled a hill of flour onto my board and made a hollow in the top with my fist. One by one, the ten eggs slipped from their shells into the hollow. I plunged my hands into their liquid, working the flour little by little into a mass of dough, exactly as Giuseppina had taught me. I didn't think as my hands moved in a pattern that was as natural to me as planting seeds or weeding a garden. The echoes of Giuseppina's instructions had found their way into my muscles.

I shaped the dough, kneading and pushing it with the rhythm I'd learned from Giuseppina's singing. Now and then, I even found myself singing again. I took my rolling pin, a thin, tapered stick that Tilly's husband had shaped for me, and began to roll out the dough. It resisted at first, a thick slab of creamy yellow that I had to tame until it was a translucent sheet light enough to rise when I blew under it. With a sharp knife, I cut the sheet into strips and then hung the strips to dry on a wooden rack. Fettucini I would serve that afternoon, with porcini mushrooms sent from Salvatore's cousin in Connecticut.

I wiped my hands on my apron and started a pot of coffee. The rest of the house would be waking soon.

That afternoon Pip and Ernesto brought Caterina to Claudio's for dinner. She was dressed in the green merino wool coat and hat they'd bought for her. The conductor lifted her from the iron steps of the train onto the platform and ex-claimed how beautiful she was, how perfect. Pip beamed and took her hand in her own gloved one and walked with her—proud, proprietary—out of the station to Claudio, waiting in his new automobile.

CHAPTER 49

Caterina Dances

Pip and Ernesto wanted to adopt Caterina.

She danced in the parlor when they came to visit, twirling in a circle with her arms outstretched. We clapped our hands to the music on the gramophone.

I remembered Salvatore's accordion and thought, *He could play for Caterina.* She could dance in his parlor. My parlor, if I marry him.

I could give her a home again.

I could give me a home again.

I sank into the chair in the corner and watched my daughter, my sister, my mother.

My mother sat in the center of the room, cooing and praising. She touched the edge of Caterina's exquisite dress. She pressed a coin into her tiny hand and Caterina held it high as she continued to circle the room. The coin glinted in the late-afternoon light; it adorned her, like a jewel on her finger or a ribbon in her hair.

Pip did not take her eyes from Caterina. She leaned toward her as Caterina laughed and floated away. There was a hunger, a longing in Pip's body. I saw her reaching out for my daughter, stroking her hair, adjusting the bow on the sash at her waist. Caterina slithered from her grasp and danced some more.

She stopped in front of me.

"Dance with me, Mama."

She stretched out her hands.

I wanted to refuse. My body had given up that lightness and freedom since Paolo's death. I had no reason to dance, I told myself. My feet trudged to the market, bore the weight of laundry baskets and sleeping children, curled up at night in an empty bed, seeking warmth and finding none. I shook my head and held up my hands in refusal.

"Dance with me. *Per favore.* The way you used to."

Caterina grabbed my hands, holding the coin between us, and tugged at me to get out of the chair.

Pip stopped clapping. She sat back and wrapped her arms tightly in front of her.

I got to my feet and smiled at Caterina as we spun around each other.

CHAPTER 50

Gardenias

Flowers. Gardenias. White with dark, glossy leaves. Salvatore bought them for me to carry at the wedding. Pip gave me a navy-blue silk dress of hers to wear. My mother offered me her ruby earrings.

In a small cigar box on my dresser lay all the letters Paolo had written me. They were much more precious to me than the jewels Papa had showered upon my mother in appeasement, as substitutes for his attention and love.

I took the box on the morning of my wedding day and wrapped it in one of the embroidered trousseau linens I'd brought from Venticano. I buried the shrouded box out of sight in the bottom drawer with my scapulars and extra votive candles, amid the packets of dried herbs and the cotton towels for my time of the month. Salvatore didn't concern himself with these things, and he had no need to know, to see the letters, to understand why I kept them, cherished them, took them in my hand to feel the weight and smoothness of the paper and to run my fingers over Paolo's words as I'd once run my fingers over Paolo's body.

Salvatore never knew those letters existed.

CHAPTER 51

Gratitude

Marrying Salvatore brought five children to sleep under his roof—Salvatore's three, no longer motherless and neglected; Paolino, and Caterina, restored to me despite Pip's bitter disappointment; and a sixth growing inside me within a few short months.

Pip knew, in giving Caterina back to me, that she stared ahead at a childless life.

"You have so many to take care of, Giulia. Why take her back when Ernesto and I can give her so much?"

But how could I not take her back? Not only my own flesh and blood, but Paolo's? Did I want her to grow up distanced from me, as I'd grown up separated from my own mother? Not only the distance from here to Manhattan—

the train ride measured not in the clack of the rails, the minutes from Mount Vernon to Grand Central, but in the journey that separates two households as different as New York and Venticano, as far apart as my mother's parlor and Giuseppina's kitchen.

Before the wedding, I took the train down, to visit Caterina and to get the blue silk dress Pip was lending me because I refused to wear the ivory wedding gown from my first marriage. What kind of an omen was that, I thought, to put on that dress again? I wanted to cut it up, burn it, throw the ashes on Paolo's grave.

I had not been to Pip and Ernesto's house in many years. They didn't entertain the family. When they wanted to see us, they came to us with a box of Schrafft's chocolates. I had forgotten the grandeur, the opulence and the heaviness that Pip had surrounded herself with. The wood was dark, the carpets a deep purple-red, the color of Chianti. The draperies were fringed, tied back with tassels the color of dulled gold. They hid the soot that filmed the outside of the windows. They cut off the light. Even in the middle of the day, she had to light the lamps.

The furniture in Pip's parlor reminded me of my mother's rooms. No comfortable place to sit, the texture of the upholstery unyielding against one's skin.

Her coffee, served in the gold-rimmed bone china my mother had sent each of us years before, was still bitter. Her cake was store-bought.

"There's a wonderful *pasticceria* in the neighborhood," she boasted, as if this made her life better than mine. She reminded me that I was still the poor, widowed sister who did her own baking.

Caterina was dwarfed in her room. There was a pale rose-colored carpet, a white bed, a doll's house that had the instantly recognizable stamp of my mother's extravagance.

How could I take her away from this, you ask? Back to a

bed she would share with a stepsister, to a table with clamoring brothers and a father she didn't know?

How could I not?

At first, for Salvatore and me, there was only our gratitude for each other. I rescued his children, who'd been fed at one table or another since their mother's death. With the baby, who'd never known her own mother's milk, never felt the warm breath of a mother's caressing lips placed in a kiss at the nape of her neck, it was easy to scoop her up into my arms. Paolino was already moving away from my skirts, eager to follow his new brothers.

I balanced Mariangela on my hip while I stirred the gravy. I dressed her in Caterina's outgrown dresses. I blessed and pinned a medal of the Virgin Mary on her undershirt.

With the boys, it was harder. Eight and twelve years old, they eyed me suspiciously when I entered their house as their papa's bride. The little one, Patsy, had nightmares and crawled sobbing and terrorized into our bed every night. The older one, Nicky, ignored me. He shrugged off my good-night kisses, claiming he was too old for such things. It was all I could do to make a quick sign of the cross on his forehead at night before he turned away from me in his bed.

Va bene, I thought. I saw that he had enough to eat, clean clothes. I walked him down the street every morning to the corner across from No. 10 School and made sure he went in. In the afternoons, he went to the blacksmith shop and helped his father. When he came home with dirty clothes and a smudged face, I didn't yell.

Salvatore had rescued me. From a life as a burden to my family, from a place in my brother's household as little more than a maid, from my silence.

This gratitude that we felt for each other held nothing of the passion that had sustained Paolo and me. But it sustained us nevertheless. To be touched again, however awkward and unaccustomed the calloused hands, to be protected within the walls of my own home, to be thanked, with eyes that took in his well-cared-for children and my growing belly, was enough.

CHAPTER 52

The Great War

O ver the next year we began to build a life together. Salvatore created a garden out of nothing in the back of the house—a vacant lot filled with debris. I sat out there in the spring, braiding Caterina's hair, a brown glistening with the red-gold lights of her father's. The baby, Giuseppina, slept in her carriage beneath the arbor that Salvatore had built to shelter the oilcloth-covered table that sat fourteen. Grapevines planted at the same time had begun their ascent up the posts supporting the roof of the arbor. The leaves formed a delicate curtain around the baby. Next to the shed at the end of the garden, Salvatore had planted a cherry tree, its white blossoms hiding the sheet-metal wall of the garage that backed up against our property. We were content.

Our first challenge together came when the American president brought our new country into the Great War that had been raging across the ocean, and Nicky ran away.

Salvatore had taken us all up to Waterbury to visit his cousin Archimedes. Nicky and Patsy were going to spend two weeks on the farm helping Archimedes with the haying, and we decided to bring the whole family for the ride and a visit with their cousins. We borrowed Claudio's car and drove up the Post Road, the children all in the back, squabbling and restless. By the time we got to the farm, I was happy to have them run off to play in the barn, climb trees, even splash in the muddy pond. We all needed to be in the country. Salvatore and Archimedes took the boys to the river to fish, while Estella and I stayed in the house with the little ones and cooked.

Down at the river, the men talked about the War. Archimedes's younger brother Sebastiano had enlisted in a regiment from New Haven that was mostly Italian, soon to sail to the front and fight for their new country. I don't know what they said, but it was the kind of talk a fourteen-year-old boy, lying on a rock in the sun, bored with his life and feeling encroached upon by his father's growing new family, would listen to. What was it—uniforms, guns, the adventure of sailing across the ocean, of taking part in the Great War? Whatever he heard that day, Nicky took it in and absorbed it, chewing on the idea as if it were a wad of tobacco.

When they all returned from the river for dinner, I noticed how quiet he was, not taking part in the children's banter. For several months, he'd been pulling away, his boy's body shedding the chrysalis of childhood. He'd already begun to shave, and he wanted nothing to do with little-boy games with make-believe swords and guns. Real guns, that was a different matter. But he kept his own counsel at dinner that day, not sharing his fascination with the conflict.

There was no sign of anything amiss when we packed up

the car at the end of the day and prepared to say goodbye. The boys, together with Archimedes's sons, were going to sleep in the hayloft in the barn and had picked out their spots earlier. We said our goodbyes and headed back to New York.

It was sometime during the night that Nicky left the barn, seized by the pull of the War and eager to be free of his father's rule. The younger boys were asleep when he left, and when they woke up and found his corner empty, no one suspected that he'd run away. So he had several hours' head start on his journey to New Haven before Archimedes realized he was gone. He walked many of those miles in the dark and must have hitched a ride with a passing truck as dawn broke.

Archimedes had searched every inch of woods and field, every nook and cranny in the barn and sheds and house, before he sent word to Salvatore that Nicky was gone. Salvatore stopped everything, shut down the forge and took the train back to Connecticut to look for his son. He spent three days combing the countryside around the farm. Sleepless, unable to eat, he was both frantic and furious. He finally gave up and came home without his firstborn, a man upon whom tragedy had descended too many times.

A month went by. Every weekend, Salvatore traveled to Waterbury and walked the streets, questioning people. Archimedes put the word out in the Italian community, hoping someone would have seen Nicky or fed him. It was his own brother, Sebastiano, who finally gave us an answer, in a letter he sent just before his unit sailed for France.

He had come across a young enlistee in his machine gunners' squadron, a boy he thought he recognized. Although the boy had tried to conceal his identity, he eventually admitted to Sebastiano that he was Nicky. Nicky begged him to keep his secret. He had lied about his age and somehow convinced the army that he was eighteen. Thank God, Sebastiano did the right thing and got word to us before it was too late.

Salvatore went to the camp where the men had been training, Nicky's birth certificate in hand. With Sebastiano's help translating, he managed to get Nicky released from service.

I don't think Nicky ever forgave Salvatore for that, robbing him of the chance to be a soldier, a man. He came home sullen and angry. Despite the discipline of the army, the regimentation and orders, he had felt free for that one month. The prospect of going to war had been a promise of excitement, not a fear of the horror and destruction that were too far away for him to understand.

For Nicky, the war had been accounts of Eddie Rickenbacker and Francesco Baracca, the Italian ace who shot down fifty-seven German planes. It was glory and ribbons, not vermin-infested trenches and mustard gas. Sebastiano did not come back. He was killed four months later, along with sixteen other men in the New Haven battalion, on a bitterly cold December day. Nicky didn't grasp that he, too, might have died that day, or another, if Salvatore had let him stay.

Nicky dropped out of school that fall, calling it a place for infants, not men. I thought it was a mistake, but kept my mouth shut. Salvatore's family didn't believe in education the way my mother had. Salvatore's only concern was that Nicky not become a bum. He put him to work at the forge, taught him how to beat and shape metal, made him sweat and ache, and let him pound out his anger with a heavy mallet on hot iron.

CHAPTER 53

Dancing On Sunday Afternoon

Over time, Salvatore and I experienced more than gratitude. Salvatore, with his reserve, his bashful admiration, never asked me what he truly wanted to know: Do you lie in our bed at night dreaming of this hand brushing against the beauty of your body? Do you long for me in ways you find indescribable, every centimeter of your skin crying out to be touched? Salvatore did not know that he had these questions, simmering beneath our everyday discussions of money and household and children. I did not know that, eventually, my answers would be "Yes."

I'd thought we would share a table in the noisy, crowded kitchen filled with our children and never feel that we were the only two people in the world, seeing and hearing only each other. I had thought I could watch him with his work-hardened hand around the cup of black coffee I made for him every night and not imagine that same hand taking shape around my breast. Or see him bring the cup to his lips and not expect to trace with my eyes and my heart every crack in that winter-chafed mouth, envisioning that mouth on my lips.

I was mistaken.

One Sunday afternoon about three years after we were married, Salvatore took out his accordion after we'd eaten dinner and I was cleaning up the kitchen. Until then, he'd let the instrument gather dust, only bringing it down to his club occasionally or taking it along in the summer when we visited Archimedes out in the country. I'd never said anything to him about not wanting to hear him play but, without asking, he had refrained from using the instrument in the house.

But that Sunday, he went down to the cellar with an empty jug. I thought he was going to fill it with wine from one of the casks that lined the wall in the storeroom. He'd begun making wine from the grapes that grew over the arbor in the garden. But instead of coming back upstairs with a full jug, he carried the accordion, retrieved from its case under the stairs.

I think he'd intended only to clean it, because he took it into the parlor with a rag and was wiping the keys when the girls, Caterina and Mariangela and even Giuseppina, began clapping their hands and begging him to play them a song. He ran his fingers quickly over the keys in a children's tune and the girls bounced with delight.

I put down my dishrag in the kitchen and stood in the doorway of the parlor, my arms folded across my breasts, listening and watching as he played and they jumped around the room. When they saw me, they screamed, "Mama, dance!"

I looked across the room at Salvatore, who had stopped playing. He looked back, then put his head down and began to play *"Starai con me."* Not a children's song, but a love song. I stepped into the room and began to glide around my daughters. I raised my arms and coaxed the air with them, swaying my hips.

Salvatore stood and walked across the room. I sensed the strain in his body as he approached me, every muscle poised, held back from an embrace by the tautest wire of will. The air between us became heated, churning, colliding with the unspoken.

I continued to dance, not for the children, but for him.

CHAPTER 54

San Giuseppe Moscati at Night
Cara Serafini Dedrick

Giulia had spent most of that Monday before her surgery recounting to me the hidden story of her love for my grandfather. Throughout the day, despite the interruptions of nurses and preparations for her operation the next morning, she had continued her outpouring, as if this were the only opportunity she'd have to make sure someone else knew what she'd kept in her heart for so long.

I thought she'd be exhausted when evening came and her words ended, her hands making a final graceful gesture in the air, echoing the dancing that had captivated so many on those Sunday afternoons years before.

But that night she couldn't sleep. The hospital had slipped

into dim light and muted sounds—the swish of Sister Annun-ziata's rosary beads against her habit as she moved down the corridor, the click and hiss of respirators, the flicker of green lights casting water-like reflections on the linoleum floors. Above these muted sounds and through the pale, unearthly light of her IV monitor, I could hear Giulia's moaning and mut-tering and could see her arms, ghostly, flailing about the sheets.

I sat up in my cot and put my bare feet on the floor. It was cool and smooth. I went to Giulia's bedside. With her right hand she was attempting to pull the IV tube out of her arm. Her lips were parched and chapped.

I placed one hand on her arm and stilled her frantic jerking. With my other hand, I pressed the bell for the nurse and waited for her to respond.

"Are you in pain, Nana?"

She tossed her head back and forth on the pillow, not in denial, but in a repetitive, ritualistic movement. She seemed not to be aware of me. Her eyes were closed and she was reciting some kind of litany.

When Sister arrived, she assessed her condition and checked her chart.

"Unfortunately, she's had the maximum dose I can safely administer tonight. Perhaps you can sit up with her for a while to calm her and help her fall asleep. Let me know if she remains agitated. I don't want to restrain her, but if she tries to pull out her IV again, I'll need to restrict her movement."

I grabbed my sweater, put it on over my nightgown and then resumed my position at Giulia's bedside. I began to stroke her arm to quiet her and keep her from reaching for the IV. I tried to listen to the words she was uttering. At first, it sounded like gibberish, or an incantation. I bent my head close to her lips and listened. Slowly, I began to recognize syllables and familiar Italian words.

I started to repeat the sounds as I heard them, setting up an echo, a reverberation of whatever, whoever, she was calling down to help her.

"*Madre Mia,* protect me. Form a ring around me to wall out evil. Cast off my pain."

Soon, I no longer had to imitate her, but could recite the words with her in unison. It was a kind of music, rising and falling in a rhythm. *Pull me close to you. Throw off this suffering. Pull in. Cast off.*

Without intention, I lifted my hand to her forehead and with my thumb, blessed her with the sign of the cross. My fingers spread out to stroke her brow in a gentle massage. Some ancient memory informed my hand; it seemed to know what to do without my direction.

I don't know how long I sat with her, my voice joining hers and my fingertips smoothing her pale temple. But at some point I heard the quiet, steady breaths of sleep. Her arms were no longer rigid and agitated, but relaxed. Her mouth formed a smile, as if whatever images were forming in her dreams were bringing her joy.

I fell asleep myself, in the chair. I was afraid to slip back into the cot for fear that she'd wake again and I wouldn't hear her. But she slept through the rest of the night.

In the early morning, just as a thin line of pink-hued light appeared at the window, I felt her stroking my hand.

"*Figlia mia,*" she whispered and then brought my hand to her lips and kissed it. "Do you know what *serafini* means in Italian?"

"Yes, Nana. It means *seraphim,* the highest order of angels."

She leaned her head back on the pillow.

"And you are my angel."

CHAPTER 55

Life After Giulia

Giulia died a little more than a year later. Oh, her hip operation was a success, and she and I flew back to New York within two weeks of her surgery on a special Alitalia flight arranged by the American ambassador to the Vatican, a childhood friend of my cousin.

She stayed with my parents at first, unable to navigate the stairs in her own home. Giulia approached her rehabilitation with the same steely drive that had kept her alive into her nineties. Every time I went to visit her, she had painstakingly made a little more progress toward walking on her own. She was determined to get back to her home.

She and I did not mention the letters again. "They are for

you," she told me before we left Italy. "You alone. You are the only one who knows what to do with them."

By Christmas, Giulia was back in her own house, giving orders to all my aunts and my mother as they hustled around her kitchen on the morning of Christmas eve, preparing the feast of the seven fishes for that evening. I had left Andrew and my kids at my brother's house so that my sister-in-law Jeannie and I could help. But even though we were grown women, we were relegated to setting the table, Giulia pointing with her cane at the drawer where the embroidered linen tablecloths were kept or instructing us to polish the silver before we laid it on the table.

It was the last Christmas eve the whole family spent together, the last Christmas eve Giulia was alive. I remember that night more vividly than her funeral, which, despite her long life, stunned us into an empty, hollow silence.

But that Christmas eve we were still together, talking over one another, raising glasses of pinot noir, my cousins and I keeping our kids from climbing the walls in anticipation of Santa Claus, our husbands—most of them not Italian—trying to avoid the *baccala* and octopus. And over it all presided Giulia at the head of the table, her oldest son—my father Paolino— and her youngest son, Sal, on either side of her. Three of her children had already passed away before her, and Mariangela had moved to Florida. Only her sons, Caterina, and the baby of the family, my aunt Elena, were still there, held together, as we all were, by the threads that bound us to Giulia.

During the following winter, a bitterly cold January and February filled with record snowstorms, Giulia began to deteriorate. She rarely left the house, and Caterina moved in to take care of her. Once a month I drove up from Jersey to spend a Saturday afternoon with her, stopping first at Artuso's bakery to pick up a cannoli. We sat at the little table in the kitchen to drink our espresso and then she led me into the living room, pushing a walker ahead of her.

The family had ordered a hospital bed and had it set up in the living room so she didn't have to climb the stairs anymore, but she still got up every day, dressed and held court with whoever stopped by to visit her.

Our ritual was the same every time I came. She sat in her chair in the corner, near the votive candles she'd moved down from her dresser in the bedroom. The Metropolitan Opera broadcast played softly on the radio. I sat in front of her as she closed her eyes and I reached up and began to circle her brow.

She was the only one I dared touch in that way, the only one who'd heard me recite the ancient incantations that had sprung from my lips that night in the hospital in Avellino. I didn't trust that what happened when I touched her was anything more than a granddaughter comforting a grand-mother. I didn't think it was anything *I* was doing. It seemed only to be Giulia placing her trust in me and feeling better simply because I was there.

I remember once watching a movie about a young woman who marries into a California wine family with an incredibly powerful matriarch who becomes the young woman's nemesis. Ultimately, the young wife triumphs, replacing the matriarch, but in doing so she takes on a striking resemblance to the older woman, even wearing her long, flowing hair in the severe wrapped braids that had been the matriarch's signature. It was as if the older woman had inhabited her.

I wasn't about to start wearing my hair in the style Giulia had favored ever since I'd known her. In a photo taken on my first birthday, Giulia hovers over me as I blow out the candle, her wavy hair pulled back in a bun at the nape of her neck. In fact, true to my baby boomer quest for perpetual youth, I still wore my hair the same way I'd worn it in my high-school

yearbook photo. No, I had no intention of imitating my grandmother's looks. But I was also uncomfortable taking on this
most mysterious aspect of her life. Like my great-grandmother,
who'd dismissed the spells of Giuseppina as so much mumbo
jumbo, I did not believe that Giulia's power had anything to
do with me.

I wasn't with Giulia when she died. It was 8:00 p.m. on
a Thursday night in early August when my mother called
me. I had just read my four-year-old twins, David and
Matthew, their nightly chapter of *The Lion, the Witch and the
Wardrobe*. Joshua, my ten-year-old, was trying to teach my
husband, Andrew, how to play Zelda on his new Nintendo,
and my only daughter, Julia, was engrossed in dressing the
Barbie doll my mother had insisted on giving her for her
sixth birthday.

"It didn't do you any harm, so I see no reason why I can't
give her one, too," she'd told me over my objections in May.

I sat alone with the news of my grandmother's death,
perched at the top of the stairs, remembering the lines of her
face under my fingertips.

We buried Giulia in Holy Sepulchre Cemetery in New
Rochelle, with Paolo and the two babies she had lost,
Carmine and Emilia. The grave is far in the back, against a
crumbling wall covered with ivy on the northern edge of
the cemetery. The plot, though remote, had been well
tended. My father told me that after Salvatore had died,
Giulia had arranged for him to be buried in Connecticut
with his first wife, the mother of Patsy and Nicky and Mariangela. Giulia made annual visits to that grave but, in her
second widowhood, it was to Paolo's grave she returned
almost monthly, restoring it from its overgrown and forgotten condition to a neat patch of grass and flowers. She had

left instructions with my father and Caterina that it was there she wished to be buried.

The dates on the headstone tell a striking story. Giulia outlived Paolo by seventy years. Carved under their names is a phrase I recognized from his letters:

Per la vita. For life.

That was twenty years ago. Although I resisted taking on Giulia's persona and her gift for healing in those last months of her life, I found I could not escape the connection that had been forged between us in our lives together. I look back now and see Giulia's imprint.

Like my grandmother, I had two husbands. Although the first one didn't die as my grandfather Paolo had, like Paolo, Jack Peyton left me with an infant and disappeared quite emphatically and finally from our lives. He might as well have been dead.

And like Giulia, I turned my culinary skills into a business, opening a catering company to support Joshua and myself. I had absorbed the drive and seriousness of purpose Giulia had called upon to survive the loss and hardship in her life, and I became as successful a businesswoman as she'd been.

When I met Andrew Dedrick, we were both trying to rebuild our lives after difficult divorces and were as tentative and cautious of new love as Giulia and Salvatore had been in their courtship. But we plunged ahead nevertheless and created a family, bringing three more children into the world—Julia, Matthew and David—to join Joshua.

Although he didn't play the accordion, Andrew brought music into my life in other ways. He filled our home with his eclectic collection of Mozart and Dylan and later, Loreena McKennitt and Jesse Cook and obscure singers from remote corners of the world whose music he'd heard on equally obscure NPR broadcasts. He encouraged Joshua to play the violin and go on to perform with the Boston Symphony Orchestra. And he enthusiastically endured the twins' experimentation with drums and electric guitars. A rock band performed in our family room throughout their years in high school, with Andrew ever at the ready to haul equipment to a gig on a Saturday night.

Although I resisted taking on Giulia's mantle as a healer, I learned something about the power within myself when David and Matthew were born early and spent the first weeks of their lives hovering precariously between life and death, health and impairment, in a state-of-the-art neonatal intensive-care unit. I sat with them every day between their Isolettes, holding one or the other in my arms, the wires attached to their many monitors draped across my lap. The NICU nurse on duty drew my attention to the monitors one afternoon. The irregularities in their heartbeats and the unevenness in their respiration disappeared as I stroked and murmured to them. When they were released a month after their births, the pediatrician told me, "I'm sending home two normal, healthy babies, and I'm not entirely sure how that happened."

The last echo of Giulia that emerged in my life came about when Andrew taught me how to dance the tango. In his arms I shed one layer of my grandmother's influence—my reserve—to discover another. Her passion for dancing.

Now, when the children return home at Christmas, after we've finished decorating the tree and before we sit down to the feast of the seven fishes, they insist on a tango. Joshua plays a haunting and vibrant tune on his violin, and Andrew and I glide across the floor as our children watch.

* * * * *

Happily ever after is just the beginning…

Turn the page for a sneak preview of
A HEARTBEAT AWAY
by
Eleanor Jones

Harlequin Everlasting—Every great love
has a story to tell. ™
A brand-new series from Harlequin Books

Special? A prickle ran down my neck and my heart started to beat in my ears. Was today really special?

"Tuck in," he ordered.

I turned my attention to the feast that he had spread out on the ground. Thick, home-cooked-ham sandwiches, sausage rolls fresh from the oven and a huge variety of mouthwatering scones and pastries. Hunger pangs took over, and I closed my eyes and bit into soft homemade bread.

When we were finally finished, I lay back against the blue-bells with a groan, clutching my stomach.

Daniel laughed. "Your eyes are bigger than your stomach," he told me.

I leaned across to deliver a punch to his arm, but he rolled away, and when my fist met fresh air I collapsed in a fit of giggles before relaxing on my back and staring up into the flawless blue sky. We lay like that for quite a while, Daniel and

I, side by side in companionable silence, until he stretched out his hand in an arc that encompassed the whole area.

"Don't you think that this is the most beautiful place in the entire world?"

His voice held a passion that echoed my own feelings, and I rose onto my elbow and picked a buttercup to hide the emotion that clogged my throat.

"Roll over onto your back," I urged, prodding him with my forefinger. He obliged with a broad grin, and I reached across to place the yellow flower beneath his chin.

"Now, let us see if you like butter."

When a yellow light shone on the tanned skin below his jaw, I laughed.

"There…you do."

For an instant our eyes met, and I had the strangest sense that I was drowning in those honey-brown depths. The scent of bluebells engulfed me. A roaring filled my ears, and then, unexpectedly, in one smooth movement Daniel rolled me onto my back and plucked a buttercup of his own.

"And do *you* like butter, Lucy McTavish?" he asked. When he placed the flower against my skin, time stood still.

His long lean body was suspended over mine, pinning me against the grass. Daniel…dear, comfortable, familiar Daniel was suddenly bringing out in me the strangest sensations.

"Do you, Lucy McTavish?" he asked again, his voice low and vibrant.

My eyes flickered toward his, the whisper of a sigh escaped my lips and although a strange lethargy had crept into my limbs, I somehow felt as if all my nerve endings were on fire. He felt it, too—I could see it in his warm brown eyes. And when he lowered his face to mine, it seemed to me the most natural thing in the world.

None of the kisses I had ever experienced could have even begun to prepare me for the feel of Daniel's lips on mine. My entire body floated on a tide of ecstasy that shut out everything but his soft, warm mouth, and I knew that this was what I had been waiting for the whole of my life.

"Oh, Lucy." He pulled away to look into my eyes. "Why haven't we done this before?"

Holding his gaze, I gently touched his cheek, then I curled my fingers through the short thick hair at the base of his skull, overwhelmed by the longing to drown again in the sensations that flooded our bodies. And when his long tanned fingers crept across my tingling skin, I knew I could deny him nothing.

* * * * *

Be sure to look for A HEARTBEAT AWAY,
available February 27, 2007.
And look, too, for THE DEPTH OF LOVE
by Margot Early,
the story of a couple who must learn that love comes
in many guises—and in the end it's the only thing
that counts.

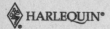 **HARLEQUIN®**

EVERLASTING LOVE™

Every great love has a story to tell™

These deeply emotional novels
show how love can last, how it
shapes and transforms lives, how
it's truly the adventure of a lifetime.
Harlequin® Everlasting Love™
novels tell the whole story.
Because "happily ever after"
is just the beginning....

Two new titles are available EVERY MONTH!

www.eHarlequin.com   ELPOS07

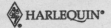

EVERLASTING LOVE™

Every great love has a story to tell™

What marriage really means…

Fall From Grace
by **Kristi Gold**
AVAILABLE THIS FEBRUARY

A surgeon and his wife, divorced after decades of marriage, discover that wedding vows can be broken, but they can also be mended. Memories of their marriage have the power to bring back a love that never really left.

For a deeply emotional story of what marriage really means, buy this novel today!

Also available this month:
Dancing on Sunday Afternoons by Linda Cardillo
The love story of a century…

www.eHarlequin.com

HEFFG0207

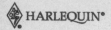

HARLEQUIN®

EVERLASTING LOVE™

Every great love has a story to tell™

Save $1.⁰⁰ off

**the purchase of
any Harlequin
Everlasting Love novel**

Coupon valid from January 1, 2007
until April 30, 2007.

Valid at retail outlets in the U.S. only.
Limit one coupon per customer.

RETAILER: Harlequin Enterprises Limited will pay the face value of this coupon plus 8¢ if submitted by the customer for this product only. Any other use constitutes fraud. Coupon is nonassignable. Void if taxed, prohibited or restricted by law. Consumer must pay any government taxes. Void if copied. For reimbursement submit coupons and proof of sales directly to: Harlequin Enterprises Ltd., P.O. Box 880478, El Paso, TX 88588-0478, U.S.A. Cash value 1/100¢. Valid in the U.S. only. ® is a trademark of Harlequin Enterprises Ltd. Trademarks marked with ® are registered in the United States and/or other countries.

5 65373 00076 2   (8100) 0 11302

HEUSCPN0407

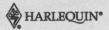

HARLEQUIN®

EVERLASTING LOVE™

Every great love has a story to tell™

Save $1.⁰⁰ off

the purchase of
any Harlequin
Everlasting Love novel

Coupon valid from January 1, 2007
until April 30, 2007.

Valid at retail outlets in Canada only.
Limit one coupon per customer.

RETAILER: Harlequin Enterprises Limited will pay the face value of this coupon plus
10.25¢ if submitted by the customer for this product only. Any other use constitutes
fraud. Coupon is nonassignable. Void if taxed, prohibited or restricted by law.
Consumer must pay any government taxes. Void if copied. Nielsen Clearing House
customers submit coupons and proof of sales to: Harlequin Enterprises Ltd. P.O.
Box 3000, Saint John, N.B. E2L 4L3. Non–NCH retailer—for reimbursement submit
coupons and proof of sales directly to: Harlequin Enterprises Ltd., Retail Marketing
Department, 225 Duncan Mill Rd., Don Mills, Ontario M3B 3K9, Canada. Valid in
Canada only. ® is a trademark of Harlequin Enterprises Ltd. Trademarks marked with
® are registered in the United States and/or other countries.

52607370

HECDNCPN0407

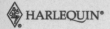

EVERLASTING LOVE™

Every great love has a story to tell™

Love always finds a way…

Daniel Brown promised to love Lucy McTavish forever—a promise he's unable to keep. Angry and grieving, Lucy tries to move on with her life, but Daniel is never far from her thoughts. Then, through a meeting with a charismatic stranger in a London park, she discovers that Daniel has kept his promise in the most unexpected way.

A Heartbeat Away
by Eleanor Jones

On sale this March!

Also available this month:
The Depth of Love by Margot Early

The deepest feelings last the longest…

www.eHarlequin.com

HEAHA0307

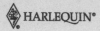

COMING NEXT MONTH

#3. *The Depth of Love* by **Margot Early**

"I'm yours. And you're mine." Eve Swango and
Tommy Baca belong to each other. Always have. Always will.
For decades now, they've shared a passion for exploring the
wild, subterranean depths of a New Mexico cave. *Their* cave.
In this fascinating, moving and original romance, two lovers
learn that the deepest feelings last the longest....

#4. *A Heartbeat Away* by **Eleanor Jones**

One morning Lucy McTavish meets a stranger named
Ben in a London park. The connection between them is
immediate and powerful, but it's also perplexing. As their
lives intersect in the weeks that follow, Lucy begins to ask
herself, has Daniel Brown, her soul mate, her greatest love—
her husband now gone—kept his promise after all?

www.eHarlequin.com

HECNM0207